How Briggs Died

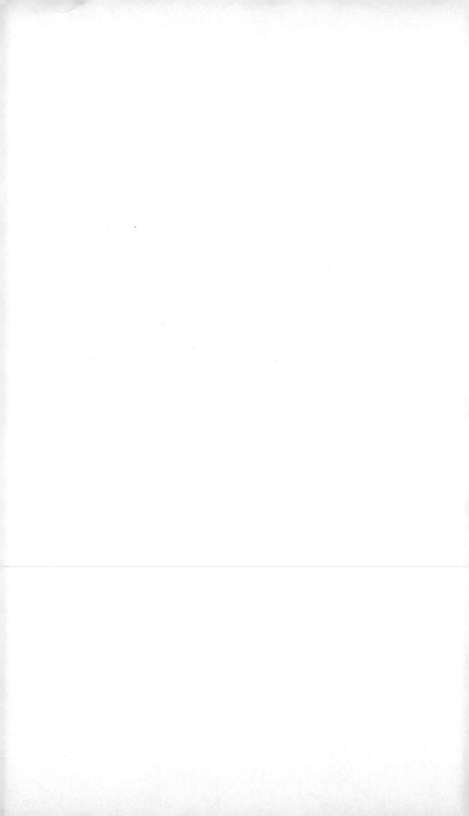

How Briggs Died

DOUGLAS HARDING

The Shollond Trust
London

Published by The Shollond Trust

87B Cazenove Road

London N16 6BB

England

headexchange@gn.apc.org

www.headless.org

The Shollond Trust is a UK charity reg. no 1059551

ISBN 978-1-914316-41-8

Preface

Douglas Harding's first book was *The Meaning and Beauty of the Artificial*. It was completed but not published in 1935 when Harding was 26 and living in Ipswich, Suffolk. Although the subject of *The Meaning and Beauty of the Artificial* is the role of the artificial in the evolution of the human species, at the heart of the book is the question 'What am I?'. This book was Harding's first attempt to answer that question. It was his first sketch of a many-levelled model of the self, a dynamic living system that functioned 'vertically'. According to this model, our human behaviour is not simply our own. It is the result of the behaviour of all the layers within us—cellular, molecular, atomic... We may think it is we who are acting but it is not. Our actions are the result of the combined actions of our cells, which are the result of the combined actions of our molecules, which are the result of the combined actions of our atoms. And of what are these actions the result? In the final analysis, science fails to identify any 'thing' at the base of this many-levelled organisation that we are. Yet from this mysterious, invisible base, this eternally creative 'fountainhead', arise all our thoughts and actions, evolving as they ascend through each level to burst into consciousness at our human level. When you think, it is not you as an individual thinking, it is the many-levelled whole thinking in and through you. How unimaginably clever this 'organisation' is! We will never fully understand how it works. How do 'you' know how to think? How do 'you' know how to do anything? The most we can do is humbly submit to the fact that deep down we are infinitely wiser than we can ever know because we are infinitely deeper than we can ever know.

After finishing *The Meaning and Beauty of the Artificial* Harding put aside his philosophical writing and, over the next year, wrote more than a dozen short stories, gathering these together in a collection he named after one of the stories, *The Crimson Tiger*. Harding had at this time two ambitions in terms of his writing. On the one hand he wanted to write a great philosophical book. *The Meaning and Beauty of the Artificial* was his first step in this direction. On the other hand he wanted to be a novelist, like his hero Dickens. These short stories were Harding's first step in that direction.

In 1937 Harding and his wife Beryl moved to India—Harding got a job in in Calcutta. Two years after arriving in the country he was writing his next book. Again, like the stories, it was not philosophy but fiction. It was *this* book. Harding wrote *How Briggs Died* in just a few months. "I gave my heart to it and when I did it, I did it. There was nothing else and I just lived it, as is my wont—had it for breakfast, dinner and tea and slept with it." Appearing during the War in 1940 it was the first book of Harding's to be published. The Sunday times reviewed it in October 1940: "D. E. Harding's detective story is very nearly first rate; it has an ingenious and by no means impossible plot, some lively character drawing and any amount of detection… I think that this is a first novel; it is a very promising one."

Immediately after completing *How Briggs Died* Harding wrote a second novel featuring the same detective. He was following in the footsteps of another of his heroes, Sir Arthur Conan Doyle, whose detective stories, of course, starred one detective throughout: the famous Sherlock Holmes. Later in life Harding described his two detective novels as detours from the main focus of his life: the working out of a credible view of "man's place in the universe". But writing the short stories and the detective novels developed his writing skills, so they played a part in terms of his overall development as a writer. "I think the detective novel brought out and exercised one's capacity if you like, for construction, for putting a whole together, fitting a puzzle together, inventing a pattern really."

As well as enjoying the story in *How Briggs Died* and, if it is of interest to you, observing how Harding was developing his ability to "put a whole together", there's something else that is curious about this novel. Harding, of course, is known for 'headlessness'. His best-known book is *On Having No Head*. Harding first realised he was 'headless' in 1943, three years after finishing *How Briggs Died*. The curious thing is that the accident, or crime, or whatever it was that happened in *How Briggs Died*, turned out to be a premonition of headlessness. Harding reflected on this many years later: "As Kierkegaard said, life is lived forwards and understood backwards. You understand things you didn't understand at the time. You understand the deeper reason for your fascination." Whilst Harding was writing *How Briggs Died* the question 'What am I?' was bubbling away in the background of his mind, even when he was not consciously thinking of it. But it seems that the answer to this question, the answer that was to emerge as 'headlessness' just a few years later, was also bubbling away in his mind, making its way up through the layers of his being. For headlessness appeared in *How Briggs Died*, though in a highly disguised and distorted form. Of course, Harding didn't know it at the time. It was only later, when he became conscious of his headlessness, that he could look back and, with the benefit of hindsight, recognise that headlessness was there, hiding in his novel. A portent of things to come. The One works in peculiar ways.

Have fun trying to solve the puzzle in *How Briggs Died* before Jethro Ray, the detective, works it out. Then look forward to the next adventure of Harding's unconventional sleuth when we publish the follow-up, *The Melwold Mystery*!

Richard Lang

PART ONE

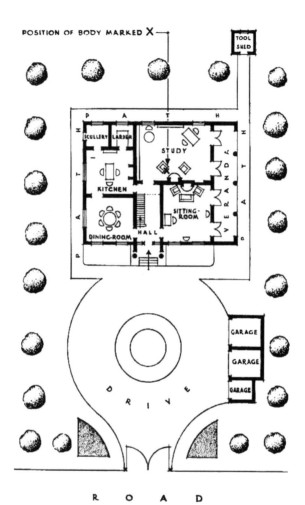

POSITION OF BODY MARKED X

TOOL SHED

PATH

SCULLERY · LARDER

STUDY

KITCHEN

VERANDA

SITTING-ROOM

DINING-ROOM

HALL

DRIVE

GARAGE

GARAGE

GARAGE

ROAD

PLAN OF THE BRIGGS' HOUSE

SCALE 0   10   20   30   40 FEET

CHAPTER I

TRADITIONALLY, like a lamb, the month of March had gone out, and April had come in with a mildness that belonged to June. Over the parish church of Bingly on All Fools' Day a warm, bright sun shone in a sky that was serenely cloudless.

Hovering round the church on this particular afternoon were two dilapidated creatures that looked rather like things that the sun had inadvertently hatched before their appointed time. They wore voluminous flannel bags with shiny seats and spotty fronts, and their tweed jackets hung about their shoulders like sacks. Their neckties were of coarse wool, and bright red and bright green respectively.

There the resemblance between Jethro Ray and his friend Joshua Briggs ceased. All the rest was difference.

The distinguishing features of the former—he of the red tie—were a massive pair of horn-rimmed spectacles and a pair of squinting eyes behind them. The combination of thick lenses, black rims, bright blue eyes looking in different directions, and jungly blond eyebrows meeting over the nose was definitely queer. So queer that to most people the combination conveyed an impression of lively craziness, or of stupidity masking a preternatural intelligence. The rest of him, which was lanky and very untidy, passed more or less unnoticed.

With a two-foot rule under his arm, a notebook in one hand, and a pencil in the other, Ray was walking round, peering at, sketching, and measuring the tower of Bingly church. To the layman the tower merely looked sombre, four-square, and graceless, but to

Ray, who had already achieved a reputation as a specialist in Saxon architecture, it was a beautiful and exciting structure, a mine of historical information, and an opportunity to indulge his flair for archaeological detection. The long-and-short work, herring-bone courses, and triangular arches, taken along with local traditions and records, were clues that, properly read, would yield a thrilling solution. Baffling, self-contradictory, and enlightening by turns, the evidence nevertheless led somewhere. Where, Ray was determined to find out.

Ray's friend, Joshua Briggs, of the green neckwear, sat among the tombstones on a little stool some distance from the tower, sketching the church. A little older, and far less grotesque-looking than his friend, Briggs was comely in an undistinguished way, with a beak of a nose separating grey, unflinching eyes. Earnestly he worked, meticulously pencilling in every stone and tile and leaf and blade of grass. The man drew as though he was possessed of an eager devil.

It was this quality of artistic zeal that had attracted Ray. The two men had met for the first time about a year back at a Bloomsbury party; at once Ray had noticed the contrast between Briggs, to whom art appeared really to mean all in all, and the dabblers and posers that made up the rest of the crowd. An eccentric and desultory friendship had sprung up between them, and they had spent, at odd times during the course of the year, many days together in the country, the one in quest of archaeological curiosities, the other of picturable subjects. Briggs had made the George at Bingly a kind of headquarters, and had engaged a room there permanently, although he was away most of the time. On this occasion he had invited Ray down from London to spend a couple of days reconnoitering in the neighbourhood. He had arrived late that morning, and they had started for the church right away with their lunch in their pockets.

Towards tea-time the wind in the churchyard began to freshen—a chill evening wind that made Ray put on a shabby overcoat and Briggs pack up his paraphernalia. Along a rut-scarred lane they picked their way to the George, while Jethro prattled of Bishop Atheston, who had built five churches, of which Bingly might or might not be one, of Bingly's tower, that might or might not have been added after 1066, and of the peculiar variety of triangular arch that flourished in the vicinity and nowhere else in the world.

Briggs, with customary patience, listened unprotesting to this discourse till they reached the George, when he announced his intention of finishing his half-completed drawing in his own room. Ray, for his part, said that this suited him perfectly, because he was about to retire to his room to write up notes on Bingly church for some lecture or other.

*   *   *   *

After dinner that night the two friends sat beside a blazing log fire in the lounge discussing Briggs' drawing, now finished. A wealth of detail, a chiaroscuro, a brilliance of light and a profundity of shadow that went beyond nature, endowed the picture with an intensity only to be found in dreams. The thing was too real, horribly real as only nightmares are real. Ray held the drawing up to the light, blinking.

He exclaimed: "You modern painters astonish me, Briggs! You don't know how to compromise. Why must you either distort things till I can't recognize them, or make them so vilely realistic that they give me the creeps?"

Briggs smiled. "Whereas the photographer does neither."

"I have it!" cried Ray. "The photographer and the average Academician depict the outward semblances, but you people are nature's Holmeses and Poirots, for ever unearthing marvellous clues to some more marvellous Mystery. Cosmic sleuths, so to say."

"The adroitness and speed with which you bring any given subject round to your own, Ray, are positively staggering," laughed Briggs. "I wonder whether you'll ever get a chance to do any real detecting. As distinct from merely writing detective stories, I mean."

"Don't be patronizing, Briggs. You painters are all the same. You think that putting blobs of coloured mud on a stretched rag is the only way to get an authentic kick out of life, unmask reality, and generally get under the epidermis of existence. But anyone who makes satisfactory patterns does the same thing. Whether the patterns are composed of notes or words or paint or clues doesn't matter so much."

"A man like my brother James, for instance, whose sole object seems to be making money—and love. What about him? Does he make satisfactory patterns?"

"There's nothing inherently evil in making money. The snag is that it merely consists of stringing units together, of piling up the shekels and not arranging them. The only thing worth doing in life is to move on the face of the waters and produce order out of chaos."

"And making love?" asked Briggs, with the air of one who has put a poser.

"A good instance of what I was saying, Briggs," came the ready answer. "A love affair should have pattern, like music. Without counterpoint, crescendo, diminuendo, and so forth, it's just a noise trailing on, a formless habit."

"What amuses me about you," laughed Briggs, "is the fervour with which you believe in something that's just occurred to you, and that you're certain to contradict with equal fervour tomorrow."

"Pattern-weaving, Briggs. But tell me more of this brother of yours."

"There's little to tell. James and I were always very different, and we always heartily disliked each other. He's an art dealer, and, dealer-like, he doesn't care a tinker's cuss about painting. He's made a packet of money at the game, and spends it on a light-o'-love called Margot and on racing. I go and see him now and then at Tiddenham and at his place in London to try to get him to sell some of my pictures. To give him his due, he's tried quite hard to push my stuff."

"Has he a wife?"

"Yes, indeed. A mournful, handsome, refined creature with a Greek profile and a flat chest. In every way a contrast to Margot, who's small, gay, plump, and naughty."

"And James's wife, how does she react to the familiar triangular pattern?"

"I really don't know. You see, I've only met Ellen once or twice. Having an affair herself, probably."

There came a lull in the conversation. The clock on the mantelshelf struck ten. Ray lay back in his easy-chair, blinking unseeingly at the capricious firelight on the ceiling. Briggs' head started nodding. Only the sound of a distant bicycle bell vibrated in the silence.

At five past ten the peace of the lounge of the George was rudely shattered. Sawberry, the landlord, bustled in with an envelope in his hand. He gave it to Briggs.

Briggs shook himself back into consciousness, and opened the telegram. He read it twice, then handed it in silence to his friend, who read:

Tiddenham, 9.0 P.M., April 1st

JAMES MET WITH FATAL ACCIDENT THIS EVENING STOP PLEASE COME AT ONCE ELLEN

CHAPTER II

NEXT morning Ray, snuggling under two eiderdowns lay curled in one of the George's luxurious feather beds, recapitulating.

Within fifteen minutes of receiving the news of his brother's death Joshua Briggs, grave and unflurried, had paid up the landlord, thrown a couple of suitcases in the back of his car, and was saying good-bye to Ray.

"It's only thirty-five miles to Tiddenham," Joshua had explained, "and I'll be there within an hour."

And Ray had added, "You faithfully promise to let me know what's happened?" Joshua had promised.

Was it possible, Ray asked himself, that at last a chance to do some real detection had come his way? Detective novels were one thing, and real bodies and police and criminals were another and, no doubt, quite different thing. He hadn't so much as seen a corpse in the course of his twenty-seven years, much less tracked down a murderer. After all, he reflected, unless one is a policeman murder simply does not come one's way. At least, not in real life. On the other hand, in fiction corpses line the sleuth's progress. Poirot has but to go to Egypt, and lo, somebody is sure to kick the bucket in peculiar circumstances. Mr Ellery Queen may elect to take a holiday, but murder doesn't. The elegant figure of Philo Vance is the starting-gun for dirty work to begin. In fact, it was arguable that the ace detective is, in some obscure way, the real author of each crime. Murder is rare, yet he runs up against it time after time, by 'accident,' as he would have us believe. Once or twice, and the matter might pass as mere coincidence. As it was, the only explanation seemed to be that the sleuth incites the villain to do his deed in order to reduce unemployment among detectives; either that, or the detective carries round with him a baleful atmosphere in which the rank weed of murder flourishes exceedingly.

"An atmosphere," Ray soliloquized, "from which I seem to be all too free."

The rotund figure of Mrs Sawberry, bearing materials for the early-morning cup of tea, broke in upon these meditations. It was the envelope on the tray, however, that intrigued him. He seized it, ripped it open, and read:

Tiddenham, 8.0 A.M. April 2nd
COME OVER AT ONCE HAVE BOOKED ROOM FOR YOU
TIDDENHAM ARMS JOSHUA

Ray wasted no time considering the hidden purport of this message, but dressed at once and snatched a hasty breakfast without stopping even to shave. Within half an hour he was at the wheel of his ancient Morris two-seater and chugging along at thirty-five—which was all he could squeeze out of her—in the direction of Tiddenham.

He reflected with a grin that his exhilaration was not wholly due to the poignant spring air in his face, nor to the sight of green-flecked, undulating woods on either side of the road, and dazzling clouds, like white behemoths swimming in a cerulean sea. How disgraceful, he thought, bending forward in his seat as though to urge forward a lagging steed, to be rejoicing that some poor devil had got himself killed, and to be hoping against hope that he was murdered! And on such a morning!

At ten past ten Ray pulled up outside the Tiddenham Arms, a mock-Tudor pub whose real habitat was a by-pass road rather than a decent village. In the place of massive half-timbers were slats of pinewood tacked on to the wall and stained the colour of gravy. A substance like spotted dog encrusted the spaces between the wooden uprights, and a salmon-pink roof fittingly crowned the structure. Jethro shuddered inwardly and pushed open the bar-parlour door.

A buxom woman of thirty-five, with pink cheeks and copper-coloured hair, came forward.

"Mr Ray?" she asked. Ray nodded and smiled. "I'll show you to your room. We've been expecting you."

She led the way upstairs to a room with an enormous brass-knobbed bed and flowery wallpaper, further bedecked with pastel pictures of pyramids, palms, and camels' rears in brilliant colours. Ray winced again and turned to his guide.

"Mr James Briggs has met with an accident?" he queried, switching to a more congenial train of thought.

"So I hear. They found him shot."

"Suicide?" Ray looked prepared to hear the worst.

Mrs Greene shrugged her wide shoulders non-committedly.

"Anyhow," Ray continued, "I must needs be getting along to the Briggses' house. Can you show me the way?"

She took him downstairs and directed him. The house was only ten minutes' walk from the Arms, in the opposite direction to the village. Ray decided to go on foot.

After a little way the road became a lane embowered with tall elms and fringed with thick hedges. No cottages or houses fronted the lane, and Ray met no one. At length he came quite suddenly upon a sedate, early-Victorian residence in stucco and green paint, almost hidden by trees. The house, though by no means large, bore all the hallmarks of comfortable respectability; a short gravel drive led through gate piers of manorial pomp, past well-tended islands of turf and daffodils, to an Ionic portal that was elegance itself.

Joshua, looking a little worn in spite of his tan, answered the door to Ray.

"So glad you've come," he said, taking Ray into a large sitting-room on the right-hand side of the hall. Ray subsided into an easy-chair, while his friend poured out drinks.

"They say it's an accident," said Joshua, with his back still turned. "But I wonder. . ."

"Suppose you begin at the beginning."

Joshua took a long pull at his Scotch and soda, sat down, and started talking.

"I got here soon after eleven last night. A police inspector and a constable were prowling round taking notes. Ellen had more or less collapsed, and Mrs Groves—that's the housekeeper—was helping her upstairs. Storr, the doctor from Stokeby, was here doing something or other. And then of course there was—the body.

"Apparently Ellen had come in at about eight o'clock and found him sitting in a chair in the study, with a shot-gun between his outstretched legs. He'd been cleaning it. At least, they found cleaning rags on the table beside him, and it seems he had intended to go shooting to-day. The thing had gone off in his face. Horrible mess. Storr says he died instantly."

"What makes you think it wasn't accidental?" asked Ray.

Damn it all!" cried Joshua. "Do you think he'd be such a fool as to clean a loaded gun, and point it at his head into the bargain?"

"Then you think he—"

"Killed himself? I don't know. It's possible, but not very likely, from what I know of James. No, I don't know what to think, except that there's something queer about it all. Something I want your help to find out."

"Was anyone in the house when it happened?" asked Ray.

"Not a soul was anywhere near. Groves, the gardener, and his wife had gone off to the pictures at Stokeby—it was their night off. Ellen was in Stokeby too. The day-girl, Alice, wouldn't be here in the evening, anyhow. And that, along with James, is the whole household."

"What about the doors and windows?"

"The French doors to the study were open; so was the drive gate. Anybody could have come in and done it."

"When did it happen?"

"I heard Dr Storr telling the Inspector that James died between five and six."

"And who last saw him alive?"

"I don't know. They were all out when he got back, and the last they saw of him was at breakfast-time. He was up in London for the day, apparently."

A telephone bell started ringing in another part of the house.

"That may be his office calling now," said Joshua, excusing himself.

In Joshua's absence Ray examined the room more closely than he had been able to do so far. Like the exterior of the house, it had an air of stolidity. Mahogany and hide furniture, dull, but not in bad taste or overcrowded, carpet of the thickest pile, heavy damask curtains—evidently James had been a man of substance.

A framed photograph on a side-table caught Ray's eye. It was of two men posed stiffly against a dark background. One of them, who was obviously Joshua with a self-conscious grin on his face, was standing with an arm resting awkwardly on the back of a chair. A little younger, but no tidier, than the present Joshua, Ray observed. The prominent nose, large, earnest eyes, and swarthy countenance were unmistakable. The other man was seated. He wore horn-rimmed glasses on a nose that bore a family resemblance to Joshua's, but his perfectly pressed lounge suit, stiff collar, and wooden expression were the very antithesis of Joshua's happy-go-lucky slovenliness.

Ray put down the photograph as his friend re-entered the room.

"That' s James and me, " said Joshua, grimacing. "I think he must have put that photo there just to draw odious comparisons. The white sheep and the black sheep.

"That was Margot on the 'phone, by the way," he continued. She says that James spent yesterday in town, and left his office at about four o'clock in the afternoon, saying that he was coming straight down here. That was the last she saw of him. She wouldn't believe me when I told her what had happened."

"Did she say whether anything unusual had occurred yesterday? Was his manner normal?"

Joshua shook his head. "Can't say. I didn't ask. She's coming down this afternoon, and we'll find out all the details then."

"Won't that be rather . . ." Ray hesitated.

"No, I don't think so. Margot's official status was James's secretary. She looked after his office in London, typed his correspondence, and made his appointments. Mrs Groves tells me that he even brought her down here now and then."

"By the way, Briggs, do you know the contents of the will yet?"

"That reminds me!" Joshua exclaimed. "I must go over to Stokeby and see James's lawyer and bank manager this morning. Ellen naturally wants to know how much he left. Her money was in his account, and he was pretty well off, so I should bring back good news. Would you care to come?"

"I'd rather stay here and talk to the housekeeper, if I may, and if she's about."

"By all means do. The house is yours, except for Ellen's room upstairs, where she's lying in bed. Incidentally, the body has been shifted to Bingly mortuary." He went over to the fireplace and pressed a bell.

"You know, Ray," said Briggs, "although my brother and I were not friends, and I can't pretend I'm prostrated by his death, I'm resolved to find out how he died. I think, between us, we shall succeed. Are you in this with me?"

"Up to the neck. You don't know what a service you're doing me, Briggs, by letting me in on this."

The door opened, and a dumpy, pop-eyed woman walked in, wiping floury hands on her apron. She raised questioning, apprehensive eyebrows.

"Mrs Groves," said Joshua, "this is my friend, Mr Ray. He would like to ask you some questions about my brother and what happened yesterday."

Mrs Groves' troubled features sagged further. "And what should I know about it all to tell the gentleman?" she complained. "And me with me cooking and all to do."

"I'll come and sit in the kitchen, Mrs Groves " said Ray soothingly, "and you can talk to me while you work. We know you don't know anything about the accident, but you can tell me about your work here and what sort of a person Mr Briggs was, and that sort of thing."

Mrs Groves shook her head doubtfully and retired into the hall, followed by the two men.

"I'll be back in an hour or two," said Joshua, on the doorstep, "and meantime I'll leave you to carry on. Good luck!"

*　　　　　*　　　　　*　　　　　*

Mrs Groves led the way to a door at the back of the hall and into the kitchen. Ray sat down and lit his pipe, while the housekeeper stood by the table, doubtful as to what to do next.

"Don't mind me, Mrs Groves, just carry on," said Ray. Still eyeing him, she started to stir the contents of a basin. "That's better," he said. "But surely you don't do everything in a house of this size? There are other servants?"

"There's that girl Alice," she grumbled, bending over the pudding-basin. "She came this morning at seven, as usual, and stayed no more'n five minutes after I told her the master's shot himself." She sniffed her contempt.

"Ah, yes!" sighed Ray sympathetically. "Whereas you, on the other hand, believe in sticking to your job, I see. Do you like being here, Mrs Groves?"

"I've known worse places. The missus, now, she's a good sort. Kind o' gloomy, but her heart's in the right place. Mr Briggs, he's different. Kind of queer he was."

"Yes?" Ray prompted.

"Nothing special, like; only queer. And treated her real nasty he did. They never used to quarrel that I know of, and yet he treated her like she was a stranger, He was more civil to me than what he was to his own wife. And then bringing that Frenchy girl down here—calling her his secret'ry. Secret'ry my foot!" Mrs Groves gave the pudding a vicious stir.

"You saw him before he left yesterday morning, Mrs Groves? What was he like?"

"Oh yes, I served his breakfast. Much the same as usual he was. Stiff like, not talking much. He tells her he's going shooting to-morrow—that's to-day, I mean—and he says he's going up to London in his car. And she says as how she's going shopping in Stokeby in the afternoon, and going to the pictures afterwards, and'll be back at eight."

"Did Mr Briggs say when he was coming back?"

"I never heard him. They never talked more'n they could help."

"What happened after breakfast?"

"Why, nothink out of the ornery. About half-past nine, Mr Briggs went off in the car, and the missus stayed in all day till tea-time, and then off she goes in the little car to Stokeby. Then Mr Groves and me have a bite o' tea in the kitchen here, and catch the bus to Stokeby, last night being our night off."

"What time was this, Mrs Groves?"

"Well, the bus leaves the Tiddenham Arms at half-past five, and it takes ten minutes to walk from here. I reckon we left at quarter after five, about three-quarters of an hour after the missus went. We went to the Majestic, and saw a lovely picture, all about a little girl whose parents was living separate."

Ray suppressed a groan.

"Just sweet she was." Mrs Groves' bulging eyes started to swim at the mere memory of it. "And then we went and had supper with Mrs Wills in Stokeby, and caught the half-past nine bus back. When we got here the place was upside down. The doctor was in the drawing-room lookin' after Mrs Briggs, and the study was full of police. I just put my head inside, and that was enough for me."

Mrs Groves went to the range, turning her back on Ray. "Horrible! Haven't seen nothink like it since the air raids. Crumpled up in the easy-chair he was. And his head—ugh! And his shirt-front all red. I just took one look, an' run in here all of a tremble. Then in comes the Inspector, and asks me questions till I'm fair fit to scream. You might 'a' thought I'd done it meself the way he spoke to me. Whew, what a night!"

Ray was about to speak when a bell started ringing.

"That'll be the front door. 'Scuse me, sir." And Mrs Groves scuttled out.

Presently from the hall there came the sound of a man's voice. Ray opened the kitchen door a couple of inches and stood listening. The visitor was saying:

"Yes, they told me about it in the village this morning. I've come to see Mrs Briggs and find out what actually happened."

"Well, I'm afraid you can't see Mrs Briggs just now, sir. Doctor's orders is she must rest. Took awful bad, she was last night, and she'll be sleeping now, and mustn't be disturbed."

"Of course, of course. . . . I hear Mr Briggs' brother is here. Is he in?"

"He's gone off to Stokeby, but he said he'd be back to lunch. You care to wait for him, Mr Sothern?"

There was a pause, and Mrs Groves added, "There's Mr Day here, sir, what's a friend of Mr Joshua's. Would you like to see him?"

"Er—yes. May as well, I suppose."

The sound of approaching footsteps in the hall sent Ray back to his seat just in time before Mrs Groves re-entered.

"There's a gentleman—Mr Sothern—wants to speak to you. He was a friend of Mr Briggs," she explained.

"Right-ho, Mrs Groves, I'll give you a chance to get on with the cooking, and go and talk to him. Take me along and introduce me, please." She preceded Ray into the hall.

"Mr Day, sir," she said to Sothern, and beat a hasty retreat to the kitchen.

"Ray, in point of fact," smiled Jethro, proffering a hand. "Won't you come into the sitting-room?"

Sothern regarded Ray with a what-are-you-doing-here look. He was a wiry man of middle age, somewhat over-dressed, and with a Hitler moustache flourishing in the midst of a rufous, pock-marked countenance.

"Sothern's my name," he said, in a strident voice. "I wanted to see Briggs' brother."

"He'll be back in a few moments," Ray lied. "Won't you sit down and wait for him? Perhaps I should explain that I'm a friend of Joshua Briggs'. I'm his—er—secretary, in a manner of speaking." Some sort of justification for his presence seemed to be indicated.

Sothern sat down and lit a cigarette. Ray said, "Are you a friend of Joshua's?"

"No," said Sothern, as though he meant it. "I've met him once or twice. I knew James pretty well. Can you tell me what's happened?

There're all sorts of rumours going round the village."

"Well, I've only just got here, but so far I gather that Mrs Briggs found her husband alone in the house at eight last night, shot dead. That about exhausts my information."

Sothern frowned, as if in deep thought.

"You say you knew him well," Ray ventured.

Sothern came out of his trance with a jerk. "Knew him well? Yes and no. I used to come here occasionally on neighbourly visits, but I haven't seen him recently. I hear the police were here half the night. Any idea what they think about it?"

"None whatever. Do you think it could have been suicide? Was Briggs that sort of man?"

"What do you take me for?" was the somewhat testy answer. "I didn't know him intimately. Accident, suicide, murder? How the hell should I know which it was?" He went on more civilly: "I was going out shooting with him to-day, and then the milkman or somebody told my servant that he was dead, so naturally I came to see what had happened."

"You arranged the outing over the 'phone," said Ray, soliloquizing rather than putting a question.

Sothern gave a slight start. "How the devil—?" He checked himself. "Of course, I've already told you I hadn't seen him lately. Yes, he telephoned me the day before yesterday and said he'd decided to take up shooting after all. We fixed up to go out this afternoon."

"Then, unless something unfortunate happened between the time he telephoned you and last night, it doesn't look like suicide, does it? Accident, possibly. The cleaning rags that they found by the gun seem to lend colour to that theory."

"Lord, what a fool! I thought Briggs had more common savvy than to mess about with a loaded gun. Especially as he knew nothing about guns."

"Oh?"

"As a matter of fact, about a fortnight back he was showing me the new gun he'd bought. He didn't know the butt from the barrel then, and I know for a fact that he hasn't had any practice in the meantime, because he told me as much when he rang me up."

"Well, if he hadn't used the gun, what do you imagine he was cleaning it for? And why on earth was it loaded, do you think?"

"You can never tell with these beginners. Probably he was messing around with the thing like a child with a new toy."

"Ah, then you think it was an accident?"

"No!" Sothern almost shouted. "I tell you I don't know anything and I don't think anything. Anyway, who the hell are you, and what do you think you are doing, cross-questioning me like a detective? Are you a detective?"

Ray mildly disclaimed that distinction. There was an uneasy pause in the conversation. Sothern looked at his watch.

"Eleven-twenty!" he exclaimed, getting up. "What am I waiting for? Ellen—Mrs Briggs can't be seen, and Briggs' brother probably won't be able to tell me any more than you . . . Good morning to you."

Sothern didn't wait to be shown out. He strode down the hallway, snatched up his hat, and let himself out of the front door, closing it none too gently after him. Ray went to the drawing-room window and watched him climb into a sports-car, rev up the engine viciously, and drive away, churning up the gravel behind him and missing the gatepost by a hair's breadth.

"Nice man!" murmured Ray.

*   *   *   *

He turned round and took off his glasses, and started polishing them, from habit rather than necessity. Putting them on again, he began to walk across the room, when something caught his eye. On the writing desk opposite the fireplace there lay a blotting-pad, and on the top sheet of blotting-paper there were ink marks.

He peered at the writing. The reversed characters and the fact that some of them overlapped made the writing difficult to decipher. Taking the pad over to the window, to throw light on it, he managed to make out the letters "Dear Mar. . ." at the beginning. The signature at the end was obviously James Briggs'. The date looked very much like March 31st—the day before James died—but he couldn't be certain.

Ray gave a suppressed whoop of pure joy. A clue! And the police had been prowling round half the night and missed it. The only pity of it was that Dr Watson was not handy to impress!

Mar looked very much like the first part of Margot, the woman in the case. The next moment Ray was cursing himself for a fool. Would James have signed a *billet d'amour* like that? No. Not unless there had been a quarrel. A quarrel, though, was a possibility. Also it was possible that *Mar* was the beginning of another name.

Ray carefully removed the sheet of blotting-paper, folded it, put it in his pocket-book, and made for the kitchen. Mrs Groves dropped a saucepan lid as he burst open the door. He addressed her in his most wheedling voice:

"Mrs Groves, I want your help, please. Do you know which of Mr Briggs' friends has a name beginning with Mar?"

"Oh, you gave me such a fright, sir!" she answered, panting. "Beginning with Mar? No, can't say as how I do. Unless . . . unless you mean that woman. I've heard him call her Margot when Mrs Briggs wasn't there. He always called her Miss Fayette when the missus was about." Mrs Groves' voice subsided into a mutter conveying strong opinions concerning Frenchwomen and wayward husbands.

"Can't you think of anyone else whose name begins with those letters? Please try hard, Mrs Groves," Ray pleaded.

Mrs Groves heaved an impatient sigh. "No, I can't. Are you doing one of them crossword things? 'Cause I ain't no good at them."

Ray shrugged his shoulders resignedly, and turned to go. "What about this Mr Sothern? What's his Christian name?" he asked, as a last forlorn hope.

The housekeeper looked up brightly into Ray's face. "Why, now you come to mention it, his name's Martin. It's often I've heard the master calling him that over the 'phone, and when he came round here."

Whistling softly and polishing his spectacles with meticulous care,

Ray walked out of the kitchen, along the hall, and out of the front door into the garden.

CHAPTER III

THE Town Hall clock was striking eleven when Joshua Briggs parked his Ford in Stokeby's market square and asked a constable to direct him to the offices of Messrs Turner, Postlethwaite, and Chamberlain, solicitors.

Stokeby is a flourishing borough in which chain-store firms, cinema magnates, and speculative builders have not yet completed their mission of destruction. Much of the square is still fronted with Georgian façades which are the essence of undemonstrative refinement, like Cranford gentlewomen lined up in a row. The old-fashioned family grocer, with his shelf of canisters and curious non-mass-produced merchandise from every corner of the earth, is not quite extinct in Stokeby. A saddler and a blacksmith still contrive to get a living.

Hatless, and still attired in grubby flannels and tweed jacket, Joshua strolled in the direction of the lawyers' office. The sight of an outfitter's show-window reminded him that he was still wearing a green tie. He went in and bought a black one, and put it on in the shop. A hat also seemed indicated, so he bought a black trilby that could be converted to the pork-pie shape at a later date. Feeling somewhat more respectable, he walked on to the far end of the square, to the building that the policeman had pointed out. He passed under a richly carved pediment into a dim and dusty inquiry office. An open-mouthed youth stared up at him.

"I would like to see Mr Turner," Joshua announced firmly, ignoring as far as possible the upturned countenance.

The youth shook his head and continued to gape.

"Not in? Then Mr Postlethwaite." For answer there came a renewed shaking of the head.

"And naturally Mr Chamberlain isn't in either?"

This time a slow grin spread over the office boy's face. "They're all dead," he chuckled, waiting to see the effect of this announcement.

Joshua was beginning to tire of this game. It was evident that the knave had mistaken him for a vendor of india-rubbers. This was not altogether to be wondered at, in view of Joshua's clothes.

"Look here, young fellow," he said severely, "is there an epidemic in this town, or do I have to kick you in the pants before I get an intelligible answer out of you?"

This threat loosened the youth's tongue. "The partners in this here firm's Mr Lucas, Mr Smith, and Mr Peabody, and they're all out unless you've got an appointment."

"Give this card to one of them, and if you don't look sharp I'll get you sacked," snapped Joshua, handing him a crumpled pasteboard.

The youth disappeared through a door in the back of the office. Presently he came back, subdued beyond recognition. "Mr Lucas will see you at once, sir," he announced. "This way, please."

Joshua walked through into a musty sanctum, occupied by a rubicund old gentleman sitting at a desk strewn with papers. Joshua took the proffered chair, and began:

"I'm the brother of James Briggs, who lived at Tiddenham. My sister-in-law tells me that your firm are his lawyers."

"That is so. We have handled some of Mr Briggs' affairs. But you say lived at Tiddenham. I trust that nothing is wrong?"

There followed explanations and expressions of sympathy.

"Did you know my brother, Mr Lucas?" Joshua asked.

"No, I'm afraid not. You see, my partner, Mr Peabody, who is away at present, always dealt with Mr Briggs' affairs, though he kept me fully informed, of course."

"Then perhaps you could tell me about my brother's will. My sister-in-law says that she believes that he did make a will. She's not very well, naturally, and asked me to see you on the subject."

"Exactly, exactly." Mr Lucas coughed professionally, and hesitated. "You will appreciate my position, Mr Briggs. Not to put too fine a point on it, I am not authorized to give information to persons unknown to me."

Joshua produced an envelope. "As a matter of fact, I have this note from Mrs Briggs. And if you care to ring up the house—"

The letter seemed to reassure Mr Lucas. He said, "We legal men have to be cautious, you know, Mr Briggs. In any case, however, the contents of your brother's will will be common knowledge before long." He rang for the clerk and instructed him to bring the will. When he had received it he resumed, consulting the paper, "Mr James Briggs bequeathed his entire estate to Ellen, his wife, with the exception of his property at Tiddenham, which he left to his brother, Joshua Briggs. In other words, to you, sir."

Joshua looked perplexed. "When was this will made?" he asked.

"In May of last year."

"Strange that James should leave me the house. He never told me about it . . . I should have thought that Ellen would have had the Tiddenham place."

"I understand that Mr Briggs told my partner that Mrs Briggs did not like the house, and in the event of Mr Briggs' decease she would move elsewhere."

"I see. By the way, you are sure that this is the last will he made? He may have changed his mind later."

Mr Lucas shifted uneasily in his seat. "I am in a very difficult position, Mr Briggs. As the deceased's brother, no doubt you should know. On the other hand, I doubt whether any good will come of my handing on such information . . . Can you give me your word that you will treat the information I give you as strictly confidential, and that you will make no use of it before referring to me?"

Joshua promised.

"Well, then, four days ago Mr James Briggs rang up my partner, Mr Peabody, and made an appointment to see him in this office to-morrow morning, regarding the will. He told Mr Peabody that he intended making a new will, and wished to discuss the matter with him."

"He gave no reasons?"

" No."

"And no indication of the kind of change he wanted to make?"

"None at all."

"Well, Mr Lucas, I'm most grateful for your help," said Joshua, rising to go. "I'll come to-morrow, if I may, and see Mr Peabody about further details. In the meantime I've plenty to do." And having reassured the old gentleman that his confidence would not be abused, Joshua took his leave.

*   *   *   *

Joshua paid a brief call at the Black Horse for a restorative, and went on to the bank where James had kept his account.

Without any delay he was admitted to the manager's private office. This time Joshua handed over Ellen's note of introduction at once. The manager was familiar with her signature and announced himself ready to give information.

"As you see from this note," Joshua began, "I've been authorized by my sister-in-law to look into my brother's affairs, since she's not well enough to do it herself at present. Apparently she knew very little about my brother's finances, and has no idea how matters stand at present. So far we've only been through a part of his papers, and his pass-book hasn't come to light yet. It's no doubt at his office. Meantime I would be most grateful if you would give me details of my brother's account. Mrs Briggs is naturally most anxious to know."

The manager offered his condolences, and rang for a clerk. "I will just send for the particulars. I'm afraid the news will come as rather a shock to Mrs Briggs, but her husband's account here is not all that it used to be."

The manager held a whispered conversation with his clerk, who went out, and returned after a few moments with a slip of paper. The manager's eyebrows rose as he read it. He said:

"Things are worse than I recollected. When Mr Briggs transferred his account to this branch about a year ago he had about £1000 in his current account, and we handled gilt-edged securities to the value of £9000 or so for him. We held the scrip, collected the dividends, and bought and sold occasionally. For the past seven or eight months there has been only selling, a good deal of it at a loss. The proceeds were always transferred to his current account, from which he frequently drew cash, often in quite large sums at a time. He always conducted his business by letter and sent his man to collect the money, so I got no chance to discuss matters with him. Nevertheless, I felt it was perhaps my duty to warn him that his funds were becoming very low indeed, and, in fact, I telephoned him recently on the subject. He said that he knew how things stood, and that lately he had had unusually bad luck at the races. He was confident that his account would be in a healthy state before very long.

"Well," continued the manager, sighing, "it's not my business to offer advice unless it's called for. I felt that Mr Briggs was acting unwisely, but so long as there was actually no overdraft I couldn't interfere, of course. About a month ago all his stocks and shares had been sold up and the money withdrawn from the bank. Not only that. His current account fell rapidly, and we arranged a mortgage of £700 on his house. The present balance of his account is only some £400."

The manager looked at the amazement on Joshua's face with surprise. "Then you had no idea of what was happening?" he asked.

"None whatever. We all thought he was rolling in wealth. I knew that James did a certain amount of betting, but not on such a scale."

The manager was sympathetic. "It's possible, of course, that Mr. Briggs had an account elsewhere. I hope so for Mrs Briggs' sake, though I think it is unlikely."

"A most forlorn hope," sighed Joshua, bidding the manager farewell.

*　　　　　*　　　　　*　　　　　*

Meantime Ray, pacing the gravel path outside the front door at Tiddenham, was taking stock of the situation.

It occurred to him that he was pursuing his inquiries in anything but the approved style. The systematic methods of the giants of detection; the mind that functions like an X-ray contraption; the vulture's eye for the hair, the speck of dust, or the spent match which magically solves all—these, Ray reflected, were lacking. He hadn't even inspected the scene of the crime.

Without further reflection he walked round the outside of the house, past the drawing-room windows, to the open veranda, which ran along the side of the building. A pair of French windows, opening on to this veranda, stood ajar. He went in.

It was obviously the study—the room in which Briggs had been found shot. A long room, with windows opening on the garden at the back of the house as well as on the side-veranda, with several well-stocked bookcases, a leather-topped desk with a swivel-chair, and a pair of easy-chairs. On the walls were half a dozen conventional oil-colours in gilt frames. An ordinary comfortable-looking male retreat.

Ordinary, except for the small brown stain, partially hidden by one of the chairs, that disfigured the carpet, and for the larger brown stain on the seat of the chair—the chair, evidently, on which Briggs had been found sprawling with the gun between his legs.

Ray turned to the bookcases. Bound volumes of the *Art Dealers' Journal*, technical books about pictures—their restoration, preservation, and identification, an *Encyclopaedia Britannica*, a dictionary, various other works of reference—nothing out of the ordinary. Another bookcase held novels almost exclusively—a mixed bag consisting of well-thumbed works as heterogeneous as *War and Peace, Ulysses, The Moon and Sixpence*, and *Marius the Epicurean*, as well as plenty of Dickens, Thackeray, Trollope, and Wells. A dilapidated copy of Wheeler's *Social Life among Insects*, a row of Fabre's books, and a treatise on racehorses filled the top shelf.

"I suppose a really first-class sleuth would be able to construct a complete character study of the owner of these books," Ray soliloquized. "So far, James Briggs is a very shadowy creature in my mind. Perhaps the desk will be more helpful."

He sat down in the swivel-chair and tried one of the desk drawers. It was unlocked. Ray drew out a pile of miscellaneous papers and laid them on the desk. Receipted bills for electric light and gas, an old driving licence, and a gun licence lay on the top of the pile. The date of the last was the 7th of March, the previous month. Ray pocketed the licence, and tackled the rest of the papers. There were more receipts and a number of letters from Joshua, bearing the address of the George, Bingly, and Stephen's Hotel, W.C.1. They were rather formal letters to write to a brother, Ray thought; apart from a perfunctory exchange of news and inquiries about health, they were concerned with James's inability to sell Joshua's pictures in sufficient numbers. One letter referred to a meeting in the latter's London office, during which there had been a tiff. Another mentioned an abortive visit of Joshua's to Tiddenham, only to find that James was away on one of his "wretched jaunts."

As there appeared to be nothing else of interest, Ray replaced the papers and shut the drawer. The others were locked.

Altogether, the spot marked X on the plan had proved unproductive. He sauntered out into the garden again.

    *   *   *   *

A little man with a creased bronze countenance and a tattered moustache was bending over a flower-bed near the garage doing something with a hoe. He touched his cap as Ray came up.

"Nice mornin', sir," he announced, in a husky voice. As a matter of fact, it was exceptionally chilly and on the point of raining.

Ray good-naturedly agreed, however, and inquired whether the speaker were not Mr Groves, the husband of Mrs Groves, the housekeeper.

The old man nodded.

"Nasty business this accident, Groves," said Ray, removing his spectacles and polishing them assiduously.

"Ay, it is that," wheezed Groves.

"You were at the pictures when it happened, I think. I suppose you didn't see anything of Mr Briggs yesterday?"

"Only when he went out in the morning, sir. I was a-workin' on this 'ere flower-bed, and when he come to get 'is car out of the garage he says to me, joking like, 'How'd you like another five bob a week, Groves?' Not like his usual at all, he wasn't. Not so stiff. So I said, 'Very much, sir,' and he laughed and drove off to London."

"Nothing else, Groves? He didn't say when he would be back from London?"

"No, sir. That was all."

Groves resumed his work, while Ray stared vacantly at the garage. For a house of moderate size it was a big garage, with three pairs of doors; evidently it was capable of accommodating three cars. The doors were all padlocked.

"Mr Briggs' car is in there, I suppose, Groves?"

"Oh, yes, sir. Leastwise, it ought to be. I don't have nothink to do with the cars."

"Cars? Oh, yes. Mrs Briggs has a car too—the one she drove back from the cinema in, I suppose."

"That's right. Hers is in the end one. Mr Briggs, he used these two."

"He had two cars?"

"No, only one, but he used both them garages. Sometimes one, sometimes t'other."

"Rather queer that. Have you any idea why?"

"No idea, sir. Don't see why he shouldn't, though. They're the same size. Same key fits both the locks."

Ray extended questioning hands to heaven. "What manner of man is this?" he exclaimed, addressing the world in general. "A man who cleans a loaded gun aimed at his head, reads Pater and books on horse-racing, and is so free from the habit-forming habit that he swops garages for no other reason than whimsy. And, unless I deceive myself, the half has not been told." He turned to the gardener. "Believe me, friend Groves, the Saxon bishops and all their long-and-short work are not as intriguing as one of these clues.

"Always assuming that they *are* clues, and not insignificant trifles the meaning of which escapes me," he added, leaving the bewildered Groves to his hoeing.

CHAPTER IV

THE brilliant weather of the previous day had broken. Dun, white-edged clouds, like surf, were rolling athwart a grey sky, and a rising wind, sweeping through the tall trees that surrounded the house, sulked and sighed monotonously.

Ray sought sanctuary in the house. As he opened the front door he collided with Mrs Groves.

"Oh, sir!" she exclaimed. "I was just a-coming to find you. The missus says would you kindly come upstairs and speak to her?"

"Of course," replied Ray, turning down his coat collar and rubbing his hands. "She's better, I hope?"

"I wouldn't say that, Mr Ray. This trouble has fair bowled her over. . . . Please come this way."

Ray followed her upstairs, and was ushered into a spacious bedroom with a cheerful fire burning in the grate. Over the bed, which was empty but unmade, there hung a crucifix and a rosary. Ray turned to the woman sitting by the fire. Clad in a red silk dressing-gown, pale and grave, with straight, jet-black hair, Ellen Briggs looked like a Rossetti painting. Not a happy face, Ray thought, lined as though with sleeplessness, eyes lacking in lustre—yet handsome, beautiful even. And when she spoke to him her voice was low and subtle.

"You are Mr Ray, I think, a friend of my brother-in-law's?" He bowed assent. Dismissing Mrs Groves, Ellen resumed: "My housekeeper tells me you have been questioning her about the death of my husband. Please do not think me rude if I ask what you are doing here."

"May I sit down?" Ray asked. She motioned him to the chair on the opposite side of the fireplace. "Joshua did not tell you about my coming here?" he resumed.

"I believe he did say something, Mr Ray, but last night I was scarcely capable of taking much notice."

"Naturally," Ray sympathized, warming his hands at the fire. "Naturally. . . Well, Mrs Briggs, the situation is this. Yesterday your brother-in-law and I were staying at Bingly together, when he got your telegram. As you know, he came here at once, leaving me behind. This morning he sent for me, and I came over to help him. We hope to clear up a few points that are not quite plain concerning your husband's death."

She looked at him suspiciously. "So you are a detective, then?"

"Not really, Mrs Briggs, I assure you. My idea is merely to help Joshua. I hope you have no objection, and that I'm not intruding?"

Ellen Briggs sighed wearily and shook her head. "No, I haven't any objection. I merely wanted to know. . . Have you any idea who"—she hastily corrected herself—"any idea how it could have happened?"

"Like you, I'm not so sure it was an accident."

"I didn't say what I thought about it," she answered sharply. "I simply wanted to know what you think."

"I've only been here for a couple of hours, and I know hardly anything yet. In fact, I was wondering whether you could help me."

"What is it you want to know?" she asked resignedly.

"Any information about your husband would be welcome." Looking at her tired, drawn face, he added, "I'm afraid I'm tiring you, though."

"I have very little to tell about yesterday. My husband and I breakfasted together. He told me he was going up to London and would be back some time before dinner. I believe he mentioned something about going shooting one day. He seemed in quite a normal frame of mind. He went at about nine-thirty, and I didn't see him again—alive."

"At the time of your husband's death you were at the cinema, I gather?"

"Yes." Ray thought her tone a little more emphatic than the question called for.

He took off his glasses, searched for, found, and removed a non-existent particle of dust from one of the lenses. "I wonder if you would mind telling me something about the character and habits of your husband, Mrs Briggs," he said suavely. "I feel it might help solve the mystery of his death if one were to know more about him."

"Well, it sounds a strange thing to say, but I didn't know my husband in any real sense, although we've been married for a year and a half. There were difficulties, you understand. Difficulties of temperament. He was interested in business and racing, which took him away a good deal. And he was never communicative. Lately he had become more reserved than ever. And his friends—what friends he had—were not my type."

"Such as?" Ray prompted.

"Sothern. The man who took a cottage in the village at the beginning of the year. A most unpleasant, drunken individual. He used to come here frequently until recently. And the odd people that used to call on him! Only the other night—three or four days ago it was—a strange, disreputable-looking man came to the house and demanded to see my husband. They remained together in the study for quite a long time, and there appeared to be a sort of a quarrel going on. I could hear the raised voice of the stranger in the sitting-room, but I didn't hear any words. As usual, my husband told me nothing afterwards."

Ray bent forward. "Did this man give any name?"

"If so, it was to Mrs Groves, who let him in. I didn't see him."

"I will ask her. . . And your husband's other friends, Mrs Briggs?"

"Except for Sothern, he hadn't any friends down here. Of course, he knew people in London, but he didn't bring them to Tiddenham."

"But I thought his secretary. . . ."

The muscles of Ellen Briggs' face tautened. "Why!" she exclaimed. "Who told you about her?"

"Joshua said he believed she sometimes brought her work down here," said Ray, fiddling with the poker.

"And told you the rest of the story, I've no doubt. . . . Well, if you don't know already, you soon will, and there's no point in making a secret of it. This woman, Margot Fayette, was ostensibly my husband's secretary, actually his mistress. No doubt he thought he was deceiving me when he explained his absences from home by saying that he was going away on business or to race-meetings. And he even had the effrontery to bring her down here, pretending he had a lot of correspondence to do—but that you know already."

"Do you chance to know how long Mr Briggs had known this Miss Fayette?" His manner was a model of discreet commiseration.

"I believe for three or four months only. But even in so short a time there seemed to be trouble enough between them. I have an idea that she had previously been connected with Sothern. One evening the three of them were here. I went to bed early, and after I had come upstairs there was a terrific quarrel, Sothern threatening blue murder and the girl crying. It was brought to an abrupt end when Sothern walked out of the house, slamming the front door behind him. That must have been in February. Since then we haven't seen much of Sothern, although they seemed to have patched things up again."

The effort of talking had apparently exhausted Ellen Briggs. She lay back limply in her chair, regarding Ray through half-closed eyes.

"I must apologize for wearying you, Mrs Briggs," he said, rising to go. "Most inconsiderate of me. Perhaps when you are feeling better we can have another talk."

She detained him with a gesture. "One thing before you go, Mr Ray. . . You aren't connected with the police in any way?"

"I can swear to that."

"Then I can tell you something I didn't tell them. There may be nothing in it, of course. And I didn't want to mention it to the police because, you understand, it might lead to unnecessary scandal. I can rely on your discretion?"

Ray reassured her.

"Well, the last time that the Fayette girl came down here there was a row. They were in the study, supposed to be doing correspondence. I was next door in the sitting-room. I overheard them mutually accusing each other. She threatened to kill him if she ever caught him with another woman—I liked that!—and kill him in a way that would put the police off her track. I'm not sure, but I thought I heard him retort by accusing her of having been to see Sothern."

Ray looked incredulous. "You heard all this in the sitting-room? How is it that you didn't hear what passed between your husband and the mysterious stranger the other night? You were in the sitting-room and they were shouting in the study, I think?"

Ellen Briggs shifted uneasily in her chair. "Well, I must confess"— she faltered—"that I wasn't in the sitting-room the whole of the time. In fact, I. . . . listened at the study door. In these matters one's code is a little different." She smiled wanly, and Ray made a sympathetic murmur.

She resumed: "As I say, there may be nothing in it, but I should be grateful if you would find out what she was doing last night and let me know. Like you, I'm interested in clearing up the mystery of my husband's death."

"With the greatest of pleasure I'll do what you ask," replied Ray, "provided you help me with any information I want."

She nodded, and Ray continued, "An extraordinary number of quarrels took place in the house, Mrs Briggs. You have already told me of scenes between Sothern and your husband, between your husband and the mysterious stranger, and between your husband

and Miss Fayette. Mr Briggs seems to have been a quarrelsome man. You, I believe, had no scenes with him?"

"It takes two to make a quarrel, Mr Ray."

Ray nodded understandingly. "Incidentally, Mrs Briggs, were you at the cinema alone last night?"

"Yes. . . . But I don't see the connexion." She sat up in her chair, and stared at him.

"I merely want to straighten everything out. . . . And you came back here immediately the show was over, arriving at about eight?"

"Really, Mr Ray, why should I answer all these absurd questions?" she exclaimed. All her previous languor had disappeared. "Surely you're not suggesting that I—"

"I'm suggesting nothing of the kind," Ray replied firmly. "And of course you needn't answer any question of mine. But you've just told me you want my help. In order to help you I must know all the details of the behaviour of the people involved, even though most of that behaviour is irrelevant."

Ellen Briggs subsided on to the cushions again. She looked worried, as though anxiously debating what to say.

"I came out of the cinema at. . . ." The words trailed off into silence. She was staring at something behind Ray. He turned to look.

Standing just inside the door, with his hand still on the door-knob, stood a tall man with a blond beard. He carried a black attaché case.

"I'm so sorry," he said, in a velvety, somewhat foreign-sounding voice. "I see that you did not hear me knock. I trust that I do not intrude?" He smiled, and walked over to the fireplace.

Ellen returned the smile. "Of course not," she said. "You startled me a little, that's all. . . . This is Mr Ray, a friend of my brother-in-law's. This is Dr Storr, my doctor."

Dr Storr bowed from the waist, smiling. Ray merely blinked.

"I'm just going," he said. He turned to address Ellen: "You were just about to say. . . ?"

In the smoothest of tones Storr interrupted. "I am sorry, sir, but I cannot allow my patient to talk now. She is very weak and upset by this horrible accident. You will excuse, please?"

As Ray walked to the door the doctor was saying: "It was very unwise of you to get out of bed in your condition, Mrs Briggs. Please get back immediately. You must sleep now. I will give you a bromide."

*   *   *   *

Ray shut the door behind him and walked heavily down the corridor to the stairs. At the head of the staircase he turned round and tiptoed back to the door of the room he had just left.

The keyhole afforded only a restricted view of the interior, including neither the doctor nor his patient. Ray applied his ear, and waited.

For minutes, it seemed, there was complete silence. Then came a rustling sound—from the fire, maybe, or from Ellen Briggs' silk dressing-gown. And then, faintly, a low voice—Ellen's—saying, "Darling. . . darling. . . ."

And then a little cough, proceeding not from inside the room, but from a spot immediately behind him.

Ray straightened up and rotated in double-quick time. Confronting him was the pop-eyed face of Mrs Groves, distorted with wrath.

He shushed her with his finger to his lips, and signalled her away from the door, following on tiptoe.

Down in the hall Ray pressed a couple of half-crowns into Mrs Groves' floury palm. He said, grinning: "Extraordinary, the things one imagines, isn't it, Mrs Groves? Just now you thought you saw me listening outside a door, didn't you, now?"

The housekeeper smiled a wry and rascally smile. "I'm beginning to think it was only me imagination. Howsoever," she soliloquized, "I think I should ask the doctor, just in case it's serious. Seein' things ain't good for a body."

Ray withdrew the five shillings and substituted a note. Sighing, he said, "Silence, to coin a phrase, is in this instance definitely golden, I see. Now run along and attend to the cooking," he added, sniffing the air. "It seems to be burning, and, hungry as I am, I don't want charcoal biscuits for lunch."

Bestowing on him something that might almost be taken for a wink, Mrs Groves tripped off into her kitchen.

CHAPTER V

RAY collapsed with a groan into one of the easy-chairs in the sitting-room

"Oh, lord," he complained to Joshua, who had just returned from Stokeby, "I'm suffering from physical starvation, mental gluttony, and spiritual diarrhoea! What I need is a mental stomach-pump and lots and lots of good stimulating food, preferably containing mushrooms, sweetbreads, strawberries, Brussels sprouts, *pâté,* smoked salmon—"

"Stop it, man, you're making me sick!" cried Joshua.

"Served in the proper sequence, I mean," Ray explained.

Opportunely Mrs Groves appeared at the door, announcing lunch.

Over the meal they exchanged news of the morning's researches. It was not until coffee was served that the conversation took a more general turn.

"Well, Ray," observed Joshua, lighting one of his brother's opulent-looking cigars, "I hope you see daylight, because I don't."

"I see nothing," Ray retorted. "I'm a blind mouth, a gaping receptacle, a sort of human pillar-box. We haven't nearly arrived at the sorting-office stage, my dear Briggs. It isn't even collection time yet, and won't be for some little while."

"Don't you dare my-dear-Briggs me! You'll be wearing smoking-jackets and deer-stalker caps next, and sneering 'Elementary' every time I open my lips."

"On the contrary, Briggs," laughed Ray, "I'm fully aware of the importance of being distinctive. It's a problem to which I shall have to give deep attention. Proper pride forbids me to ape any of the old masters of detection. The difficulty is that they've explored every avenue of eccentricity and left no impediment unturned. There are the maimed, the halt, and the blind, females, persons so fantastically ordinary as to be incredible, and geniuses whose omniscience is such that they can detect the brand of a cigar from one whiff at a hundred yards, date a scarab, and chat nonchalantly about the more intimate mating habits of the seven-toed Siberian pine-siskin. There are lean, dark, tall, lantern-jawed, inscrutable demigods of noble—nay, royal—mien; and there are funny little old men with hirsute growths and insanitary habits. There are creatures that have the insufferable habit of dropping their final g's on the slightest provocation, and are always ordering meals that sound like Radio Paris in spate. And finally there are policemen. I'm confidently expecting to read about the detective who is bedridden, writes lyric verse in Bengali, and is able to distinguish three hundred and twenty-seven varieties of the lesser or rufous-bellied domestic cockroach.... Yes, Briggs, I'm fully alive to the necessity for a high coefficient of craziness in the detective. I do not wish to shirk my responsibilities in this direction. The difficulty is to know how to fulfil them."

Joshua's only comment was to discharge a thick screen of cigar-smoke.

"I count my blessings one by one, however," Ray went on. "For instance, heaven has bestowed upon me that which in an ordinary man would be considered a blemish. But in me, qua detective, it is a characteristic of peculiar charm, like the moustaches and pipes and disgusting habits of my rivals. It constitutes, as it were, my membership card of the Detectives' Union. In addition, it puts murderers off their guard. They never can be sure whether I'm looking at them or the other chap."

Joshua threw his cigar into the fire with a gesture of disgust.

Ray took up the implied challenge. "Oh, admittedly, being cross-eyed is only a start, but I'm beginning to develop secondary characteristics. Have you noticed, Briggs, how assiduously I polish my spectacles, blink, peer, squint, and pry? Also my ties?"

"God knows I have!" growled Joshua. "But do I have to go on listening to this?"

"Only while I sum up by saying that, until I get my man—or woman—in this case, I'm in my pre-natal stage *qua* detective; and I can't blossom properly before parturition, if you get my meaning."

Joshua looked up eagerly. "Then you think it was murder?"

"How often," Ray sighed, "do I have to tell you, Briggs, that I do *not* think until the situation is ripe for thought. Premature ratiocination results in bias, which is reason's enemy. . . . If I were to hide the pieces of a jigsaw picture puzzle round this house—in the bedrooms, living-rooms, kitchen, and odd corners—how would you set about reconstructing the picture?"

"Another rhetorical question. You tell me."

"Well, supposing you confined your activities to this room, collected all the bits of the puzzle that you could find here, and started fitting them together—"

"I would be certifiable."

"Precisely. But that's what you're expecting me to do. If I started at this juncture to make patterns of the evidence, I would *(a)* be wasting my time, and *(b)* be developing dangerous prejudices. The pale cast of thought will become me when I've collected all the data. Before then all contributions are thankfully received and salted down for inspection at a later date."

"And you don't allow yourself to speculate one little bit?" Joshua asked sceptically.

"To err is human, Briggs, and I've not yet graduated into the pantheon of super-sleuths. Wherefore my inability to refrain from a certain amount of premature conjecture."

"For the Lord's sake spill the beans!" said Joshua peevishly.

"I shall do nothing of the kind. But I don't mind telling you that the items that fascinate me most to date are the mysterious stranger who called here one night shortly before the shooting and quarrelled with James; your brother's peculiar tastes in literature; and his habits—or rather lack of habits—in the matter of garaging his car."

"I'm damned if I can see anything in that. The two garages, you say, are identical. I don't see why he should use only one of them."

"I'll tell you why. There's nothing to choose between the left-hand side of your face and the right, so far as contours, area, and repulsiveness are concerned. Yet I'll bet you always start shaving on the same side. I don't know whether you clean your teeth before shaving or after—always assuming you clean them at all—but whichever it is, I'll bet you don't vary the sequence. If we had no habits we would spend all our energy making petty decisions about matters that are properly left to the subconscious to take care of. When your brother started swopping garages, believe me he had a reason for doing so. Perhaps he was taking one of those mind-training courses."

"I wouldn't put it past him," Joshua grinned. "Are you weak-willed, unable to concentrate, unsuccessful in business? Build a master-mind in thirty easy lessons!"

"Your brother, Briggs, was a complex character. Tell me more about him."

Joshua shook his head. "I think one knows less about one's relatives than anyone else. I mean about their minds."

"For once I agree with you, Briggs. Consanguinity seems to make mental intercourse almost impossible. Relationships remain more or less at the animal or material level. Nevertheless, you know something about your brother."

"Of course. I know that he was respectable, the sort of fellow who wears a wing-collar because he likes it. When he looked at a picture he thought in terms of cheques and sales commissions. He studied the form of racehorses—unsuccessfully it seems. He even read the *Daily Mail*."

"*And* Pater," Ray cut in.

"I doubt it. You never can tell people's tastes from their libraries."

"The sort of man who knows the gold from the dross by reputation only, fills his bookcases with uncut first editions as an investment, and keeps his Gertrude Page out of sight?"

"Yes," laughed Joshua. "Of course, Margot was rather a blot on his respectability."

"And not the only blot, Briggs. But, since you mention her, what's *she* like?"

"Full of life. Absolutely Ellen's opposite. Not overeducated, I should say, but intelligent. And easy on the eyes. . . . However, you'll judge for yourself in a very little while. In fact, her train's almost due now. Come with me to the station to meet her."

"No, thanks," replied Ray. "I shall potter here. The scullion, it appears, is playing truant, and I wield a pretty dish-cloth."

"Well, *chacun á son goût.* So long!"

*   *   *   *

"A gentleman like you didn't ought to do this sort of thing," remarked Mrs Groves.

"Which sort of thing?" asked Ray, manipulating a handful of silver.

"Wiping up. Take Mr Briggs now. He wouldn't 'a' done such a thing. Beneath his dignity."

"Do you mean to suggest, Mrs Groves, that I'm undignified?" said Ray, in a grieved tone.

"Oh, no, sir. I allus know a real gentleman when I see one." She felt in her apron pocket to make sure that the note was still there. "I've me doubts that Mr Briggs was a real gentleman. As for that drunken Sothern—"

"Some of his friends *were* queer," Ray agreed. "For instance, the strange man who called a few nights ago."

"Ah, he was a rum 'un, if you like! Nasty bit of work. Been drinking, if you ask me. Said he wanted to see Mr Briggs, gruff like. 'What name shall I say?' says I. 'Hogg, Mr Hogg,' he says, 'and tell him not to keep me waiting.' And then he swore somethink horrible. Mr Briggs seemed upset when I told him who wanted to see him. And after I'd shown this here Mr Hogg into the study and shut the door I heard him shouting fit to bring the house down."

"Did you accidentally overhear what he said, Mrs Groves?" Ray asked, grinning.

"Oh, sir, you're not suggesting I would—" They both laughed. "Well," she went on, "I didn't hear anything to signify, only I heard him—Hogg—say as how he'd like to wring the master's neck, and he called him a double-crosser and I don't know what. I couldn't hear what Mr Briggs said, he speaking low and quiet."

"You showed him out again?"

"No. Mr Briggs did."

"And what did friend Hogg look like?"

"Common type of man. Dark, middling height, shabby."

"Congratulations, Mrs Groves!" cried Ray enthusiastically, patting her on the back with a plate. "You're wasting your time washing dishes, with a talent like yours for observation…. Now tell me, what sort of a face had this Hogg?"

"Well, sir, what with the light in the hall not being overbright, and him with his coat-collar turned up, and me rattled like, I didn't see much of his face, and what I saw weren't exac'ly Clark Gable."

"How did he come to the house? On foot or in a car?"

"Well, I didn't see or hear no car. Unless he left it outside in the road, I reckon he walked here."

"You're quite sure he was a stranger to Tiddenham?"

Mrs Groves shook her head emphatically. "I never set eyes on him before. Nowadays we get all sorts coming down from London. Trippers, charabang parties, and week-enders with sixpenny wedding-rings. Riff-raff!" She gave vent to her feelings by blowing her nose violently.

"Tut, tut, Mrs Groves! And do those merrymakers patronize the Tiddenham Arms?"

"Yes. There ain't no other hotel in this place."

"A very appropriate hostelry for the purpose," observed Ray, recalling the architecture and the furnishings he had seen that morning. "I wonder if Mr Hogg stayed there. Or possibly he came straight down from London by train. How far is the station from here, Mrs Groves?"

"A good half-hour's walk. Up and down trains every half-hour, seeing as how it's on the main line to St Pancras."

Ray looked at her admiringly. "Mrs Groves, you are positively the sleuth's Baedeker and the answer to a detective's prayer.... But observe, madame"—he pointed at the heap of clean crockery on the kitchen table—"I have earned my keep, isn't it?"

Mrs Groves' stolidity almost melted into kittenishness. "Go on, Mr Ray!" she cried. "You're a caution, you are, imitating the doctor like that."

Ray beamed at the tribute of this recognition. "Ah, yes, the good doctor. Sit down, rest your weary limbs, take this cigarette, and spread yourself on the subject of the family physician."

After an unequal struggle Mrs Groves gave in, accepted a cigarette from Ray's case, and sat down at the table. "And what should I know about the doctor, except that he lives in Stokeby and he's one of them foreigners?" she demanded, pulling at her cigarette as though it were a lemonade straw.

"Xenophobia is unworthy of you, Mrs Groves," Ray admonished.

"Who's she? . . . Well, as I was saying, he's an I-talian or German or somethink outlandish, and he's been looking after Mrs Briggs ever since she came here. Her health ain't too good at the best o' times and he comes here pretty often."

"He's a friend of the family's?"

"Well, he don't stay here to dinner, if that's what you mean. I don't think Mr Briggs liked him very much. Anyway, they didn't hardly ever see each other, Mr Briggs being hale and hearty and needing no doctor."

"The doctor is a bachelor?"

"Er. . . .yes."

"You hesitate, Mrs Groves. Why?"

"It ain't for me to say nothink, sir. I never listen to no scandal nor repeat what folks tell me. What's more, they may be wrong when they say as how Dr Storr ain't all he oughta be. Him and his French ways!" The housekeeper got up and crushed out her cigarette in the sink-tidy.

Ray turned shocked eyes heavenward. "Terrible. But I thought you said he was an Italian?"

"They're all the same. Polyganders!"

"Ah, Mrs Groves, what it is to be British and above these things! . . . I agree with you that repeating rumours is disgraceful. Do these scandalmongering public nuisances mention any names in connexion with our good doctor?"

"No, I've never heard of no names, though many's the time I've asked Emily Bates, what does for him."

"Ha! The doctor's housekeeper?"

"Yes. Lives out. Goes in at eight of a morning and stays till after lunch. Has his evenings to himself, he does. And Emily Bates don't have to be no detective to know he don't spend them alone, neither, having to tidy up afterwards in the morning."

"Dear me! . . . Tell me, when does the doctor go on his rounds?"

"Morning. Starts at ten or eleven; gets back at one."

"Excellent. . . . There's the doorbell, no doubt portending the arrival of Miss Fayette. . . . No, Mrs Groves, you stay here. I'll let them in."

CHAPTER VI

THE two men sat on either side of the sitting-room fire, with Margot Fayette in the middle. Outside, in a slate-coloured world, rain was streaming down and swishing, with every gust, against the windows. The trees overshadowing the house contributed to the gloom indoors—a gloom that accentuated the bright comfortableness of the fireside.

Margot was pouring out tea. Ray, with head thrown back, contemplated her behind enigmatic spectacles. He was hunting in his mind for the right epithet. Charming? Vivacious? Coquettish? All three, and more. A demi-mondaine? Hardly. A lady? He thought not. A little of both, possibly. Anyhow, a girl to throw a man off his rocker—if he were that sort of a man. Genuinely rosy cheeks for once (unless he were deceived), eyes really alive, thick, luxuriant brown hair. And a figure, clad in black silk, that was perhaps too plump to please the dispassionate eye. Ray's eye was not dispassionate.

Joshua and Margot were talking. Their conversation drifted into the arena of his consciousness. Margot was saying:

"Oh, yes, he was quite all right yesterday when I saw him." Her voice was 'French'—either a genuine accent or a very good imitation, the result of long practice, Ray decided.

Joshua requested: "Will you run through yesterday's events again, please, Miss Fayette? You've told me what happened, but Mr Ray would like to hear."

Margot bestowed a smile on Ray's recumbent figure—a smile that did not suggest a state of mourning for the deceased—and started talking. "I went to Jimmy's—Mr Briggs'—office at ten o'clock, as usual. He came in between half-past eleven and twelve—I can't remember the exact time. After looking through the letters and dictating some replies he went out to lunch with some gentlemen. It was a long business lunch, I guess, and it must have been almost three-thirty by the time he got back. He signed the letters he had dictated that morning and left soon after."

"About what time would you say?" Joshua queried.

"I don't think he stayed much longer than half an hour in the afternoon, so that makes it about four when he went."

"Anything unusual about his manner? Did he say or do anything out of the ordinary?"

"No. He was nice and cheerful. I think he was pleased about some business he transacted with the gentlemen he met at lunch."

"Are you quite sure you don't know who these gentlemen were?" Joshua inquired earnestly. He turned to Ray. "If only we could find out what passed at that meeting—"

"No," said Margot. "I don't know who they were, and I've no idea. He didn't say."

"What a pity! If he had only mentioned their names we might have cleared up the mystery by now . . . . But you must know where he went to lunch?"

Margot shook her head. "He used to go to many places. I don't know which it was."

"And the letters he wrote? Don't tell me you don't know what they were about."

Her eyes flashed. "If you talk to me like that I shall answer no more of your questions. . . . Of course, I know about his letters. They were ordinary business ones. One of them was to you. You didn't get it?" she exclaimed, seeing the startled look on Joshua's face.

Ray sprang to life. "Hell!" he cried, fishing a letter out of his pocket, and handing it to Joshua. "I'm damnably sorry. Never occurred to me it was from him, or I'd have remembered to give it to you."

They stood looking over Joshua's shoulder while he tore off the cover, and read:

> *54 Fitzwilliam Street*
> *London, W.C. 1*
> *April 1st*

Dear JOSHUA,

Thanks for your last letter. I have had no luck with your last batch of watercolours. Why don't you try painting more traditionally, and holding an exhibition? Then I could probably be of more use to you. I am sorry I was out when you looked in at the house the other day. Come along again some time.

JAMES

"It arrived for you this morning at the George," Ray explained, "and Mrs. Sawberry asked me to give it to you." They sat down again and continued drinking tea in silence. Ray pocketed the letter unobtrusively.

"Well, that doesn't get us much further," Joshua remarked. "Any questions for Miss Fayette, Ray?"

"Yes. I find it a little odd that James Briggs should have his letters to his brother typed. A little unfraternal."

Joshua laughed. "That was quite characteristic. He regarded me as a business connexion—which I was, of course."

"That's right," Margot agreed. "He always kept carbons of his letters to you. He said one should be businesslike, even with relations."

"I guess that's good enough," replied Ray. "Question number two is: how long does it take to motor from Fitzwilliam Street to this house? And, incidentally, I suppose he did motor down?"

"Well," replied Margot, "there was a good deal of traffic about at that time, so he would take about two and a half hours, I should think. Last time I motored down with Mr Briggs I think that's how long it took us."

"And," Joshua added, "he did motor down, because the police found his car in the garage last night."

"Good. Question three: Forgive me for being so rude, Miss Fayette, but were you on the best of terms with Mr Briggs? Did you ever quarrel with him?"

Margot appeared to hesitate whether to be annoyed or amused. She said, "No. We never quarrelled."

"Are you quite certain that last time you were down her you had no sort of row with him?"

"Why are you saying these things?" she cried angrily. "I tell you

I never quarrelled with him. Anyhow, what's all this to do with you or the. . . . accident?"

"Not mere idle curiosity, Miss Fayette," answered Ray firmly. "James Briggs may have taken his life or he may have been killed. In either case, it is essential to know what sort of a man he was, and what were his relationships with other people. You are one of the other people."

"Well, you're wrong if you think that because of me he—"

"I'm dealing with facts, Miss Fayette, not theories," Ray snapped.

There was a brief silence. Ray lay back, watching Margot, who was biting her lip and frowning.

"Any more questions?" Joshua demanded drily.

Ray hesitated. "No. . . unless Miss Fayette could tell us—But I'm afraid she would misunderstand my motive."

"Come on, Ray, let's have it. Miss Fayette realizes it's a matter of routine, don't you?" He appealed to Margot, who paid no attention.

"Well, then, here goes." Ray sat upright in his chair and confronted Margot with a challenging stare. He said, evenly, "Miss Fayette, where were you between half-past five and half-past seven last night?"

She laughed loudly. "That's an easy one. I was in the office till six, and then went straight to the flat of a girl friend of mine in Kensington. I was with her there the whole evening." She gave a slight start. "Here, what are you insinuating now?" she cried.

"Nothing whatever," Ray grinned. "When a detective can't think of any sensible question to ask he asks a few irrelevant ones, just as padding. You can't expect him to ring the bell every time."

"Well," Margot commented acidly, "you're the first detective I've ever had the honour to meet, and so far I'm speechless with admiration at the way you conceal your master-mind."

Ray smiled his sweetest smile. "Naturally. We sleuths prise up our bushels gradually, you know, to avoid dazzling our victims. Makes people dashed uncomfortable if you reveal your brilliance in one blinding flash. I mean to say, *noblesse oblige*, the Public School spirit, and—"

Margot started laughing in spite of herself.

Joshua groaned. "For God's sake," he pleaded, addressing Margot, "don't encourage him! When he starts talking about himself heaven, earth, and hell won't stop him."

"Hush, Briggs. I am about to ask Miss Fayette a question which is positively my last. Would you be so kind as to tell me the name and address of the friend with whom you spent last evening?"

This time there was no hesitation. "No!" she shouted. "I'll see you damned first! What the hell do you mean by dragging me here"—she turned to Joshua—"to be cross-questioned by this . . . this lunatic, who calls himself a detective? You said you wanted my help, instead of which this boss-eyed goop practically accuses me of—"

"Murder in the first degree!"

She stared at him open-mouthed. Joshua stood spluttering.

"Sh! Not just yet!" Ray took off his spectacles beamed, pushed his face to within a foot of Margot's, and said, "Not just yet, Miss Fayette . . . . I may be as boss-eyed as a chameleon, but I swear that, within the next forty-eight hours, I'll expose you and what you're hiding.

"And that, ladies and gentlemen," he added, on his way out, "is not Jethro's rash vow."

*　　　　*　　　　*　　　　*

Joshua followed him out into the hall.

"Look here, Ray," he expostulated, "what did you want to say a thing like that for?"

"Briggs," admonished Ray, "you're biased. A pretty girl comes along, and in two shakes you're practically a moron, incapable of consecutive thought."

"But surely you don't really think she—"

"Never mind what I think. I've got work to do. Now, you stay here and get that name and address out her—I don't care how you do it—while I amuse myself elsewhere."

"Sothern?"

"Very likely."

"Now you're talking sense," said Joshua. "And I'll extract that name and address or succumb in the attempt."

"Or both," Ray added, as Joshua retreated into the sitting-room.

*　　　　*　　　　*　　　　*

Ray switched on the hall light. Taking from his pocket the piece of blotting-paper that he had found in the sitting-room that morning, he held it up to the hall mirror.

The words on the paper constituted three distinct sections, placed at different angles and partially superimposed. Evidently the blotter had been applied three times during the writing of the letter or letters.

A thick nib had been used, and the characters stood out fairly boldly, except where the ink had partially dried before blotting.

Ray wrote the words down one by one in his notebook as he deciphered them. When he had finished the entry read :

March 31st

DEAR MAR

I'm s   y you feel   o about Margot
me. I'm afraid   done about it and it
       ot my fault   me.
should remain frie   s
 I will be in   6.45   orrow night.   and
me and have a ch   ll be alone

Yours,

JAMES BRIGGS

He slowly folded the blotting-paper and replaced it in his notebook. As he did so he heard a small sound, a sort of creak, coming from upstairs. Turning quickly, he was just in time to see something white vanish over the landing balustrade. Somebody had been watching him.

Putting his notebook in his pocket, he walked deliberately to the study door, opened it, and closed it again with a bang. Then, after waiting a few seconds, he walked noiselessly back to the stairs, mounting them on tiptoe. The landing was empty. He came to the door of Ellen Briggs' room.

A line of light showed underneath the door. He put his eye to the keyhole. There was nothing to see, only the drawn curtains of the window and a chest of drawers. He tried listening. The only sound was a kind of scratching, as of a pen-nib on coarse paper. After a few moments the scratching ceased, and there came the sound of footsteps approaching the door.

Ray rushed for cover. Providentially a large clothespress stood near the corner of the landing, providing a convenient recess between itself and the return wall. Into this niche Ray slipped, and waited.

The bedroom door did not open, but he heard a faint ringing in one of the downstairs rooms. Presently there came a ponderous footfall on the stairs. Ray peeped. Mrs Groves' head appeared at the head of the stairs and bobbed across the landing. She knocked at Ellen Briggs' door and went in, obligingly leaving it ajar.

Ray strained to hear what passed, but he caught only the sound of the housekeeper's voice as she departed, saying, "Yes'm, he'll post it." She carried a letter in her hand.

As soon as he heard the sound of the kitchen door closing behind Mrs Groves Ray came out of his hiding place and crept down to the hall, where he put on his overcoat and let himself out by the front door.

CHAPTER VII

IT was twilight. Ray stood on the doorstep, getting what shelter he could from the canopy that projected over the entrance. To fill in time he fished out his pipe with half-numbed fingers, filled it, lit up, stuffed his hands deep into his pockets, and awaited developments.

After ten minutes that seemed twenty came the wished-for footsteps crunching on gravel. Groves, clad in mackintosh and cloth cap, rounded the house. Ray waited till he had got on to the road, then followed.

As he approached Groves looked round. "Oh, it's you, sir," he said. "Dirty night for a gentleman to go walking, ain't it?" he added, as Ray joined him.

"That goes for you too, Groves," retorted Ray. "What brings you forth?"

They walked on together. "I'm going to the post, sir, up in the village," Groves explained.

"Ha!" cried Ray. "That's splendid. Lend an ear, Groves. I feel disturbed with a strange internal conflict."

"Meaning indigestion, sir?"

"No levity, Groves. Listen. My lower self says: 'Don't be a sap. Why shouldn't you let him trudge all the weary way to the post, loud though the tempest rage? Why not let him suffer? He probably deserves to!' And then, Groves, my higher self says: 'No. Give! Give of yourself till it hurts!' Groves, I'm glad to tell you that my better self has won. I consent. I will do it for you."

"Do what, sir?" asked Groves apprehensively.

"Post your letter," said Ray, putting out his hand.

"Oh, no, sir, thanking you all the same."

"What?" cried Ray. "You spurn this self-sacrificing offer? Groves, I'm deeply grieved. Embittered even."

Groves apologized: "Sorry, sir, but Mrs Briggs was very partic'lar I should post it myself."

"Why this absurd request?"

"Well, it's like this 'ere. Mrs Briggs told my missus as how the doctor wanted to know extra special how she was feeling, and this 'ere letter's asking 'im to call in the morning, 'cause she ain't feeling very good."

"Very interesting. But I still don't see why I shouldn't undertake this errand of mercy."

"She said as how the letter were very important and I was to post it myself," said Groves stubbornly.

They walked on together for a few moments in silence.

"Just where is this pillar-box?" Ray inquired suddenly.

"Just arter we get to the pub."

"Ah!" murmured Ray, and there was another silence.

They stopped while Ray relit his pipe. "Groves," he said, scrutinizing the gardener's face with the help of the lit match, "how much do you get a week?"

"One pound fifteen. And me missus gets the same, making three pound ten in all, and free lodging thrown in."

Ray groaned. "I'm shocked. For a man of your sterling worth

to get so little is disgraceful. An apt commentary on our so-called economic system."

"Well there's folks what's worse off."

"Too true. But has it never struck you, Groves, that wealth is distributed without reference to merit, or services rendered to society, or even common sense? Why is my pocket-book dripping with dough and yours an aching void?"

"I ain't got a pocket-book."

"Don't quibble. I'll tell you why. Because my father floated dud companies and snitched your father's savings. My late revered parent was a social menace; yours a pillar of society. Mine left me wads of the stuff; yours left you none."

"My father weren't no pillar of society."

"Immaterial. You don't get my drift, Groves. I propose to adjust, if ever so slightly, this anomaly, this gross injustice. Groves, accept this trifling tribute from the bloated capitalist's offspring."

Groves put out an eager hand.

"One moment. I ask nothing in return but—"

"No, sir." Groves put his hand back in his pocket. There was no more conversation till they got within sight of Tiddenham Arms.

"Bearing in mind your general character," Ray observed sadly, "I should put you down as a staunch teetotaller. What a pity!"

Groves began to hum and haw. "Well—er—I ain't what you'd call a reg'lar drinker, but—"

"Good enough!" cried Ray, thrusting wide the door of the public bar and shepherding the wavering gardener across the threshold.

*　　　　　*　　　　　*　　　　　*

The *clientèle* of the Tiddenham Arms were already present in some force. A knot of customers, enveloped in a haze of tobacco-smoke was engaged in desultory conversation and in propping up the bar counter behind which officiated the buxom Mrs Greene.

"What's your fancy, Groves?" asked Ray, beaming upon their hostess. "An angel's kiss, pink champagne, a starboard light? Name it!"

"Mild and bitter," said Groves bathetically.

"Make it two pint pots," Ray sighed, bestowing a pitying look on his companion.

"Excuse me one minute, Groves," he said, as soon as the drinks arrived. "I'll be with you anon." He disappeared through the door leading to the hall, Mrs Greene following.

"Will you be in to supper?" she asked.

"Hope so, but can't say," replied Ray breathlessly. "Mrs Greene, will you do me a tremendous favour? Don't let old Groves go. I'll be back with him in three minutes. Meantime keep him, on any pretext. And lend me the local telephone directory, please."

Mrs Greene opened the drawer in the hall table, took out a telephone directory, and handed it to him.

"You *are* funny," she laughed, and went back to the bar.

Three minutes had elapsed, and Ray had not yet returned. Groves plonked down his pint pot and got up to go.

"That will be one and tuppence, Mr Groves," said Mrs Greene in a matter-of-fact voice.

Groves wheeled round and confronted the landlady of the Arms with a face in which bewilderment and rage struggled for mastery.

"The gentleman appears to have gone, and I must ask you to pay for the drinks," said Mrs Greene.

"What?" he spluttered. "For 'is too?" He pointed an unsteady finger at Ray's full tankard.

"Well, he hasn't touched it. You may as well drink it and get your money's worth." She pushed the beer over to him. "Of course," she added, "he may very likely come back. Why not wait a little while?"

At that moment Ray walked in. His face wore a look of bliss. Smiting Groves on the back, he sat down on a stool and asked Mrs Greene for a gin-and-lime.

To Groves he said: "Confoundedly sorry. Slight indisposition. Finish that one and have another. . . lots more."

"They wanted me to pay," Groves grumbled.

Ray shot an inquiring glance at Mrs Greene, who winked back.

"Ah," he exclaimed, "I see! A slight misunderstanding. Don't sulk, Groves, nobody wants you to pay. Hostess, kindly give the gentleman a double-X to cheer him up."

Ray directed his attention to the rest of the company. A swain in a bowler and a double-breasted serge suit was demonstrating a trick to an appreciative audience. He held a ten-shilling note tight against his glass, and pressed the lighted end of a cigarette against the paper, which was not even scorched. A murmur of approval greeted this performance.

"Superb!" cried Ray. "Excellently well done. I see you are skilled in the magical art. Do me the honour of accepting a half-pint of the best as a small token of appreciation."

The youth's self-congratulatory grin gave place to a look of embarrassed wonder. Mrs Greene executed the order, and the crowd drifted into a circle round Ray and Groves.

"As one magician to another," continued Ray, still addressing the young man, "you know the Sergeivitch-Borakovsky levitation trick, of course?"

"No," the youth faltered.

"You astonish me. For an illusionist of your calibre not to know the celebrated S-B trick is a minor tragedy. A state of affairs that must be remedied at once. . . . Gentlemen," Ray cried, "would you like to witness this remarkable feat?"

There was a chorus of ayes, ahs, and yesses.

"Then watch me closely. For this trick I must have any small object." He turned to Groves. "Let's see what this gentleman's pocket contains."

Before the gardener, who was by this time half-way through his double-X and slightly fuddled, could resist, Ray had thrust his hand into Groves' mackintosh pocket and removed the letter. Without looking at it he held it up in front of Mrs Greene.

"Be good enough to describe this object," he said.

"It's a letter addressed to Dr Storr at Stokeby."

"Very good." He turned up his cuffs, bent down, pulled up a trouser-leg, and tucked the letter in the top of his sock.

"Now stand back and watch me very closely."

Ray extended his arms, shook down his trouser-leg, and started revolving slowly.

"Now, sir," he said to the young man in the double-breasted serge, "kindly feel in my right-hand jacket-pocket."

The awed youth promptly obeyed, felt in the pocket indicated, and extracted a letter.

"Why, it's the letter addressed to Dr Storr!" he gasped.

"'Ere," growled Groves, rising unsteadily, "gimme that letter, d'yer hear?"

Ray handed it over to Groves, who made for the door, grumbling. Ray saw him out into the road. "That's right, Groves," he said. "Post your letter before it's too late, and then, I think, you had better go home."

"You bet I will," Groves snorted indignantly.

Ray bent down, attended to his sock, and re-entered the bar. A heated discussion was going on.

"I tell you he might a been in league with the bloke what's just gone out," a man in dungarees was saying.

"What if he was?" retorted the serge suit. "How did the letter get from 'is leg to 'is pocket? Answer that one."

"Easy," cried the dungarees. "There was two letters. The toff 'ad one of 'em in 'is coat-pocket all the time."

"You mean the letter didn't go from 'is sock to 'is pocket at all?"

"That's right. What's more, I bet it's still there."

Ray coughed, strolled back to the counter, and finished his gin-and-lime. An unnatural quiet filled the bar.

"That'll be exactly three shillings," observed Mrs Greene.

He laid the money on the counter and turned round. Every one's attention was respectfully but insistently directed upon the lower part of his person.

"We was just wondering, sir, if you'd mind showing us your sock. This here gentleman"—the serge suit pointed to the dungarees—"is septic."

"*Mot juste,*" Ray commented.

"Please," the serge suit pleaded, "show 'im where 'e gets off."

"Doubting Thomas," said Ray witheringly, and hoiked up both trouser-legs to the knee. "Now, after that disgusting exhibition, I really must tear myself away."

"And let that be a lesson to you," he said over his shoulder to the dungarees, "O ye of little faith!"

CHAPTER VIII

TWO men under umbrellas stood on the up platform of Tiddenham Junction Station, watching the rear lamp of the six-fifty to St Pancras glide into the mouth of the tunnel.

One of them was Joshua Briggs, who had just been seeing Margot off to London. He held in his hand the piece of paper she had just given him. On it she had written:

> *Miss P. Starke,*
> *13 Pilchester Terrace,*
> *S. Kensington*

Joshua pocketed the paper and walked off the platform. At the station entrance he encountered the other man.

"Good evening, Dr Storr," greeted Joshua. "What brings you this way?"

The doctor bowed stiffly. "I have been accompanying a patient of mine to the station. She is an old lady who lives in Tiddenham, and she is going to the South Coast for her health. What a horrible climate you have!" He smilingly indicated the rain-drenched darkness that confronted them.

"Filthy," Joshua agreed, buttoning up his coat-collar. "By the way, doctor, we had practically no opportunity to talk last night, and there are some points I should like to go over with you when you can spare the time."

Dr. Storr shrugged his shoulders and made a deprecatory gesture with his hands. "You mean in connexion with the regrettable accident? I doubt whether I can be of assistance to you, Mr Briggs."

"Just one or two points," Joshua cajoled. "Come along with me now to the house and have a drink—it's more or less on your way."

"I am very sorry, but I am expecting to be called to a case at any moment. You understand?"

"I tell you what. We'll look in at the Tiddenham Arms. It's on the Bingly road. And we can have a chat over a glass of beer. My friend Ray is probably there, and I'd like you to meet him."

At once the doctor looked interested. He said: "Mr Ray? Ah, that is the gentleman I met this morning, with strabismus and untidy clothes, I think! Yes, I will come with you for a few moments."

A short while later their cars pulled up outside the Tiddenham Arms. Joshua led the doctor through into the hall, where Mrs Greene appeared after a moment.

"Mr Ray went out a little while ago," she explained "and he asked me to tell anyone who wanted him to wait in his room. He said he'd be back in five or ten minutes."

"We'll go up and wait for him," said Joshua.

Mrs Greene summoned a boy, who showed them up to Ray's room, where they ordered drinks and made themselves as comfortable as possible on a settee with broken springs.

"Well, doctor," Joshua began, after two slender glasses of lager had arrived, "what's your frank opinion about my brother's death?"

"Mrs Briggs is my patient. I hardly ever saw her husband, and I know hardly anything about him. How can I express an opinion?"

"But," Joshua persisted, "you saw the position of the body and the gun, and you examined the wounds. What conclusion did you come to as to the cause of death?"

"I saw nothing to contradict the belief that he was shot with the gun that was found lying at his feet."

"Of course. But from the nature of the wounds do you think he could have shot himself, accidentally or intentionally? Because, if he couldn't have done so, it's murder."

Dr Storr drained the remainder of his glass at one gulp, and wiped his beard nervously with a silk handkerchief.

"As you are the dead man's brother, I feel I can give you my unofficial opinion. But it is quite confidential, please."

Joshua gave the desired assurances, and the doctor continued: "Well, then, take the theory of accident. Mr Briggs is killed while he is cleaning a gun, a loaded gun, aimed at his head. But Mr Briggs is not a child; he is a man of the world—a business man. If it is true that he knew little about firearms, it is also true that he knew that they are dangerous when loaded. It follows that it was not an accident—yes?"

"Go on," Joshua prompted.

"Next, take suicide. As I said before, I know very little about Mr Briggs' private life, and I cannot imagine what the motive could be, unless it was something to do with money—I have heard he was a betting man. Let us assume that he has lost very heavily and decides to kill himself. The only convenient weapon is the gun. He puts the cleaning materials at his side, in order to stage an accident—he does not like it to be thought that he committed suicide. Now, the gun is a large and heavy object. One could not level it at one's head conveniently, so—But it is quite easy to put the gun between one's knees, so"—he demonstrated with a cushion—"to bend down, point the barrel at one's head, and pull the trigger, so."

There was an ear-shattering report, followed by the tinkle of falling glass.

The doctor sprang up, collapsed in mid-air, and fell in a heap on to the sofa.

*   *   *   *

From somewhere near the door there came a small chuckle. Joshua wheeled round.

By the open door stood Ray. His hair was dripping, and his overcoat was soaked. An insane smile irradiated his face.

"Such bad nerves," he said, in a matter-of-fact voice, taking off his overcoat and draping it over the head of the bed.

Ray went on: "Just run downstairs, Briggs, and fetch a double brandy for the doctor. Can't you see the poor devil's fainted?. . . And you look as though you could do with one as well."

Joshua stared at the doctor, who had revived to the extent of rubbing his eyes, and then at the smashed table-lamp on the floor.

"Yes," Ray apologized, "damnably careless of me."

Dr Storr sat up and drew a white hand across his forehead. "What happened? . . . .Where's Briggs?" he cried.

"He's gone to get you a drink," replied Ray, sitting down on the bed. "Everything's all right. Sit back and rest."

"But the gun . . . . the shot?"

"Regrettable accident on part of self. Knocked over table-lamp owing to undue haste to join party. Sincere apologies."

A somewhat restored Joshua appeared at the door, bearing a couple of brandies and a soda siphon.

Ray, sitting on the bed drying his hair on a towel, watched the two men on the sofa, gulping down their brandy in silence.

"Ray," cried Joshua, putting his empty glass on the floor, "you're the most infuriating, facetious, and infantile ass I've ever had the misfortune to meet!"

Ray stopped rubbing his hair. It stood up in a halo of blond spikes, like the crown of the figure of Justice on the Old Bailey. He smiled that broad smile which he reserved for more stressful moments.

"Briggs," he purred, "within the next, let us say"—he paused to make a brief calculation—"forty-five hours I'll make you eat those words. Like David in Gath, I may look a fool and behave like one, but—"

"You see what I mean?" snapped Joshua, addressing the doctor. "Come, I think we'll get out of here!"

Ray held up his hand. "I believe you were discussing the possibility of suicide, doctor, when I rudely intervened. Pray continue."

"Really, I must be going. I have a patient." He stood up.

"Talking of patients, how is Mrs Briggs?"

"Not at all well, I fear. Her husband's—"

"Suicide?" Ray cut in.

"Yes, I think it was very likely suicide. Her husband's death has upset her nerves very much indeed. She does not appear to be very ill, perhaps, and she is physically quite strong. But psychologically"—he sighed—"I am afraid she may become a neurotic subject. Perhaps having delusions, even."

"Very sad," said Ray sceptically, watching the doctor's face in the mirror, in front of which Ray was combing his hair.

Dr Storr buttoned up his overcoat and pulled on his gloves. At least six feet two, massively built, and not unhandsome, he cut an impressive figure. "All the same," said Ray to himself, "you passed out as easily as a Victorian miss." Aloud he said: "Just one question, doctor. When did James Briggs die?"

"It is very difficult to say. In detective stories they can tell so easily, but in real life. . . ." He spread his hands.

"Come, now," Ray insisted, "you must have some idea. You were second on the scene, and you were the first medical man to view the body. If you can't help us, who can?"

"So much depends on the conditions. There was a fire in the grate, but it had burned out. No one knows how long the fire was alight after he died, and how long it was may make a great difference to my estimate. Also his state of health, with which I am not familiar, would affect the time it took for rigor mortis to set in. Allowing for all these factors as far as I can, I would still put the death at not later than six o'clock."

Ray made a note in his pocket-book. "You're sure of that, doctor?" he asked.

"As sure as one can be in these matters."

Ray accompanied the doctor as far as the stair-head. Joshua went downstairs with him, apologizing for Ray's behaviour.

"It was entirely my fault," said Dr Storr politely. "It was ridiculous to have fainted. I have been working too hard." He bowed. "Good night, sir."

Joshua shut the door and mounted the stairs with a purposeful tread.

*　　　　　*　　　　　*　　　　　*

He found Ray lying on the bed, convulsed with internal laughter.

"Ray, you're fired!"

There came no answer.

Joshua resumed: "You think murder's a joke, an opportunity to play schoolboy tricks on people. You put every one's back up with your facetious prattle, accuse the wrong people, and waste your time on wild-goose chases when there are important clues to follow up. Sothern, for instance. Have you been to see him about that letter?"

The prostrate figure on the bed shook its head.

"Well, I'm sorry I asked you to help me. What have you done so far, except find a bit of blotting-paper that would have been found anyhow, and mess up things generally?"

For answer Ray stretched out a hand, in which he held a piece of folded notepaper.

Snorting with annoyance, Joshua turned his back and made for the door. Ray, who was there before him, planted himself in the opening and proffered the paper again.

This time Joshua took it and read:

Tiddenham,

April 2nd

R. is still here spying. M.F. came this afternoon. I heard R. ask her whether she quarrelled with J., and of course she denied it. It was too risky to stay and hear more of their conversation. I'm sure the police think it was accident or suicide, but R. isn't satisfied. For God's sake stick to the F.D.S. theory. Also think of a way of getting R. away from here without arousing suspicion.

E.B.

Before Joshua had finished reading Ray was back on the bed, snuggling in the eiderdown.

Joshua sat down on the sofa. "This is your writing. Another of your little games, I suppose?" he said hoarsely.

"My little games, Briggs, have more point to them than you would imagine. One of them produced this true copy of a letter written by your sister-in-law to our good doctor this evening. The original is now in the post."

On this occasion Ray could not complain of any lack of appreciation. His friend's Adam's apple was working up and down like a piston.

At length Joshua found his voice and said: "I can't see how you—"

"We have our little methods."

"What do you make of it?"

"It seems fairly clear. Let's have your version," said Ray.

"R. obviously stands for you, M.F. for Margot, J. for James. What do you make of the F.D.S. theory?"

"Not much doubt about that, I think," replied Ray. "The doctor was very keen on the suicide idea. F.D.S. suggests *felo de se* to me."

"But if she tells the doctor to stick to the suicide theory, and to get you out of the way because you suspect it wasn't suicide—it means . . . . murder!"

"You go too fast, Briggs. A little while ago you were sure that Sothern was our man. Now you switch over to the doctor—or is it Ellen? To-morrow it will be someone else. We haven't gathered together all the bits of our jigsaw puzzle yet. You can amuse yourself piecing together the bits we've collected so far, if you like. I'm after new ones."

"But," Joshua persisted, "this letter almost amounts to a confession. We've more or less caught them red-handed. Whereas, in Sothern's case, how do we know he got that letter? There's no conclusive evidence against Sothern so far. This letter is real evidence."

"Oh, really? Of what?"

"Murder, of course."

"Nonsense, Briggs. I can think of at least two other explanations of this note—neither of which I'm going to discuss now."

Joshua sat on the sofa, reading and re-reading the letter, with a perplexed look on his face.

"And that's not the only letter the doctor will get in the morning," Ray announced idly.

"What! You intercepted another letter? From her?"

Ray, ignoring the interruption, went on, "The envelope bears a Tiddenham postmark and was posted by Groves. . . . I'd give a lot to see Storr's face when he opens it!"

Joshua cried in an agonized voice: "For God's sake, Jethro, please!"

"It contains three sheets of thin brown paper. And at the bottom of each is a printed testimony to the effect that it has been impregnated with disinfectant!"

CHAPTER IX

DON'T you agree with my description of this place?" asked Ray, wrestling with a chop.

Joshua surveyed the dining-room of the Arms with a somewhat jaundiced eye.

"Observe, Briggs, the abomination of tessellation underfoot," Ray continued, pointing with his fork at the jazz linoleum. "And the unkindly light, encased in a contraption that looks like frozen lightnings secured with chromium-plated trouser buttons. If you can bear it, glance at the maculated wallpaper, and note the noxious weeds, tied with pink ribands, that sprout from every corner. And finally, if you want to lose your appetite altogether, notice this photogravure, in a gravy-coloured frame, entitled Sunset over Loch Lomond; or, Love's Delight."

"It's the sort of room," said Joshua, "that my brother would probably have liked."

"Odd, these family differences. For instance, I have a brother who's practically brainless."

They both burst out laughing.

The dining-room door opened. Ray recognized Mrs Greene's voice saying outside, "Your usual table, Mr Sothern, in the corner."

Sothern, in a smart dark suit, walked in, and, recognizing Joshua, came over to their table. Bestowing a curt nod on Ray, he said to Joshua, "Tried to see you this morning, Briggs, but missed you."

Joshua invited Sothern to join them. After a moment of hesitation he accepted and sat down.

"Sorry about your brother. Nasty business," he said.

"I didn't know you two knew each other," Ray lied.

"We've met in town," Joshua explained, "at James's office occasionally and at a party once, I think."

A somewhat uncomfortable silence followed.

Joshua was the first to speak. Turning to Sothern, he asked casually, "By the way, did you get a letter or a note from my brother yesterday or the day before?"

Sothern looked surprised. "No," he said. "What makes you ask?"

Joshua glanced at Ray, who was absorbed in the act of interring breadcrumbs in the salt-cellar.

"Nothing," replied Joshua lamely. "It merely occurred to me that if you had heard from him the letter might have thrown some light on his state of mind."

Ray patted a neat mound of salt into shape, marking the site of the burial. "Being a bachelor, Mr Sothern," he said, without looking up, "I suppose you dine here pretty often."

"I do. What of it?" came the curt reply.

"You made an exception of last night, Mrs Greene tells me," Ray lied again.

"Why not?" he demanded truculently. "I don't come here regularly every evening. What are you driving at, anyhow?"

Ray stared at him intently. "Not what you think," he said. "I asked whether you dine here often because it occurred to me that you might have met a man who, I believe, was staying here. Name of Hogg."

Sothern was in the act of raising a glass of beer to his lips. For a split second—but long enough for Ray to notice the fact—Sothern's hand stopped in mid-air. He took a long draught, and set down the glass on the table. His face betrayed no interest in what Ray had said.

"No," he said evenly, "I haven't come across this—what did you say his name was? Is he a friend of yours?"

Ray shook his head. "Of the late James Briggs. And since you were also one of Briggs' friends, it seemed possible that you might know each other."

"Never heard the name. I wasn't so intimate with Briggs that I knew all his friends." Sothern's truculence had now disappeared; he seemed preoccupied. "Well," he inquired, after a long pause, "have you solved the mystery? Was it accident, suicide, or murder?"

Ray grinned. "The house is divided on the question. Briggs here is in favour of murder. His sister-in-law apparently adheres to the suicide theory. So does her physician, Dr Storr. As for Margot—yes, I think Margot believes it was murder. And I half gathered from our interview this morning, Mr Sothern, that you had leanings towards the accident school of thought."

"Me? No. I don't know what to think. I'm not at all sure that it wasn't suicide."

"You mentioned," said Ray, "that he had made an appointment to go shooting with you today. He would hardly have done so if he were contemplating suicide. I think you said he rang you up to make this appointment the day before yesterday?"

"That's right. But something may have happened meanwhile to

make him want to do away with himself."

"Possibly.... possibly," mused Ray. Abruptly changing the subject, he said to Sothern, "Nice place, Tiddenham. Do you bask in its rural delights, Mr Sothern, or does the Metropolis claim you daily?"

"Unfortunately it does."

"Ah!" Ray exclaimed. "That might explain why James Briggs wrote a note rather than phoned you—because when he rang you up you weren't in. A little point that had been puzzling me."

"Note? What note?" Sothern demanded furiously. "Hell! Haven't I told you Briggs didn't send me any note?" He laid down his knife and fork with a clatter.

Ray put his notebook on the table in front of Sothern. The book lay open at the page on which were transcribed the words on the blotter.

Once again Ray watched Sothern's face intently. It was not a pleasant sight. It had the pinkness not of health, but of heavy drinking. The black smudge of a moustache and the thin mouth lent a sort of ferocity to the ordinariness of the remainder. It was not a face that lacked control, Ray thought. Anyhow, if fear or guilt lay behind that countenance they were, at that moment, well concealed.

Sothern turned to Joshua in exasperation. "What the devil's this fellow up to?" he cried. "Is he mad, or is this a newspaper competition?"

"Neither," replied Joshua. "This is a copy, taken from the blotting-paper he used, of parts of a letter that James wrote you the day before he died—on March 31st."

Sothern returned Ray's stare with interest. "I tell you this letter was never delivered."

Ray pounced. "Ah, then, it was written to you!"

For a moment it seemed that a chink had been found in Sothern's armour. "Er . . . . no!" he stammered. Then more collectedly, "You're trying to trap me. But you won't, see?" He got up. "I think I've had enough of your company for one day. And as for this"—he indicated Ray—"I've had far too much."

Ray laughed. "You haven't finished your pudding," he called out after Sothern's retreating figure.

The only reply was a slamming of the door.

Joshua broke the silence. "A typical conclusion to an interview with Jethro Ray," he commented drily.

"It's getting quite monotonous," Ray chuckled, taking a big handkerchief from his pocket. "Which is all to the good. For remember, Briggs, that the angry man is vulnerable."

Sothern's empty beer-glass lay on the table. Ray wrapped it gingerly in the handkerchief and transferred it to his pocket.

"And that, Briggs," he said, "is the professional touch, that was."

*   *   *   *

"No," said Ray emphatically. "I will not talk to you about the doctor and Ellen Briggs. I will even restrain myself from tackling Mrs Greene tonight on the subject of Hogg. And I flatly refuse to go out into the tempest again to investigate the alibi, if any, of Mr Sothern. Sufficient unto the day."

"Extraordinary thing," observed Joshua tritely, lighting a cigar, "that this time last night we were sitting round a fire just like this in a pub, talking and smoking. It seems about six months ago."

"There are differences, Briggs. For instance, you were wearing a red tie—now it's black. Why, I don't know, for you don't seem prostrated with sorrow. Last night's was an aromatic log fire; tonight's is made of stinking coke from Stokeby gasworks. And this room! How does your painter's soul react?"

"Not so unfavourably. I make my best pictures of the worst-designed buildings. Beautiful architecture makes a dull subject for the painter."

Ray agreed. "You find your best material in disgusting slums and industrial areas, and would sooner paint a refuse destructor than the Parthenon. And quite right too, Briggs. The Parthenon is quite capable of standing on its own aesthetic plinth without your help. Whereas the incinerator needs you. . . . . You're pretty keen on your job, aren't you?" he added.

"I guess so."

"Nothing else matters?"

"Hardly anything. A little wenching, a little boozing, and a little reading occasionally. But painting's the thing. I'd sell my soul to paint as well as Picasso, or De Chirico, or even Dali and Ernst. In fact, as soon as this affair's settled up I'm off to Paris to get down to things thoroughly. There's more real art in Paris than in the rest of the world put together."

"Well," said Ray, "let's see what the morrow brings forth. By this time tomorrow night I hope to have collected the remaining evidence. I shall then spend several hours in travail, ending, I trust, with the birth of my first-born solution. And you, Briggs, who are, so to say, its father-elect, will gather together a large audience for me to exhibit my beautiful creation to. And when that ceremony is over you can desert me as soon as you like and dash off to Paris."

"And if you fail?"

"I'll be faithful to archaeology, and never so much as glance at crime again."

PART TWO

CHAPTER X

ON the morning of April the third the parish of Tiddenham lay beneath a wind-swept and cloud-garnished firmament in which a well-intentioned sun strove vainly to shine.

Groves pondered his daffodils with the eye of sorrow. Bent, mud-bespattered, and bedraggled, their appearance corresponded exactly with the gardener's mood—a mood compounded of a hang-over and a domestic squall.

"Double-X," he muttered, in a tone of withering contempt.

"Don't!" said a voice behind him. "It's a bad habit."

The gardener looked round with an anguished expression on his face.

"Why this *de profundis* look?" asked Ray gaily.

Groves, feeling that this question called for no reply, started plying a rake. At this juncture Joshua Briggs strolled up, whistling.

"Unlike Groves," said Ray, "you don't seem weighed down with *Weltschmerz*. I trust you've fuelled yourself for a strenuous morning?"

Joshua nodded. "I'm Watson and Hastings rolled into one. What are my orders?"

"First, address yourself to Groves, who for some reason looks upon me with distaste, and cause him to produce tools?"

"Tools? What sort of tools?"

"Any convincing-looking implements not of the gardening kind —hammers, screw-drivers, pliers, gimlets, bradawls . . . ."

"What for?"

"Wait and see."

"More mystery," laughed Joshua. "This doesn't seem exactly the time to start a new hobby, but the great must be humoured, I suppose . . . . Well, Groves, what about it?"

The gardener sighed, and led the way to a shed at the back of the garden. A bench littered with woodworking instruments stood in the midst of a heap of shavings.

"Splendid!" cried Ray, collecting a handful of tools. "And this bag will do nicely to put them in."

"Now," he continued, having dumped the tool-bag in the back of Joshua's car, "off we go. Goodbye, Groves! And try a small tomato-juice laced with Worcester sauce. The entire school of Philosophic Pessimism owes its existence to neglect of that particular restorative!"

"Where to?" demanded Joshua, when they had driven out on to the road.

"First stop Sothern's cottage," rapped Ray.

After a few hundred yards they pulled up outside an ivy-mantled thatched cottage. Rambler roses, not yet in flower, threaded the trellis-work that garnished the front door. Leaded windows peeped from under mantling, shaggy eaves.

"Our friend is in love with the quaint, the picturesque?" queried Ray, swinging the wrought-iron knocker. "Somehow he struck me as hardly the type. Been reading Beverley Nichols, possibly."

The door slowly opened some nine inches, revealing the features of a slatternly maid-servant.

Ray's inquiry for the master of the house elicited no more than a gape and a slow shaking of the head.

Ray looked disappointed. He said: "What a pity! Er—we represent the—er—Eastern Counties Benevolent Society, and we did so want to see him about the money that's due to his domestic servant."

"That's me," said the maid, revealing a dawning intelligence. The door opened a further nine inches.

Feigning astonishment, Ray said, "Surely you're not Miss . . ."

"Ivy 'all."

"You are? Why, that's splendid!" He turned to Joshua. "This is Miss Ivy Hall, whose name we have down here for five shillings." He pointed to an imaginary entry in his notebook.

At the mention of the money Miss Hall's face showed increased evidence of life, and her hand, palm upward, started a forward movement.

Ray stroked his chin doubtfully. "It's rather irregular, Miss Hall, to pay the servant direct, and not through the employer. In this case, however, I think—" He appealed to Joshua. "Yes, I see that my friend agrees with me. As a special case, we can make payment direct to the party. You will, of course, have to sign a receipt."

Joshua butted in. "We can't deal with the papers, out here," he observed, rising to the occasion.

Miss Hall, taking the hint, admitted them to a low-ceilinged parlour, smelling pleasantly of old oak.

Ray seated himself at a table and started writing in his notebook.

"Of course, Miss Hall," he said, "we must ask one or two questions before handing over the five shillings."

The girl nodded.

"Just lay the money on the table," he said to Joshua, "while I talk to Miss Hall. That's right . . . . Now, then, how long have you worked for Mr Sothern, Ivy?"

"Ever since 'e come to Tiddenham, 'bout three months ago."

"Good. And what are your hours?"

"I get 'ere six of a mornin' an' make 'is cup o' tea what 'e 'as in bed. Then I cook 'is breakfast, an' when 'e's gone I wash up an' make 'is bed an' tidy everythink up. That's all."

"What time do you go as a rule?"

"That all depend on when I finish. Sometimes one o'clock; sometimes, I reckon, it's earlier."

"What about the day before yesterday? What time did you go on that day?"

"Day afore yesterday? I—er—"

"Roughly will do."

"Well, Mr Sothern, 'e told me to . . . I mean—" She fiddled with her apron. "Mr Sothern 'ad 'is dinner at 'ome that day, an' I come 'ere an' cooked it for 'im."

"What time did you get here and leave, Ivy?"

Ivy appeared to be in trouble. "What're yer askin' me all them questions for?" she demanded tearfully.

"It's the regulations," said Ray soothingly. "We have strict instructions not to part with the bonus until we are satisfied that the conditions of work and the hours are perfectly O.K. We are also empowered to increase the bonus in deserving cases."

In response to Ray's wink Joshua added a couple of shillings to the silver that lay on the table.

Cheered by this sight, Miss Hall resumed, "Well, Mr Sothern told me partic'lar not to talk to any gen'lemen."

"And," Ray added, "he told you that if you had to talk you must say that you were here with him the evening before last, though, as a matter of fact, you were elsewhere." It was a statement of fact rather than a question.

"Why, 'ow did yer know?" Miss Hall blurted out, then pulled herself up. "I mustn't answer any more questions. Mr Sothern said as 'ow I mustn't."

"Quite, quite. We always make a practice of respecting employers' wishes. I think, my friend"—he turned to Joshua—"we might hand over the money now. Here you are, Miss Hall."

Miss Hall, duly thankful, signed a receipt. Ray lingered.

"Did a gentleman ever call here named Mr Hogg?" he asked.

· "Yer don't mean the dark gen'leman what called 'ere one mornin', do yer?"

"I certainly do. I ask you because he's a particular friend of mine. What did he say?"

"Nothin', except as 'ow I was to tell Mr Sothern as 'ow Mr 'Ogg 'ad called."

"Which you did, of course."

"Oh, yes, sir."

"What day was this, Miss Hall?"

"Lemme see. 'Twern't yesterday, an' 'twern't the day afore that. I reckon it were the day afore that."

"Which, being translated, means three days ago and the day before Mr Briggs died."

"I reckon so."

"Just one other thing, Miss Hall, before we go. You remember the letter which came for Mr Sothern two or three days ago? An unstamped letter?"

Miss Hall shook her head slowly. "No, I don't. Mind yer, I don't say no letter come, an' I don't say it never. What with them circ'lars an' bills an' all, 'ow should I remember?"

Ray said gravely, "The Society will be very disappointed at your failure to remember, Miss Hall."

Miss Hall stared at him perplexedly. "What should they wanna know a thing like that for?" she asked. "Seems funny to me."

"Ah!" sighed Ray. "Officialdom, red tape, proper channels, and correct procedure. We can't help ourselves. Why, only the other day we had to ask a second footman whether his maternal great-aunt had ever been to Brighton. Only after we had elicited the required information were we able to make over the thirteen shillings that the Society had sanctioned."

"'Ad she?"

"What? . . . . Oh, you mean the great-aunt. Yes, I'm afraid she had. Badly."

Shaking his head sadly, Ray wished Miss Hall a good-morning and joined Joshua in the car.

*　　　　　*　　　　　*　　　　　*

"And now to Stokeby, please, Briggs, and if you can listen carefully and drive safely at the same time I will post you with the latest information regarding our mystery man, Hogg.

"I have this from Mrs Greene," he resumed, when they had got through the village. "Hogg arrived at the Tiddenham Arms five or six days ago, carrying a small suitcase. Apparently he'd walked from the station. He booked a room for a few days—period indefinite—and his room, incidentally, was my room. As to person, he was of middling height, darkish, moustachioed, and ill-favoured. His clothes were shabby-ordinary rather than shabby-genteel, and he spoke with a rich Cockney twang. Probable age thirty-five to forty-five. Liked his bottle—adored it rather . . . . You see, Briggs, that while you were swinishly slumbering I was snooping—not unpleasantly, I must admit."

"The widow of the Tiddenham Arms," observed Joshua drily, "is passing fair."

"Litotes. She is also possessed of a fine sense of hospitality—but let that pass . . . . To continue: this Hogg did not vouchsafe any information as to the purpose of his stay, and he talked very little to anybody. He usually got up near to lunch-time, soused, smoked black shag, and played patience till the evening, and then went out for walks. Since he paid, these minor eccentricities were overlooked."

"When did he leave?" Joshua asked.

"I was coming to that. On the evening of first inst.—that is, on the evening of the accident, suicide, or murder—he announced his intention of departing, paid his dues to the uttermost farthing, and walked out of the Arms carrying a little suitcase. That was at about quarter-past six."

"Did he say where he was going?"

"Yes. To London by train."

"Rather a coincidence," Joshua remarked.

"There are interesting features. Hogg knew both Sothern and your brother—he called on both of them. He came down here for an obscure purpose. He left at about the same time as your brother's death."

"A quarter of an hour *after*," Joshua corrected.

"According to Dr Storr, Briggs. But *rigor mortis* is an erratic phenomenon, all doctors make mistakes, and some men are liars."

CHAPTER XI

MAJOR GEORGE FITZHERBERT WIGLEY, Chief Constable of Stokeby, had spent a large slice of his life upholding Imperial law and order. According to Ray, the Major's sojourn amid lesser breeds had left him with an infra-red complexion, a liver that needed decarbonizing, and the temperament of a gorilla that had been crossed in life. This estimate, though founded on fact, did the Major less than justice. Apart from the fact that he wore khaki shorts on the slightest provocation, smelt faintly but permanently of curry, and believed in things like Pukka Sahibs, Major Wigley was tolerably human.

At nine-thirty on April the third Inspector Hines knocked at the Major's door, edged up to the presence, deposited four sheets of typed matter on the desk in front of the Major's nose, and stood by for action.

"What the devil's all this, Hines?" growled the Major, screwing in a monocle.

"The Tiddenham case report, sir."

"Humph. D'you expect me to plough through all this drivel?" He picked up the sheets and flung them down again. The Inspector, aloof and patient, said nothing.

"Well?" the Major went on. "Don't stand there like a dummy, man. Sit yourself down and tell me what you've done. Make a verbal report. Save me reading this." He prodded the report with a paper-knife.

Inspector Hines sat down on the edge of a chair. "At 8.15 P.M.

on the 1st inst.," he intoned, "an urgent telephone call was taken by Constable Cameron. The call was made by Dr Storr, speaking from the house of Mr James Briggs, at Tiddenham. Cameron and I at once proceeded to the above-mentioned—"

"For the Lord's sake, man," broke in the Major, "talk like your reports if you must, but spare me words like 'above-mentioned'!"

"Very well, sir. Cameron and I proceeded at once to the premises referred to, where I found Dr Storr, Mrs Ellen Briggs, and the body of the deceased, who was identified as James Briggs by those present. The body was found in a sitting position in a chair in the study, which is at the rear of the house. The head showed severe wounds, which appeared to be the cause of death. On the floor, between the outstretched legs of the body, lay a shotgun containing a spent cartridge."

"Fingerprints on the gun?" asked the Major.

"Excuse me, sir, but that comes later," the Inspector reproved mildly. "Before examining the scene of the—er—shooting in detail I questioned those present.

"Ellen Briggs, who was in a state of collapse, was at first unable to make a coherent statement. Later she said that she had returned to the house at about 8 P.M., when she had found the body, and telephoned immediately to Dr Storr, who had arrived about fifteen minutes later.

"Dr Storr stated that he had received a telephone call from Mrs. Briggs at 8 P.M., and had proceeded at once to her house, where he found Mrs Briggs in a state of collapse, and the body of James Briggs. Life was extinct. He telephoned the police forthwith.

"At about 8.30 P.M. I telephoned to Police Surgeon Simpson, who arrived about half an hour later."

"Disgusting," commented the Major.

"As you say, sir," agreed the Inspector. "Questioned as to the cause of death, Dr Storr gave it as his opinion that it was due to gunshot penetrating the brain. There were complicated fractures of the cranium, and death, in his opinion, had been instantaneous. Questioned as to the probable time of death, Dr Storr expressed doubt. *Rigor mortis,* he stated, had already begun to set in at about 8.20, when he first examined the body. He declined to make a definite statement, but was of the opinion that the deceased had died between 5 P.M. and 6 P.M. On arrival Dr Simpson concurred with Dr Storr's opinion as to the cause of death, but placed the time of death between 6 P.M. and 7.15 P.M. He thought that death had not occurred before 6 P.M."

"That's odd," observed the Major. "Their times don't even overlap. ... This Dr Storr—he's a newcomer to Stokeby, isn't he?"

"Yes, sir. But I understand that his medical qualifications are very good," replied the Inspector, and continued with his report. "Dr Simpson concluded from an examination of the powder-marks on the face that the gun had been fired at very close range—only a few inches. The position and direction of the wounds indicated that, at the time of firing, the gun had been held in a position between the legs of the deceased, and had been aimed upwards at his head. Lead shot removed from the body was later identified as the kind used in the type of cartridge found in the gun.

"Ellen Briggs affirmed that the deceased was wearing the clothes in which he had left the house that morning. She identified the gun as the one the deceased had purchased some time previously.

"An examination of the body by Dr Simpson revealed no further wounds or marks, excepting a scar on the right forearm, which, Mrs Briggs stated, was the result of a cut sustained some weeks back."

Inspector Hines paused for breath and consulted his notebook. "The following articles were recovered from the pockets of the deceased:

"1 half-hunter gold watch and chain.

"1 stylo pen.

"1 leather pocket-book containing £5.

"Loose change totalling 6s.

"1 bunch of keys.

"1 Press cutting of racing fixtures.

"4 bills, totalling £137 4s.

"2 Dutch guilders.

"1 silk handkerchief."

"Look here, Hines!" cried the Major. "This sort of thing may be good routine, but it isn't getting us any further. Who cares whether his handkerchief was made of silk or calico? Let's have something about fingerprints on the gun, and who saw Briggs last. Leave out the non-essentials."

"Yes, sir. I'm just coming to fingerprints. I found finger and thumb impressions corresponding to those of the deceased on the butt and the barrel of the gun. Further prints, blurred and not yet identified, were also found. Three pieces of rag, slightly stained with oil, were found on a table next to the chair on which the body was discovered.

"On my arrival at the house the drive gate was open, the front door was locked with a night-latch, and the French windows leading from the study to the veranda and garden were open. Dr Storr said that on his arrival the same conditions had obtained. Mrs Briggs was unable to remember whether the French doors had been open or closed, but she recollected that the front door had been locked when she arrived at the house.

"The room was searched for fingerprints. In addition to those I have already mentioned, fingerprints of the deceased and of Mrs Briggs were found on the handle of the door leading to the hall. In several places the prints of Mrs Groves the housekeeper were found. No fingerprints could be traced on the handle of the French doors.

"A search of the room revealed a tumbler containing the remains of a whisky-and-soda, a soda siphon, and half a bottle of Scotch whisky. All these bore the fingerprints of the deceased only. A gun licence and a number of unpaid bills were found in the drawer of the desk. Further inspection of the study failed to reveal anything appearing to throw light on the tragedy, and the remainder of the house and grounds were searched without yielding anything of interest. The deceased's car, in which (it transpired later) he had left that morning for London, was found in a garage in front of the house."

"Half a minute, Hines," interrupted the Major. "These other prints on the gun: did you compare them with the prints of everybody in the house?"

"Yes, sir. Including those of Dr Storr and Mr Joshua Briggs."

"Carry on, and let's hear about Briggs' doings on the fatal day."

"I was just coming to that, sir. Questioned as to the movements of the deceased on April 1st, Mrs Ellen Briggs said that she last saw him between 9 and 9.30 A.M., when they had breakfast together. Mr Briggs, who seemed to be in a normal state of mind, told her of his intention to drive to London and to return early in the evening. Mrs Briggs stated that she knew of no reason why the deceased should take his life. She was not aware of any financial difficulties."

"No?" exclaimed Major Wigley.

"No, sir. Apparently her husband did not discuss his monetary affairs with Mrs Briggs."

"Incredible! What sort of married life did they lead? Happy?"

"I have made a few inquiries, sir. The general impression is that it was not a happy marriage, although I heard of no definite quarrels."

Major Wigley nodded, and the Inspector went on: "Dr Storr, who was present during the interview, intervened at this stage and asked that Mrs Briggs be questioned no further, as she appeared to be on the verge of collapse.

"At about 10 P.M. George Henry Groves, gardener, and his wife Elizabeth Groves, the deceased's housekeeper, arrived at the house. Questioned, Elizabeth Groves said that she and her husband lived in the Briggses' house and had just come from Stokeby, where they had spent the evening. She said that Mr Briggs had left the house in his car at approximately 9.30 A.M., since which time neither she nor her husband had seen Mr Briggs. She and her husband had gone out that evening at roughly 5.15 P.M. They left the place empty, and before going they saw that all the windows on the ground floor were closed and fastened, and that all the doors, including the French windows of the study, were locked. They were unable to throw any light on the tragedy.

"At about 11 P.M. Mr Joshua Briggs, the brother of the deceased, arrived at the house, having come from Bingly in response to a telegram sent earlier in the evening by Mrs Briggs."

Inspector Hines folded his notebook, heaved a deep sigh, and said, "That, sir, concludes my investigation on April the 1st."

"Not bad, Hines. You seem to have covered the preliminaries pretty adequately. What did you do yesterday? Make it brief, if you can."

"Checked up his movements in London, sir. Nothing much came to light there—he left for Tiddenham at about four o'clock. I have made various inquiries in Tiddenham village, with negative results so far. As a matter of routine I have checked the alibis of the gardener and the housekeeper. They are apparently sound. Mrs Briggs states she was at the Capitol Cinema here in Bingly from six o'clock, but I have not been able to get confirmation yet."

"After all that, what is it, Hines—accident, suicide, or murder?" asked the Major.

Inspector Hines pursed his lips and frowned. "Well, sir," he said ponderously, "if it hadn't been for the cleaning rags being beside the gun, and the fact that his state of mind was apparently normal,

I would have said it was suicide. He was a ruined man. As regards murder, there is nothing pointing that way. It *looks* like accident."

"You emphasize the word *looks,* Hines. You have your doubts?"

"Well, sir, I think it may have been an accident, though how a man could be so foolish—"

"Not at all improbable, Hines. Fellow had no doubt hardly set eyes on a gun in his life, much less handled one. Very likely didn't know the business end of the thing from t'other end."

"Possibly, sir," Hines agreed grudgingly.

"Hines, you're hedging. You tell me you don't think it's suicide for a double reason. You're pretty sure it isn't murder. And you doubt the accident theory. What the hell's left? Don't tell me you can think of a fourth alternative."

"No, sir. I can't make up my mind between suicide and accident."

"Fifty-fifty either way, hey?"

"Yes. . . . May I ask what you think, sir?"

"Hm. . . . inclined to take your view, Hines. Coroner'll probably minimize the financial trouble, concentrate on the cleaning rags and the normal state of mind, and direct the jury to bring in a verdict of death by misadventure. Pleasanter for all concerned."

Hines stood up. "Further instructions, sir?" he inquired.

But at that moment the door opened, admitting the statuesque form of P.C. Cameron, followed by Joshua Briggs and Jethro Ray.

*　　　　　　*　　　　　　*　　　　　　*

"Well, sir?" said Major Wigley, in a you-don't-get-any-change-out-of-me sort of tone, after the introductions and preliminaries were over.

Joshua hesitated. Ray had inconsiderately insisted on this visit; insisted also that he, Joshua, should start off the talking, and had advised him, in case of emergency, to refer in passing to a near relation in the Poona Light Horse. The Major's manner was making matters difficult.

"You will understand, sir," he began, "that I'm very concerned about my brother's death, and anxious to get at the truth."

"Obviously, sir," was the somewhat curt reply. "But I'm afraid you will have to wait for the verdict of the Coroner's Court."

Joshua glanced at Ray, whose attention was unobtrusively riveted on the report that lay before the Major.

"Of course, I understand that," Joshua replied diffidently. "But it did seem to my friend and me that you might be willing to give some indication—"

"I'm sorry, gentlemen, I can't help you," interrupted the Major, in a manner that admitted of no dispute. "I am here to collect information, not to impart it without proper authority to do so. Have you anything to say that will throw light on your brother's death?"

"Well..." said Joshua, and stopped. Major Wigley's ample eyebrows ascended half an inch.

"Yes!" interjected Ray, smiling broadly.

The Major had hitherto paid scant attention to the lanky young man with the thick spectacles and the queer taste in neckties. Now he described a quarter-circle in his rotating chair and confronted Ray with a pink expanse of startled countenance.

There was a pause in which Ray sensed that he had been weighed in the balance and found wanting.

"Let's have it, then," snapped Major Wigley.

Ray smiled. "With the greatest of pleasure, sir, if you will kindly let us have a little information."

The colour of the Major's face deepened a shade or two. "Blackmail?" he snorted.

"Not at all, sir. We feel that you will not refuse to pass on a few unimportant details in return for the very considerable help we believe we will be able to give you." Ray felt that he had achieved a new high record in conciliatory unctuousness.

This speech did not appear to mollify the Major. "I must warn you," he said, in a bottled-up voice, "that to withhold evidence likely to have a bearing on the case is an offence."

Ray lifted a protesting hand. "Forgive me, sir. You misjudge me. I wouldn't dream of obstructing the course of the law. On the contrary, I have, of my own accord, come to you with important evidence. All I want in return are a few facts about fingerprints."

"Why?" The Major's voice made the furniture rattle.

Ray adopted the tactics of a snake-charmer confronted with an intransigent cobra. "Because, sir, armed with this information from you, I feel sure I shall be able to assist the law to catch a dangerous criminal."

"What? . . . Criminal?"

"Yes, sir. Murderer, to be more specific."

Ray mentally likened the Major's face to molten lava trying not to erupt.

"Are you mad, sir?" the Major bellowed. "Who *are* you, anyway? One of these private detectives?" Words could not convey the contumely which accompanied the last of these questions.

Ray's appeasing smile was worthy of the Diplomatic Corps. "I'm merely Mr Joshua Briggs' secretary. We want to get at the truth, sir, just as you do. And I have information that can help you."

There followed a brief interval during which the Major lay back in his chair writhing mentally. Emerging from this ordeal a somewhat calmer man, he inquired: "How do I know this isn't a trick merely to get the information you want?"

For answer Ray extracted from his pocket an object wrapped in a handkerchief, and set it carefully on the table. Major Wigley instinctively edged away a couple of inches. Was it a bomb? He saw nothing in Ray's appearance to discourage the idea.

"What's this?" he demanded, in a strained voice.

"You found fingerprints on the gun I imagine, sir?"

"Odd if we hadn't," came the retort. The Major continued to eye with suspicion the object in the handkerchief.

"In addition to the deceased's, I mean?"

The Major wriggled uncomfortably in his chair.

"Trying to trap me?.... Hm.... well, supposing we did?"

"Major Wigley"—Ray leaned forward earnestly—"wrapped in this handkerchief is a tumbler, and on the tumbler are fingerprints. Compare these fingerprints with those on the gun, and if the two sets don't correspond you can ring the bell for your chucker-out. Or, rather, we will walk out unaided and trouble you no more.

"On the other hand," he added, observing that the Major seemed somewhat impressed, "if they do happen to correspond I must ask you to regard that fact as security for good behaviour and evidence of our good faith."

Major Wigley pressed his buzzer three times. Constable Cameron reappeared. The Major pointed at the tumbler. "Give this thing to Inspector Hines," he commanded, "and tell him to compare any fingerprints on it with the prints on the gun in the Tiddenham case, quickly. Ask him to come to me with the results at once."

A temporary calm followed the constable's departure.

Ray, with closed eyes, appeared to be taking a well-earned rest, Joshua scrutinized his fingernails, and the Major fidgeted. He was the first one to speak.

He addressed Joshua: "What exactly do you want to know?"

Ray woke up. "Firstly, when did James Briggs die, according to the police surgeon?"

"Hm!"

"Secondly, fingerprints."

The Major gave Ray a suspicious look: "I thought you were the one who knew all about the fingerprints!"

"Not *all*, Major Wigley. Thirdly, any other matter of interest."

The Major sniffed. There seemed to be nothing more to say for the present. Ray relapsed into his trance.

"Supposing," said the Major guardedly, after a few moments, "I were to answer your questions. What use would you make of the information?"

"We would use it," Ray replied, "to help you to solve the Tiddenham case, and we would treat it as confidential."

Major Wigley looked curiously at Ray. "You do fancy yourself as a detective, then. . . . Well, now we'll see," he added, as there came a rap on the door and Inspector Hines came in.

The Inspector's face displayed as much excitement as his lugubrious features were capable of registering. Before speaking he cast a doubtful glance towards the two visitors. The Major signalled him to proceed.

Inspector Hines coughed impressively and announced: "The fingerprints on this glass, sir, seem to correspond with some of those on the gun."

Major Wigley darted a quick look at Ray, who was absorbed in the act of polishing his spectacles. "Hm…." The Major grunted, addressing the Inspector. "Seem to? What d'you mean, seem to? Do they or don't they?"

"Well, sir, the prints on the gun—I don't mean the fingerprints of the deceased, but the other ones—are not very clear. I think, however, there is little doubt that the man who handled the glass also handled the gun."

The Inspector made as though to depart. Major Wigley detained him with a gesture.

"Well, sir"—the Major turned to Ray—"perhaps you will tell us whose fingerprints these are? Who handled this glass?"

Ray replaced his spectacles. "I'll tell you immediately, sir, if you promise to answer my questions."

The Major fought a last and hopeless mental battle, inevitably ending in capitulation.

"Right," he sighed, "on condition you promise not to tell."

Ray assured him, and continued: "The fingerprints are those of one Martin Sothern, bachelor, of Honeysuckle Cottage, Tiddenham."

"Sothern!" The Major and the Inspector exchanged swift glances.

"I see you know our friend, Major," commented Ray.

"We know *of* him," corrected Major Wigley. "Have you any more to tell me, Mr Ray?" he continued. "For instance, how you connected these two sets of fingerprints?"

"I'll tell you that to-morrow, sir. In the meantime, if I might. . . . "

The Chief Constable consulted his watch and got up hastily. "Good God!" he cried. "I'm ten minutes late for a committee."

"I'll investigate Sothern's alibi, Hines, and check up his fingerprints at once," he exhorted, as the Inspector helped him on with his overcoat.

Ray coughed obtrusively. The Major was already at the door.

"And before you do so, Hines," Major Wigley added over his shoulder, "tell this extraordinary gentleman what he wants to know."

*   *   *   *

". . . . There is no evidence of murder; there is only circumstantial evidence of an uncertain nature pointing to suicide; there is evidence—not conclusive, perhaps, but definite evidence—indicating accidental death. So far as my investigation has gone, therefore, I believe that the last of these three alternatives provides not only the most charitable solution, but also the one which best fits the facts of the case."

Inspector Hines read this, the concluding paragraph of his report, not without a certain sense of satisfaction. He felt that his literary labours, which the Major had treated so coldly, had at last met with their meed of appreciation.

Ray, beaming whole-hearted admiration, said: "Inspector, believe me to be sincere when I say that that is the most lucid, well-phrased, and logically constructed police report I have ever listened to." He did not add that it was the only one.

In face of this barrage of compliments Inspector Hines strove hard, but unsuccessfully, to maintain a facial expression of becoming professional dignity. Ray divined that the psychological moment had come to put his question:

"Will you please tell me, Inspector, what you know about Sothern?"

"I'm sorry, Mr Ray, but the Chief only instructed me to give you information regarding the Tiddenham case. . . . This is a different matter."

"Out with it, Inspector! And I'll give you a tip on this case which will surely help you to honour and glory."

After a few moments of hesitation Hines gave in.

"Well. . . . very confidentially, you understand, sir. We have warnings from the Metropolitan Police now and then regarding suspicious characters. They have nothing on—pardon me—nothing definite against these people. Nothing, I mean, that a good defence counsel could not demolish in five minutes."

Ray nodded. "The cops know, but they can't do anything about it."

"Precisely. You see, confidence men and tricksters are extraordinarily difficult to pin down. They're very careful, and it's only the victim's word against the trickster's. The cumulative evidence of many such cases ought to be sufficient legal evidence, but it isn't."

Ray got up and shook hands warmly with the Inspector. "I'm very grateful to you," he said, "for all your help, and I wouldn't dream of asking you to tell me anything, Inspector, without the proper authority. . . . Come, Briggs, we have work to do!"

"And, Inspector," Ray confided in a whisper, on the way out, "my hint to you is to ask the Department who tipped you off about Sothern whether they also know of one Hogg, dark, sinister, of middling height, moustachioed, and frequently bottled. Probably connected in some way with Sothern, and possibly the murderer of James Briggs, Esquire, of Tiddenham."

CHAPTER XII

OUT in the square Joshua Briggs looked over his shoulder. "The Inspector's still standing on the steps of the police-station, staring into space," he laughed.

"But why," he added, turning to Ray, "didn't you show them the letter to Sothern—I mean the bit of blotting-paper?"

Ray shook his head. "My dear Briggs, use your noddle. What did I go to the police for: to give information or get it?"

"Why not both?"

"Heavens! Briggs, do you really think, now that at last I've got my teeth into a nice juicy case, I'm going to hand it over on a plate to a bunch of coppers?"

"Haven't you practically done so?"

"I hardly think so, somehow. As you say, I still hold the blotting-paper. I had to cast one or two pearls, but not this one of great price, to get what I wanted."

Joshua chuckled. "You're as vain as Satan. Saving it all for the great showdown of to-morrow, like a small boy nibbling the pastry edging off a jam-tart. Jethro, you've been reading too many detective stories!"

Ray seized his friend's arm impatiently: "Come along," he said, "time's slipping away. Find me a clothes-shop where I can buy you a cap with a shiny peak."

"What's wrong with my present hat?" Joshua took off his black trilby, which he had bought on the previous day at Stokeby, and examined it.

"Everything. No time for argument. I want a shop that sells officials' peaked caps."

"You're nuts !" cried Joshua. "Anyhow, you can't buy that sort of cap in Stokeby. No demand, except from gas companies and suchlike, who would buy theirs in London."

"Think, Briggs. Stokeby is just the place to buy such things…Let's try this shop now."

Ray hauled him into an outfitter's that bore unmistakable hallmarks of the county's patronage, and addressed the young man behind the counter in a distant voice.

"I require a peaked cap for my chauffeur." He pointed a superior finger at Joshua, who stood swallowing hard.

"Microcephalous," Ray added.

The shop-assistant stared. "Pardon, sir?" he said.

"Small cranium."

The assistant glanced at Joshua. "Of course, sir " he said. "We have an excellent range of sizes. Would you come this way, please?"

Ray, ignoring his friend's furious glances, guarded the line of retreat to the street door.

"And now, sir," said the shop-assistant, after the cap had been chosen and paid for, "may we make a uniform?"

Ray surveyed his friend's clothes with a critical eye.

"Hm. . . .He certainly could do with some decent clothes, couldn't he? However, he'll probably make a rotten chauffeur, and I'll have to sack him. So no uniform at present."

"One more crack like that, Ray," cried Joshua "and I'll—" He turned and made for the door.

"Democracy—what?" cried Ray, laughing outright at the assistant's horror-struck face. "None of the good old feudal spirit in him, young man."

Ten yards down the street he caught up with Joshua.

"Unless you tell me right now what you're up to, and stop being mysterious and insulting by turns," the latter cried, "I'm through with you! And even if you do tell me I think I've had enough."

"Joshua, old man," Ray wheedled," don't take it to heart. Don't you trust me?"

"No!"

"Listen, Joshua. I've got to buy one or two things in this grocer's shop. As soon as I've done that I'll tell you all."

"Well, make it snappy, or you won't find me here."

In three minutes Ray was back with a brown-paper parcel under his arm.

Shepherding Joshua towards the spot where the car was parked, he started talking earnestly: "Now listen carefully, Briggs, this is what you do. First…"

*   *   *   *

Mrs Emily Bates sloshed wearily with her dishmop at the breakfast things. For her the alimentary functions were a matter of sorrow—of disgust even. Had she not wasted her best years, and this the autumn of her undistinguished career, in bestowing earnest thought and much labour on the preparation of meals which a succession of ingrates had swallowed in two jiffies while thinking about something else? And particularly men. Men, according to Mrs Bates, believed vaguely in miracles of the loaves-and-fishes kind. They seemed to labour under the impression that meals went through no embryonic stage, involving bother to their author, but arrived full-fledged. As for the meal's wearisome obsequies, no man she had ever heard of had shown the slightest awareness of their existence.

On the other hand, on one fine morning an omelette would turn out with the consistency of a bit of liver, or a bit of liver would turn out like a boot-sole. And then men who for weeks hadn't noticed what they were eating—five minutes after a meal fit for a king they didn't remember whether the soup had been thick or clear—would fly into a rage and curse the wretched cook, who was probably the blameless victim of circumstances, anyway.

Such a morning was this one. Was it Emily Bates' fault that the milk had burned, that the toast had charred, that the poached eggs had over-poached themselves? No. It was the fault of that villainous newspaper tout who had held her in conversation while the breakfast literally went up in smoke. As a consequence Dr Storr had said some unpleasant things, some really objectionable things, that no woman ought to stand, especially from a foreigner. She had felt like handing in her notice then and there, giving the doctor an unexpurgated piece of her mind on the subject of British morals, and walking off the premises in high dudgeon. She had felt like it, but she hadn't done it. The money was too good.

She sighed deeply, flung the dish-mop into the washbowl in

disgust, and subsided into a chair. As she did so the back-door bell rang.

Breathing curses on all touts, meter inspectors, and vacuum-cleaner salesmen, she got up and opened the door.

Confronting her was an unbusinesslike looking official in flannel trousers, a black tie, and a cap with a shining peak. He carried a bag of tools.

She eyed him with scorn. "The gas-meter were read yesterday," she said.

"Telephone, ma'am," explained the official, in a mild voice.

"There ain't nothin' wrong with the 'phone neither. The doctor used it 'arf an hour ago, just afore he went out." She started closing the door.

"Something must have gone wrong after then, ma'am, because he's just rung up the exchange to say he couldn't get through to his house, and would they send somebody round to put it right."

Mrs Bates sniffed and flung the door open. "All right, come in and 'ave a look at it."

"You're a funny sort o' workman," she added ungraciously, observing Joshua's clothes.

"Inspector, ma'am," he corrected.

She turned with a sigh of resignation, and led the way through the kitchen and the hall to a small room furnished as a study, at the front of the house. On the open roller-top desk lay a telephone.

"May as well see if you're telling the truth," she snapped, and picked up the instrument.

Joshua was already on his hands and knees, busy fiddling with the connexion box, where the flex joined the fixed cable. He wrenched at the flex. Something gave.

"The junction box seems all right," he said, getting up again.

"'Ello 'ello 'ello!" Mrs Bates was bawling into the mouthpiece. She tapped the lever vigorously.

"No reply?" Joshua asked innocently.

She replaced the receiver with a bang. "All right," she grumbled. Carry on. . . . An' I'm stopping 'ere to see you don't take nothing." She sat down heavily and watched Joshua sorting out his tools.

"P'raps it's the junction box after all," he said, making futile attempts to remove the cover with a screw-driver several sizes too large for the job. He felt that the housekeeper's interested silence was worse than her conversation.

Presently a ringing of the back-door bell came to his rescue, and Mrs Bates retreated to the kitchen, fuming.

*   *   *   *

The cross-eyed young man smiled and said ingratiatingly: "Madam, this sample packet of—". Before he could get any further the door swung violently to. It did not shut, however, because Ray's foot was wedged against the threshold. He continued as though nothing had happened: "This large sample packet of the finest Darjeeling tea is presented, *free of charge*"—at these words the door opened a little— "by the East Himalayan Tea Planters' Association."

"What's the snag?" inquired Mrs Bates, eyeing the one-pound

packet covetously.

Ray looked hurt. "No snag, madam. I am instructed to give you this packet of excellent tea. However, I see you are not a tea-drinker." He turned to go.

"Ere, come back, you!" cried Mrs Bates. "What's the idea giving away bloomin' great parcels o' tay? Tain't done—leastwise, not to me."

"It's rather parky out here, madam, and it's starting to rain. If you can spare a second I'll just step in and explain." Before Mrs Bates could protest he was inside, and the door was closed. He continued: "I've been giving hundreds of these away. Yesterday I gave one to Mrs Groves of Tiddenham, who, I believe, is a friend of yours. As a matter of fact, it was she who suggested that you would appreciate a packet. Nice lady, Mrs Groves. She spoke very highly of you."

"Did she? That ain't like 'er," was the gruff reply.

"Oh, yes. She said to me: "Take Mrs Emily Bates, now. There's a really good woman, who works terribly hard to support her family and never breathes a word of complaint. And her devotion to Dr Storr—""

Mrs Bates gave a snort that would have made a lesser person's nose bleed.

Ray's face was a picture of sympathetic but discreet inquiry. He put the packet of tea on the table in front of Mrs Bates, and waited.

"Devotion . . . I like that! I 'ate 'im. What with 'is carryings-on of an evening and 'is grumblin' at the cookin' an' cleanin', an' 'is foreign 'abits! Mister, 'e's awful. It fair makes me sick to talk abaht 'im."

Ray shook his head slowly and clucked his tongue in disapproval.

He said in a shocked voice: "I expect you find traces of these goings-on next morning."

"I do. 'E can't deceive Emily Bates, what's done for gen'lemen for twenty year. Why, last time she was 'ere—night 'afore last it were—'e thought 'e'd taken me in, 'e did. But 'e forgot abaht the fag-ends with 'er lipstick on 'em. An' the glass what she used an' washed up an' put away again, just so as I shouldn't know anyone'd been 'ere. But she put it on the wrong shelf, see?"

'You've no idea who the young lady is?" Ray asked.

"No I ain't. Allus comes on Wednesdays, she does—day afore last was Wednesday—and she'll be 'ere again next week, I reckon."

"Does the doctor always take such trouble to conceal the fact that he's had a visitor? I mean, surely, he often has other guests in of an evening?"

"Course 'e does. Funny thing, on other Wednesday nights 'e never took no trouble to make out 'e was alone 'ere. I reckon 'e must a guessed I knew about this 'ere girl, an' got the wind up."

"Undoubtedly that is the explanation, Mrs Bates. "Well, now, I mustn't stop your work. There's the tea, and if you like it—er—buy some more. If you don't, throw it down the drain. I would. Personally, I hate Indian tea. Like treacle."

Mrs Bates gaped at him. "This 'ere society what you represent, d'they *pay* yer to talk like that 'bout their tay?"

"Handsomely, Mrs Bates. They believe in truth in advertising. Truth, we hold, pays in the long run. You see, if I go about saying that Indian tea is a kind of rat-poison the people who dislike me will automatically be prejudiced in favour of the stuff. On the other hand, those who like me will say, 'How frank, how enlightened, how different!' and they will drink Indian tea to encourage honesty in sales patter."

"Mister," cried Mrs Bates, "I gets all sorts comin' 'ere. Fellers like this 'ere chap what calls 'isself a telephone inspector, looks like a—"

Ray appraised the figure in a peaked cap that had just entered the kitchen. "A junior porter's assistant on one of the lesser light railways," he suggested.

Mrs Bates ignored the interruption. "—looks like a toff, speaks like a toff, an' dresses like a bloomin' gasman. What was I a-sayin'? Ah, yes! I gets all sorts 'ere. But you"—she turned to Ray—"you're the rummiest what I ever set eyes on." She looked at them in turn. "In fac', you're *both* rum."

Addressing Joshua, she said: "Let's 'ave a look in that there bag o' yours, in case you've pinched anythink."

Joshua resolved her doubts on that particular score, only to raise them on another.

"Rum tools for a telephone man," she remarked suspiciously.

"I'm with you there, Mrs Bates," agreed Ray, looking over her shoulder at the contents of the bag.

"If, sir, you managed to put the telephone right with these primitive weapons you're a genius with your hands."

"If 'e's a genius with 'is 'ands, young Alf what's semi-paralysed's a bloomin' miracle," sneered Mrs Bates.

Joshua said through his teeth, "Anyhow, I mended the blasted thing," and let himself out at the back door.

"Now I really *must* tear myself away," said Ray, following. "And remember, Mrs Bates, there's no tipple on earth to compare with a cup of good China tea taken with a slice of lemon. Not milk, remember. Lemon."

*   *   *   *

"In other words," commented Joshua ponderously, "the answer is a—"

Ray thumped him on the back and cried: "Brilliant, Briggs! Now, you stay here a minute while I pop down these steps again, creep past Mrs Bates' window and the door we've just come out of, and investigate."

Joshua started pacing the pavement, feeling more uncomfortable every moment. He lit a cigarette and tried hard to ignore the wondering stares of two small boys. At last a panting and grubby Ray arrived.

"For God's sake," pleaded Joshua, "let's get to the car and get rid of this... this... disguise!" He sniffed, and edged away from Ray. "Ray," he exclaimed, "you smell—I mean that literally this time!"

"I know," Ray concurred complacently.

"And, what's more, you stink of decayed fish."

"Right again. Congratulations on your olfactory sense, Briggs. But it was worth it. See here." Ray opened a grimy palm, in which lay two cigarette butts with scarlet-tinged ends.

Joshua gazed. "Ellen Briggs?" he queried.

Ray carefully put them in his wallet.

"Possibly," he said. "We owe these exhibits, Briggs, to the lethargy of the so-called Public Cleansing Department of Stokeby. That cod—it was practically nimble. Whew!. . . . I see by the distance you're keeping you agree with me."

"And here's the car at last. Now you can park your ridiculous tools and your even more ridiculous cap, and come with me to get a really thorough wash and brush-up and a quick refuelling for a strenuous afternoon."

CHAPTER XIII

THE interior decoration of the Capitol Cinema Restaurant had been contrived in the late Teashop-Gothic style. Poker-work mottoes of a non-controversial nature (the management insisted on this) hung in profusion on walls which, as Ray remarked, "consisted of dirty-linen-fold panelling." That particularly noxious colour, teashop orange, had broken out in patches all over the room. Even the waitresses' headdresses were smirched with it.

"Well, Briggs," sighed Ray, "I trust you have news which will make me oblivious of my environment."

Joshua put an envelope on the tablecloth. "Judge for yourself."

Ray was in no hurry. He read the address:

> *Dr Storr,*
>
> *7 Fortescue Avenue,*
>
> *Stokeby*

"Handwriting obviously Ellen Briggs'. Postmark clearly: *Tiddenham*, 9 P.M., *March 31st.* Envelope ripped open with paper-knife." He looked at Joshua. "So far, good. Where did you chance on this, Briggs?"

"Top right-hand drawer of desk, hidden under a lot of other papers," Joshua replied, not without a note of pride in his voice.

"You found no other letters from her in the desk?"

"No."

"And none of the drawers was locked?"

"None."

Ray drew out the letter. "Now let's see what she writes." He read:

> "*Tiddenham,*
>
> "*March 31st*

"I've had that awful headache again, and I can't sleep. I shall go to the pictures to-morrow night. May I, doctor? I must have some recreation. You *will* come and see me the day after to-morrow, won't you, as usual, and bring some of that medicine with you?

> "In haste,
>
> "E. B."

Ray replaced the letter in its envelope and put it in his pocket, laughing loudly.

"You're making yourself conspicuous," reproved Joshua.

Ray's unseemly merriment had created something of a stir among the diners.

His mirth subsided. He said: "Now's your chance, Briggs. Think hard. Show what you're made of. Here, read it again, study it. I'll give you three minutes while I order lunch!"

Ray turned to the waitress. "Let me see. Something quickly served, quickly eaten, and sustaining, please…. Briggs, what would Vance order? . . . Oh, never mind, I couldn't pronounce it, and the Capitol most certainly couldn't produce it. Let's say tomato soup, double sausage on mash, caramel custard, and coffee, all twice…. Rather a come-down, Briggs—what? I rather fancy that the Detectives' Union would require me to hand in my card if they got wind of this."

But Joshua was not listening. He was staring hard at the letter, frowning. "No," he said, shaking his head, "it beats me." He grinned ruefully at Ray. "Go on, say: 'You disappoint me, Briggs.'"

"You take the words out of my mouth. . . . Well, here's a hint. You see the way the paper is folded?"

"Apparently it was folded wrongly at first and wouldn't fit the envelope. So Ellen Briggs refolded it properly."

"Can't you think of another explanation?"

"No . . . but one thing's queer. This letter—or note, rather—is much more formal than I would have expected from what we know, or think we know, about the relationship between the doctor and his patient. Of course, there may have been a quarrel. And another thing: this letter doesn't *prove* she was at the pictures. It merely increases the probability that she was."

"Er—yes . . . yes," said Ray, in a preoccupied voice. "Briggs, I can't make up my mind about something."

"So *you* can't see daylight, either."

"Blinding daylight, my dear boy. It's so glaring that it calls for blue spectacles and an eyeshade…. No, that's not what's troubling me. I can't make up my mind whether to tell you now or wait till the day of judgment, meaning to-morrow…. On second thoughts, if you can't solve the little mystery of this letter now, and stand on your head and work out a problem in differential calculus at the same time, you deserve to have to wait."

"Ray," said Joshua, stabbing a sausage as though he were at bayonet drill, "I know you're a cocksure ass, a smart Alec, and a self-styled genius, but I'm damned if I can see how even you can be certain that you will run the criminal to earth to-morrow."

Ray finished his second sausage, removed his glasses, and peered at his friend through eyes blinking with amusement. "I like you best," he said, "when you're furious with me. It's the only time when you're really amusing. Work on it. It's a tiny seed of the sense of humour. Dig it about and dung it, and it'll grow to be a great tree one day. . . . No, sit down, man. I take it all back, including the tiny seed. That's right. . . . I was going to make a confession to you, Briggs. A confession—believe it or not—of weakness."

"Sometimes, Ray, you remind me of the other great ones. 'Mr X, the famous politician, is, in many little ways, just like other men,' says Mrs X.' Or of royalty: 'A charmingly human touch was when Y dropped a glove.'"

"Good Lord! If the sapling isn't flourishing already!" Ray exclaimed. "Excellent, Briggs! . . . Now, as I was about to say, I confess to you that to-morrow worries me. Actually I haven't any reason for saying that I'll clear up everything by then, except that to-day, Briggs, I'll collect all the remaining pieces of the puzzle. And tonight I'll try fitting them together. . . . But I have a horrible fear that they may not fit."

"Then?"

"I'm sunk. Because *(a)* I'll have let you down, and *(b)*—what's more important—let myself down; *(c)* you remember how I swore to the Fayette girl that I'd find her out by to-morrow morning, and *(d)* I must be in town to-morrow afternoon to lecture to a crowd of distinguished septuagenarians on some of the lesser-known aspects of Carlovingian architecture. . . . But, Briggs, we dawdle. *Tempus fugit,* as this execrable piece of poker-work announces with such devastating originality. Where is our beautiful blonde?"

He signalled frantically to the waitress. She came.

"Could we have our bill, please? . . . Yes, he will pay. By the way, I thought I would have met Mrs Briggs of Tiddenham here to-day."

The blonde shook her head. "She doesn't often come to lunch, sir. She's often here for tea, though. Of course, since that horrible accident to her husband, she hasn't been in."

"Pity," said Ray. "She was in here last on the very day he died, I believe."

"Why, yes, that's right!" she exclaimed. "I served her tea myself, and we talked about the weather. It must have been almost six o'clock before she went, we were talking so long."

"I expect she was going to the film. I see the programme starts at six o'clock."

The waitress frowned. "I don't think so, because I seem to remember her going through the door to the street, and not that door over there, which leads to the cinema."

"Ah, well, it doesn't matter," said Ray, getting up to go. "I shall have to go over to Tiddenham and see her and express my sympathy, I suppose. Good morning, miss, and"—to Joshua, when they had got outside the door—"I could do with less poker-work in your dirty-linen-fold, less *embonpoint* in your blondes, and less breadcrumbs and beef in your pork sausages, O Capitol Management!"

CHAPTER XIV

FITZWILLIAM STREET lies on the western frontiers of Bloomsbury. Its magnificent Regency façade—the street was planned as a unit—has for long been partitioned among a crew of landlords, each of whom has painted his front elevation as seemed right in his own eyes, so that half a pillar is white, the other half blue, the front doors are green, red, and turquoise, the railings variegated. If the front of St Paul's had been let out to a dozen highly individualistic house-painters, the result could not have been more unhappy. No one notices, however. For the street is no longer quite respectable.

At least, so far as its nocturnal inhabitants are concerned. These are painters, delicatessen store-keepers of doubtful nationality, unsuccessful writers, models, and a nondescript tribe which includes amateur occultists, nudists, confidence men, tarts, and vegetarian poetasters. In striking contrast are the handful of respectable individuals that still linger by day in Fitzwilliam Street, remnants of its former glory. These solicitors, picture-dealers, and business men pursue blameless callings by day in the offices of the street, arriving at nine-thirty, departing at five-thirty sharp, and holding no truck with their neighbours.

To James Briggs Fitzwilliam Street had provided the perfect environment for making the best of both worlds. Chambers, an imposing brass plate, and sombre office furniture gave an air of prosperity and clean living. The dim little bed-sitting-room that opened out of the general office had inscribed upon its door the word "PRIVATE," which in no way detracted from the austerity of the general atmosphere.

In this inner room Margot Fayette, clad in black silk, lay on the bed reading a thriller and smoking Turkish cigarettes. A heaped-up ash-tray and half a glass of gin-and-lime stood on the table beside her. Stacked against the wall were dozens of canvases, framed and unframed. Clothes—Margot's—were draped over the chairs and the dressing-table.

The telephone bell started ringing. Margot cursed, flung down her book, drank the rest of the gin-and-lime, and strutted on four-inch heels to the desk in the adjoining room. She lifted the receiver.

"Hello…. Yes, speaking…. Oh, *you!* What, you're bringing that creature? Why? . . . Oh, *all* right. . . . In twenty minutes. . . . Yes, I'll be here."

She replaced the receiver slowly, frowning.

*　　　　　*　　　　　*　　　　　*

"Ah, *good* afternoon, Miss Fayette." Ray was determined to let bygones be bygones. "Still at it, I see."

He sat down and observed the unsheathed typewriter, the pile of papers, and the files that lay on the desk. Then he turned his attention upon Miss Fayette, grave and efficient, seated at the desk, in horn-rimmed spectacles and low-heeled walking-shoes. "*Rôle* of the perfect business girl," he registered mentally.

Joshua, sitting opposite, was explaining to the girl:

"Insisted on coming. Thought we might find something here—

papers and so on—that would throw light."

Margot smiled demurely. "I hardly think Mr Ray will find much to interest him. However, he's welcome to look. Where will you start, Mr Ray?"

Ray returned the smile with interest: "Well, now, that's awfully nice of you," he said. "Supposing, to begin with, we take a general look round. This I take it, is the office, and this room here"—he opened the door marked "PRIVATE"—"is the—er—residential accommodation." The room had undergone rapid transformation—the bed was made, the clothes put away. "And beyond this we have a kitchenette. Excellent!"

Ray turned to the stacked canvases, Joshua looking on. "That one's mine," the latter said, as Ray exposed a large picture in the Surrealist mode—a grey, meticulously vivid dream-world. "So's that . . . . and that. All unsold, you see."

"Did Mr Briggs spend the night here often?" Ray asked, still bending over the pictures.

"Offhandedly Margot answered: "Sometimes once a week, perhaps, sometimes more often."

"Well, Ray, what d'you think of 'em?" said Joshua. Ray started: "Oh, your pictures! How long have you been painting?"

"Only two or three years."

"Well, for what it's worth from an outsider, I'd say you were a real painter, which probably means you'll never sell a picture till you're dead. If you were like your sensible brother James you would paint extremely flattering but otherwise realistic portraits of feline hostesses and porcine millionaires, get yourself elected A.R.A. at forty-five and R.A. at fifty, and make a cool two thousand a year. Being a painter, and not a man of business, however, you'll starve. Or, rather, you would starve, if it weren't for your private means."

"Picasso sells," said Joshua.

"There is one Picasso to a thousand other good painters, Briggs. And think how long it took him to get where he is."

Ray picked up a small unframed picture—an oil-colour of enamel-like smoothness, depicting a system of intersecting and heavily shaded cones, cubes, and spheres, almost frightening in their complexity. He said:

"Briggs, how much do you want for this?"

Joshua laughed: "Oh, ten guineas to you! But I'll make you a present of it as soon as you quit playing around and net our man."

"It's a bargain!" They shook hands on it.

Ray walked to the desk and turned over the papers in a tray. "I see these are carbons of the letters he dictated and signed on the fatal day. Are these all of them, Miss Fayette?"

She nodded.

"Hm," said Ray, reading. "Here's the copy of that letter he wrote you, Briggs. Nothing very interesting in that." He picked up the three remaining sheets of paper. "And here's one to Sir Patrick Flinders, Bart., about a certain Degas which somebody wants to sell and Sir Patrick wants to buy for his superb collection . . . . A letter to the landlord, cursing the people upstairs, who *will* throw their furniture about . . . . and a long screed to an insurance company about some accident to his car."

"Not exactly the sort of letters a man writes a few hours before he kills himself," Joshua observed.

"Quite," Ray agreed. "Nevertheless, Briggs, you must remember that your brother was not exactly an average man. At least, I find in him promise of a fascinating personality."

"As far as I'm concerned, he was only too average," said Joshua.

Ray wandered into the bed-sitting-room again, the others at his heels. He went up to the dressing-table and pulled open the top drawer. It was full of tubes of paint, brushes, palette knives, and painters' bric-a-brac.

"Whose are these?" the two men demanded simultaneously.

There was a slight pause before Margot answered. "Well, I don't know whose they are now, but they used to belong to a young fellow your brother put up here once. He left them behind."

Ray closed the drawer slowly, watching Margot's face in the dressing-table mirror. By all ordinary standards it was still fresh and lovely, but paler and more tired than the face he had admired so much the previous day. There was less vivacity and more worry in her magnificent dark eyes. He turned and offered her a cigarette, which she took with red-nailed nicotine-stained fingers that were, he noticed, just a trifle unsteady. He said:

"How's business been lately, Miss Fayette? Good?"

"He didn't discuss his money affairs with me."

"But you wrote his letters and saw his clients and you must have got a general idea."

"Of course. I don't think things were very good. He was getting keener on racing, you know, and he gave very little time to business."

Ray knocked out his pipe in the grate and filled it.

"Let's go back to the office and be comfortable," he said, leading the way.

"Now," he continued, when they had sat down, "just one more thing, Miss Fayette—"

He was interrupted by a knocking at the door leading to the hallway.

Margot excused herself, and went to answer the door. Presently the two men could hear a girl's voice saying:

"Hallo, dear, are you alone? I've come round to talk about to-night."

And Margot replying, "I'm sorry, Pat, but I've got two people here—one of them's Mr Briggs' brother. They'll be gone soon. . . . Look, I'll meet you for tea at the usual place at four o'clock."

There followed farewells and the sound of the door closing.

A second later Ray was on his feet. past Margot, and opening the door again. He caught up with the girl, a tall, beautifully turned-out blonde, on the doorstep.

"Miss Starke, I think?" he said, breathless but grinning.

"Why, yes!" Her stare gave way gradually to a look of amusement at this strange young man.

"You don't remember me?" he asked, pulling vigorously at his pipe. She shook her head.

"Strange," he continued. "Thought I had the sort of face people

don't forget. . . . However, I called at your flat"—he consulted the slip
of paper in his hand—"in Pilchester Terrace the night before last, at
half past six, but you weren't in."

She looked puzzled. "That's odd. Because I was in then, and
Margot was with me. You must have called at the wrong number,
instead of thirteen. But what did you want?"

For a moment Ray was stumped. Then, smiling broadly, he said:
"I admired you at a party the other day, and someone gave me your
name and address."

Miss Starke's well-rouged lips narrowed into a thin straight line.
Ray, slow to take warning, ducked a split second too late and took a
resounding slap on the cheek-bone. Before he had recovered from
the shock Miss Starke was walking quickly down the street, peroxide
head in the air.

A titter behind him made Ray turn. Margot, with exaggerated
politeness, was holding open the office door for him.

"Fortunes of war," he said ruefully to Joshua, who was trying not
to smile. "A muscular dame." Massaging his cheek, he went back into
the room. "Thought I'd run into her at a party once. My mistake."

Margot, in her sweetest business-girl manner, said: "Is there
anything else, sir, we can do for you this afternoon?"

"Let me see," said Ray, sitting down. "Briggs, can you think of
anything?"

"Sothern," Joshua suggested.

"Good. Miss Fayette, kindly take the stand. Briggs, your witness."

Joshua gripped his coat lapels and addressed Margot after the manner of the bar.

"Miss Fayette, how long have you known the deceased?"

Margot sat with her hands folded in her lap and a demure expression on her face. She answered: "Three or four months, sir."

"And how long have you known Mr Sothern?"

"Oh, a long time. At least eighteen months, probably longer."

"Thank you. You were—excuse me—very friendly with Mr Sothern?"

"Yes"

"And when you became—er—very friendly with the deceased, what was Mr Sothern's reaction?"

"Unfavourable, sir. Definitely negative, if you know what I mean."

"Ah, then there were quarrels?" Joshua stole a look at Ray, who nodded encouragement.

"There were."

"You ceased to know Mr Sothern?"

"Oh, yes, sir."

Ray interrupted: "I wish to put a question to witness. Thank you. . . . Miss Fayette, will you please tell the court what you know about Mr Sothern's relationship with the deceased? Was its basis business or social intercourse?"

Margot hesitated: "Well . . . . I don't think Mr Sothern is interested in pictures. It was a sort of social relationship, I think."

"Now Miss Fayette, you knew Mr Sothern, as you say, for quite a long period. Please tell us about him. How he earned his living, for instance."

"I always thought he had a private income. Anyhow I know very little about his money affairs."

"Amazing!" Ray exclaimed. "Ma'am, for a lady, of your obvious intelligence, what you don't know staggers me. . . . Sir, your witness."

"As far as I'm concerned," said Joshua, "the witness can stand down."

"Right," said Ray, "then we'll adjourn. You two can go and have a cup of tea with that muscular young lady while I pay a duty call on a neglected but wealthy aunt. I'll meet you, Briggs, in an hours' time, on the appropriate platform at St Pancras."

* * * *

The train was chugging wearily through grey, rain-lashed suburbs. In spite of the cold Joshua insisted on opening the carriage window.

"Believe me or believe me not," he explained to Ray, who sat huddled up in his overcoat, shivering, "that cod still lingers. . . . Didn't your aunt notice it?"

"Such a disappointment! She was out," sighed Ray. "So I went on to Pilchester Terrace and had an interesting talk with the porter."

"Was the alibi a fake?"

"I'd like your opinion on that question after you've heard what I've got to say. . . . Pilchester Terrace turned out to be a multi-storied structure in the wedding-cake style of the nineties, divided into innumerable flatlets, which are rented out by an avaricious, but not unduly inquisitive, landlord. William, its porter, likewise turned out to be a survival of the nineties, both in person and mind. For a small consideration he talked. I believe that for no consideration at all he would have harangued me all night on his favourite topic, which is the love-life of Pilchester Terrace.

"With some difficulty I weaned him from the grosser irrelevancies of this enthralling subject, and got him to concentrate upon Miss Starke. It seems that this young lady hits the high spots fairly continuously. She goes out almost nightly in evening dress and is driven home in the early hours by assorted young men. On those occasions when she spends an evening at home she is not alone, nor is she with girlfriends. William had given the subject much study, bringing to bear upon it a mind nurtured on the more lurid Sunday Press.

"The night of April the first had been exceptional. So far as he could remember, Miss Starke had returned to her flat at about six-thirty with a friend. Because it was a girlfriend William had not been particularly interested, and did not look at her face. He didn't recognize the photo of Margot that I had pinched from the dressing-table in Fitzwilliam Street—it might have been that girl or another; he couldn't say. Anyhow, the two girls had remained in the flat the whole evening, and nobody had called on them. William was so surprised at this fact that the circumstances were ineradicably engraven on the tablets of his mind. He was sure of them."

"Well," Joshua observed, "I guess that's a reasonably good confirmation of the alibi."

"You see nothing odd about it?"

"You mean that the girl friend might not have been Margot, but somebody else?"

Ray sighed. "Never mind, let's drop the subject and talk about something improving. For instance, what do you think of those amusing composite drawings called *Cadavres Exquis?*"

CHAPTER XV

THE leaded windows of the Tiddenham Arms chattered in the night wind. Every time a new customer came in at the door a chill gust swept through the bar, diverting the darts from their true courses and filling the room with strong language. It was to just such a gust that Ray secretly attributed the double twenty he had scored.

This feat, which concluded the game in favour of Ray's side, was followed by appropriate applause, and the company settled down to its beer-mugs and conversation again. Ray ensconced himself in a corner near the fire, the warmth of which was not sufficient to allow him to discard his overcoat. Sitting in the shadow, with turned-up collar, above which sprouted, like queer plants from a pot, a pair of thick spectacles, a pipe, and a quantity of hair, he became as the evening advanced practically a piece of furniture, attracting no more attention than the aspidistras.

The conversation, having touched on foot-and-mouth disease, Hitler, the morals of Miss Hall, and the incidence of German measles in the village, and bounced off each in turn, lighted at last on the Briggs affair.

The young man in the bowler was saying: "I tell you there's something funny about that business. Folks is all saying it was an accident, but folks as use their heads isn't so sure."

This roused an old fellow with a walrus moustache. "You ain't got a right to speak like that, Percy, afore the verdick. Any'ow, what reason come you to have to speak so, knowing no more'n present company?"

He appealed to the rest.

"That's right, Perce, tell us what you know, or shut up," piped a small voice from the rear.

Thus heckled, Percy lost some of his assurance of manner. "Well, what I mean to say," he said, "a man don't clean a gun the way he did. When you clean a gun you lay it across your knees, don't you, Bill?"

They all laughed. Bill had a reputation as poacher. He said:

"Yer never knows with toffs."

Encouraged by the success of this sally, Percy continued: "That isn't the only funny thing, either."

He paused for a drink.

"No? Let's 'ave it, Perce," piped the voice in the rear.

"I don't know as I ought to tell you. There might've been a mistake."

Cries of "Be a sport," "Come on Percy," "You can trust us," greeted this announcement.

"All right, then. Only, mind you, it wasn't me that saw him." Percy was determined not to be rushed.

"Saw who?"

"Sothern, in the Briggses' garden between seven and half-past, night before last."

"Well, I'll be damned!"

Some one whistled, *Tell Us Another One, Do*, and there was a general crowding round the gratified Percy. The walrus moustache led the opposition.

"Now then, Percy, it were mighty dark then, an' there ain't no lights in that road."

"Maybe not," countered Percy, "but the Briggses' house have got electric lights, ha'nt it? And the light can shine from the house into the garden, can't it?"

Unable to challenge this, the opposition shifted the direction of its attack.

"When yer tell us who saw 'im, we might believe yer."

"It was a friend of mine what's known to everybody in Tiddenham, only I can't tell you who, because he made me promise. He doesn't want to be dragged into a police case, and, anyway, it was pretty dark, and he might've made a mistake."

"There y'are," exclaimed the walrus contemptuously. "What did I tell yer? Rather dark. Mighta been some one else. An' who saw all this? A feller what can't be named. It's this sort of talk what does a lot of 'arm to innocent folks."

"Shut your trap!" cried Percy, nettled by this onslaught. "I never said I knew anything, did I? I only told you what I'd heard said by some one what's not quite sure himself what he saw."

"Never mind 'im, Perce," cried one of his supporters. "Tell us some more. Tell us what 'e was a-doin' in the garden."

"There isn't any more to tell," replied Percy. "He was coming out of the side of the house, and the light of the room shined on his face. . . . That's what I've been told, see? Maybe it isn't true."

Out-manoeuvred, the opposition held its peace. The conversation drifted on to the subject of Londoners.

"Every year more of 'em comes to live 'ere," some one was saying.

The man with the walrus moustache wagged his head. "Ah, an'

a pity it is! The place ain't nothin' to what it were when I was a boy. Then it were peaceful like, an' everybody in the village knew each other. Goin' to Lunnon once of a year, or maybe once in five year, were a rare treat. Work was 'ard, but life was 'omely. . . . An' now look at us. Are we 'appier? The electric's laid on from Stokeby. The road's like a table-top, an' the buses is grand. But we ain't. And the folks what come 'ere in the buses and charabanks an' cars is worse still."

"Old miserable," a voice commented.

"What I say," said Percy, "is that these here Londoners may be a rum crowd, but they bring work, and work brings money."

"An' money brings bowler 'ats," cut in Bill, the poacher.

There was general laughter. Percy reddened.

"Got 'is own back there, Perce," piped the man at the rear.

"Speakin' o' folks from Lunnon," began the man with the walrus moustache, addressing Mrs Greene, "is that bloke still 'ere what goes walkin' of a night?"

"Mr Hogg, you mean?" Mrs Greene shook her head. "No, he left for London the night before last."

"That's right," said Percy. "I saw him walking along the road to the village carrying his bag."

Mrs Greene stopped polishing glasses and looked at the speaker with surprise. "Why, that's queer!" she exclaimed. "He said he was going to the station. What should he want to go in the opposite direction for?"

"He was going to the bus stop, of course," said Percy.

"Use yer 'ead," Bill admonished. "The bus don't go to Lunnon. An' what's more, there ain't no bus after six o'clock till the nine-ten. . . . What time was it you see 'im?"

"How should I remember?" replied Percy. "It was after six, anyhow. He may have lost his way."

"Use yer head," Bill admonished again. "Ain't there a new signpost outside this pub what points the way to the station?"

Percy retorted: "Clever, aren't you? But it was getting dark when I saw him. I reckon he never saw the signpost."

Somebody had a bright idea. "P'raps, Percy, the man that your pal saw at the Briggses' was this here Hogg, only he mistook him for Sothern."

"Maybe." Percy shook his head doubtfully. "But Sothern's tall and all dressed up, and this other chap's middle height and sort of untidy."

"I tell yer what," announced the voice at the rear. "I reckon they were both in it. Between 'em they did this Briggs chap in, an' fixed it so as it looked like an accident."

There was a stirring in the corner, and Ray's face emerged from its encircling collar.

"Lord!" said Percy. "I clean forgot you were there."

Ray stood up and stretched his limbs. He said: "They also serve who only—in this case—sit and wait. . . . But come, gentlemen, in some twenty minutes Mrs Greene will shoo us all out of here. Order your drinks—on me this time, for I'm more indebted to you than you realize—and we'll play a return game of darts. . . .Let me see whether I can start off with another double twenty."

*   *   *   *

Ray sat in his bedroom at the Tiddenham Arms, behind closely drawn curtains. He had pulled a chair and a bedside table as close as possible to the inadequate electric fire. Instead of his overcoat he wore a thick woollen dressing-gown over his suit, and his feet were encased in an ancient pair of sandals. On the table lay neatly arranged papers, an enormous ashtray, three boxes of matches, a glass of cold coffee, and a plate of Marmite sandwiches to ward off night starvation. He had turned face to the wall the pictures of pyramids, camels' backsides, and palm-trees.

"We've practically reached the sorting-office stage," he said to Joshua Briggs, who had just come in, "except for—"

"These," cut in Joshua, handing him three cigarette butts. "I had no end of difficulty in getting them. Ellen has a habit of pitching them into the fire."

Ray laid out the cigarette-ends on the table, ranging them alongside those which he had retrieved from Dr Storr's dustbin. After a brief scrutiny he said:

"Interesting, Briggs, if not exactly surprising. The chances that the same person smoked these five cigarettes must be several hundreds—if not thousands—to one. Work it out for yourself."

Joshua bent over the table. "The lipstick is certainly the same colour," he observed.

"That's only one factor. There are at least five respects in which the two groups are practically identical. One: as you say, the lipstick on all five cigarettes is the same dark shade. Two: if you look closely at the grain of the paper, the diameter of the tube, the width of the lap of the paper, and the cut and the colour of the tobacco, you will see that all these are identical in each instance—indicating cigarettes of the same brand. Three: they have all been smoked to within about an inch and a half of the end—and the length of an individual's cigarette butts is a surprisingly constant factor. Four: notice that they have all been crushed out pretty violently; the charred end is split and telescoped. And five—the most important of all—is an invisible similarity; they were all smoked by a person who knew Dr Storr."

"In other words," said Joshua, "if Ellen Briggs wasn't at Dr Storr's some time during the evening of James's death you'll eat your hat."

Ray laughed. "Leaving aside the fact that I haven't got one, and any such oath would therefore be null and void, I would never, Briggs, be guilty of such a non sequitur. Remember the letter you found. Remember that the cigarette butts retrieved from the doctor's ash-can may have been smoked not on the night of your brother's death, but on some other occasion. . . .You must distinguish between certainties and probabilities."

"Oh, all right!" replied Joshua pettishly. "Do I go to bed now, or continue to function as a foil to your brilliance?'

"You can go to bed, Briggs, when you've furnished the final item of information. What was Ellen Briggs before she married your brother?"

"She was an engraver."

Ray's eyes narrowed. "Now, that's darned interesting," he said.

Joshua helped himself to a Marmite sandwich. "All this is very impressive, Ray. In the best fictional traditions, no doubt. But to a mere satellite like myself it looks like flogging a dead horse. Of course, I don't mind your all-night vigil, your little games with cigarette-ends, and your air of plumbing the bottomless abyss. I don't take violent exception to your dressing-gown, if it makes you happy. For limited periods I can even tolerate your oracular manner. But you can't expect me to be utterly overwhelmed."

"And why not?"

"Because, to me, the solution of the case is crystal clear."

"Whereas to me, Briggs, it's as opaque as a mud pie. As a mud pie that's a tangle of loose ends—if you can do that sort of thing with mud."

Joshua sighed. "You're making mountains out of molehills, Ray. The loose ends you're worried about no doubt have a perfectly simple explanation which will come to light in due course. You can't expect to master every detail of a case like this in two days. Concentrate on the essentials."

"Briggs," replied Ray, "it's an appalling thought, but you may turn out to be right after all. Perhaps I'm trying to be over-subtle. Perhaps, because I loathe the idea of an easy solution, I see non-existent complexities. Perhaps my mind is projecting wish-fulfilments."

"Decent of you to admit it, Ray. First thing tomorrow morning, then, we go to the police, hand over the piece of blotting-paper, and tell them about the interview we had with Sothern's servant girl. As it is, we'll have some difficulty in explaining why we hung on to the evidence so long."

"What about Ellen and the doctor, Briggs?" Inquired Ray. "Do we maintain a discreet silence?"

"I think not. After all, there is evidence which might be construed against them. For myself, I haven't any doubt about the murderer's identity, but the police ought to know all the facts before they make an arrest. It's been amusing to play detectives with you, and, as a matter of fact, I think you've done marvellously. But I'm sure the time's come for us to tell the police what we know, and retire gracefully."

Ray got up and started pacing the carpet. "I'm in your hands, Briggs," he said. "You called me in, and you tell me when to get out. What's more, you know all that I know—except that I haven't told you that Sothern, or some one like him, was seen outside your brother's house on the fatal night between seven and half-past, and that Hogg appears to have lost his way to the station. And now you know everything that I know, and I can't prevent you from going to the police with it even if I wanted to."

Joshua got up to go. "That's agreed, then, Jethro. To-morrow we let the cat out of the bag. I'm really grateful to you for what you've done. So grateful, in fact, that I don't mind if you gather together all the suspects and finish the case, as far as you are concerned, in the approved torture-chamber style, like a small boy pulling off a fly's wings and legs one by one."

Laughing somewhat joyously, Ray saw his friend to the hall door. "That's really nice of you, Briggs," he said. "I confirm the bargain. To-night, however, merely for the sake of amusement, I shall sift and sort, piece together and pull apart, synthesize and analyse, and generally try to tease the truth out of the evidence. Futile, very likely. Briggs, my friend, I shall probably emerge from this, my first, and possibly my last, case with a thumping great inferiority complex. For which I shall hold you responsible."

To which Joshua Briggs replied: "You make me laugh. . . . Go to bed, and to-morrow morning you'll be able to strut up and down before a thrilled audience, and tell them how cleverly you found the blotting-paper, tricked Sothern's maid, found out the doctor's little game, discovered the cigarette butts, and intercepted Ellen's letter. And we'll all be speechless with admiration. What more could a detective want."

"A depilatory for loose ends," said Ray.

*　　　　　*　　　　　*　　　　　*

By the time the clock on Ray's mantelpiece struck one his ash-tray was half full of spent matches and dottle from his pipe, the Marmite sandwiches were eaten, and the coffee was drunk. And Ray felt like Henley—bloody but unbowed.

Ray held that thinking was best done on paper or in conversation. Reasoning, without an audience to keep one to the point, or without notes and diagrams to focus one's attention, quickly degenerated, in his experience, into wool-gathering and finally slumber. In pursuance of this belief, he was now engaged in tabulating, collating, drawing up schemes, making lists and time-tables. He drew a sketch plan from memory of the ground floor and the garden of the Briggses' house. From the jottings in his notebook he made a time-table, as far as possible, of the actions of each of his suspects on the day of the tragedy; then he combined the separate time-tables into a comprehensive one. He considered the case from the point of view of each actor, listing in each instance the possible motives, and analysing the opportunity or lack of opportunity. He drew up a list of loose ends in the case. With utmost care he combed the evidence again, looking for some hint, some unconsidered trifle that he had missed, some additional loose end which could be made to knit together all the other loose ends and resolve the whole into an intellectually satisfying pattern.

At four o'clock the ash-tray was overflowing onto the table, the room had developed a rich fug, and the floor was littered with rejected lists and schemes and time-tables. Ray sat back and sighed. He took off his spectacles, revealing shadows under his eyes. His hair stood out spikily at all angles, and his tie had been discarded long before.

"Four o'clock and all's ill," he groaned.

At six he suddenly threw his pipe on the table, jumped up, and went over to the window, where he drew back the curtains and flung open the casement. Polished pinks and yellows, smooth and pure like ceramics, diffused the eastern sky. Streaks of apple-green threaded like needles a roseate embroidery of cloud-tufts that looked infinitely remote, yet as distinct as if they had been within arm's reach. The air itself, strong, chill, and perfectly still, seemed impregnated with a throbbing presence. In a cherry-tree a blackbird started to sing. . . .

At seven he shaved with unprecedented care, took a scaldingly hot bath, and put on a pair of flannel trousers which, while they were by no means new, were at least virginal from the dry-cleaners. He spent at least five minutes brushing his hair and his tweed jacket, while from the recesses of his suitcase he unearthed a gamboge tie made of material like sacking.

It was expressive of his mood that, having at length completed his toilette and arrayal, he should turn face-outwards the Egyptian pictures on the bedroom wall, slide down the banister rail, and solemnly execute a fandango in the hall.

PART THREE

CHAPTER XVI

"SUPPOSING," said Ray over the breakfast-table, "this were a detective story, Briggs."

"That sort of remark goes well with your tie."

"The match is perfect: they are both parts of an amusingly baroque façade behind which lies an interior that is Gothic in its solemnity. But as I was saying, supposing this were a detective story, who, among the numerous starters, would you back as the murderer?"

Joshua Briggs pondered. "Well," he observed, "Sothern's far too obvious, don't you think?"

"Go on."

"Ellen and the doctor have an excellent motive and lots of opportunity, so it's pretty safe to count them out."

"So it would seem."

"On the whole, I'm inclined to think that Groves is the safest bet in the field. Or Mrs Groves."

"Yes," Ray agreed. "Old Groves and his wife are well in the running. Gardener and wife plan murder of daughter's seducer, shall we say? As for Sothern, has it occurred to you, Briggs, that the time is ripe for the most suspected character in the story to turn out to be the criminal after all? It's become painfully easy to spot the villain in a detective story on *a priori* grounds alone. He or she is the one person against whom there is hardly a shred of direct, honest evidence. You can safely say that all the goats will turn out to be sheep, and that the most virtuous-looking sheep will, in the penultimate chapter, be shown up for the goat he is."

"Consequently the experienced detective fan puts his shirt on that apparently innocent animal, and ranks the pseudo-goats as a flock of outsiders. Realizing this disturbing fact, it's high time the detective-story writers used their brains and double-crossed their more intelligent readers by making the obvious villain the real villain, by disguising their wolves in wolves' clothing. In other words, I'm not so sure that, in fiction, Sothern would of necessity be written off as an 'also-ran.'"

"Good idea, Ray," Joshua replied. "A dodge that would no doubt take in the experienced reader. But the other customers would be terribly disappointed to find that they hadn't been fooled. After all, they pay seven and sixpence, or whatever it is, for the thrill of being bamboozled, tricked by fair means and foul, and made to feel daft. The author is under a sacred obligation to play the game according to the accepted rules of deceit, and give his public what they pay for. In an orthodox detective novel the villain who slew James Briggs would be a man like the blameless-seeming Groves, I think, and not Sothern, who has guilt written all over him."

"You may be right, Briggs. Perhaps the wheel hasn't yet come full circle, and the majority of the public are still duly astounded to find the villain amongst the characters with snow-white records. Assume, then, that our hypothetical detective story is of the kind which caters for such a public. What have we? Sothern is plainly not our man. Nor is the doctor. Groves, as you say, would be an intelligent bet. I can think of an even more promising horse to put your money on."

"Margot?"

"I should have thought that the evidence against Margot was strong enough to rule her out. Try again."

Joshua laughed. "I know—myself!"

"Right! You have practically all the necessary detective-story qualifications. You look as harmless as a new-born lamb, and your behaviour is more or less in keeping. Your probable motive—murder for gain—hardly works, because you would surely have found out that your brother was broke before going to the trouble of wiping him out. And the suspicion that falls upon you throughout the investigation is practically *nil.* All of which makes it practically certain that you murdered him. . . . There's only one snag."

"I'm sorry to hear that. What is this unfortunate flaw in the argument, Ray?"

"That I happen to know you didn't, Briggs. I mean in real life." They both laughed.

"Ha!" cried Joshua. "So you did have me down on your list of suspects, after all."

"Certainly I did. Everybody's suspect until proved innocent."

"Well, Ray," sympathized Briggs, "I hope you'll find it in your heart to forgive me. . . . . There are others, you know. Hogg, for example. But perhaps there's too much against him. What about Major Wigley or Inspector Hines? And what about yourself?"

"Good again, Briggs. My motive is as obscure as the most fastidious fan could desire. Or shall we say that my motive was to provide myself with the opportunity to do some snooping. Come to think of it, Briggs, it was rather a coincidence that I should be on the spot pining for a chance to play detective (as you tactfully put it), when along comes a nice little mystery, straight out of the hat. Suspicious circumstance, that. I must leave you to develop the notion, Briggs—I am obviously disqualified to do so myself. I would point out one snag, however. It is that, unless the author intends permanently to retire, he must at all costs keep his detective alive to conduct further cases. To hang him for the murder he had investigated is an excellent idea in itself, but in the long view it is uneconomic. To hang his Dr Watson is similarly unwise. Unless, of course, the author finds one or other of them so unsatisfactory that he decides to put him out of his misery forever. Even so, remember that Sherlock did return from a point that was, if I remember rightly, at least half-way across the Styx."

"Since, unfortunately, we're eliminated, Ray, it seems that the guilt must lie at the door of one of the other characters. But, to revert to our theme, I think a really subtle detective writer might very well compromise nowadays and make his most suspected character the real criminal, but for unsuspected reasons. Thereby the writer would lead up the garden path not only the common or gullible reader, but the connoisseur as well."

"Now that, Briggs, is really clever of you. If it were not for the fact that I must now tear myself away and go to see the fire-eating Major, and that you, by hook or by crook, must gather together the suspects and near suspects in this case, I would beseech you to continue. As it is, however, we are not writing a detective chronicle—that will be the privilege of my biographer hereafter."

*   *   *   *

Spring had returned from her two days' banishment with increased freshness. A gentle air, smelling of rain-soaked earth, lapped against responsive green things. The sun, unchallenged by a cloudlet, ruled a wide sky.

Ray's ancient motor chugged along the highway between Tiddenham and Stokeby at a rate not exceeding twenty miles an hour, but with rattle enough for thrice that speed. As a further insult to a morning of frisking lambs and bursting buds, his car came trailing clouds of blue and evil-smelling vapour. Of this Ray was unaware. He was equally oblivious to the scene around him, except that he felt vaguely in tune with it. In his present frame of mind he was prepared to feel in tune with anything or anybody.

He passed the speculative builders' villas on the outskirts of Stokeby without a qualm. His unseeing eye rested on Stokeby's new super-cinema and did not blench. Perseus, in such a mood, would have been able to dispense with his mirror-shield in dealing with Medusa.

Having parked his car in the shadow of the church, Ray strode into the police station. Inspector Hines admitted him to the Major's office without ceremonial. Even the Chief Constable of Stokeby, on this morning of mornings, appeared an amiable old gentleman.

Ray felt that he had hitherto misjudged him.

"Marvellous morning, sir," Ray trilled.

The austere expression on the Major's face brought Ray back to earth with a bump. "Pardon me, sir," he said. "Fact is, I feel happy."

Major Wigley made indeterminate noises in his throat and puffed out his cheeks.

"Well," Ray resumed, "did you make any headway with the information I gave you yesterday?"

"Yes, sir, we did!" exclaimed the Major. "But this is all very irregular. . . . I still don't understand how you came to know . . . . If you're still hiding something from me, young man, I must point out that—"

"I know!" cried Ray. "I shan't obstruct the workings of the law much longer. In point of fact, I was about to strike a bargain with you. My lowest terms for the one and only genuine solution of the Tiddenham case are—"

"What!" roared the Major. "More blackmail?"

"Ugly word, chief. Let's go in for euphemism and call it *quid pro quo,* mutual aid, reciprocity."

The Chief Constable rose from his seat with dignity. He said in a carefully controlled voice:

"Young man, I'm bound to acknowledge that you gave me useful information yesterday, though you did so in a way that was discreditable and not above suspicion. However that may be, the information that you lodged, along with the outcome of our own investigations, is yielding results, and we're getting along quite satisfactorily without your further help. We'll solve this mystery all right; in fact, we've practically done so already. But, incidentally, I shan't regard the case as entirely cleared up till I have a satisfactory explanation of your conduct, sir."

Major Wigley pressed the button on his desk, and almost immediately Inspector Hines appeared at the door.

"Inspector, please show Mr Ray out."

Ray stood his ground.

"Did you hear me, sir?" the Major bellowed.

Ray started, as though this outburst had recalled him from thoughts that had wandered far. He bowed with exaggerated politeness, turned round, and began walking towards the door, accompanied by the Inspector.

"Inspector Hines," said Ray, in an unnecessarily loud voice, just as they reached the door. "Will you please give me the 'phone number of the Chief Constable of the county at once? It's extremely urgent, and much harm may be done by delay."

The Inspector closed the door and whispered in Ray's ear: "Cowbridge double-three double-three."

A moment later Ray was out in the street striding towards a public telephone booth.

He had already lifted the receiver when he felt a heavy hand laid on his arm. Turning, he found himself confronted with Inspector Hines' agitated countenance.

"To what, Inspector, do I owe this molestation? Am I under arrest for attempted blackmail, or the murder of James Briggs, or for some third misdemeanour?"

In a troubled voice the Inspector strove to explain. "The Chief wants to see you, sir, urgently."

Ray replaced the receiver and shook his head. "That's odd, Inspector. I gathered that I was the unbidden guest. Why this sudden change of front? Anyhow, I have a 'phone call to make."

"Please, Mr Ray," the Inspector pleaded, "come and see the Major now. Between ourselves, sir," he added, with something approaching a wink, "the Major and the Chief Constable of the county aren't on the best of terms, and if—"

"I understand perfectly. Lead on, Inspector."

*   *   *   *

"Take your seat," said Major Wigley to the returned Ray.

Ray sat down and took out his pipe. "Any objection?" he asked.

"No." The Major's face bore marks of recent suffering, but his voice was calm. "Now," he said, "tell me exactly what your—er—proposition is."

Ray was in no hurry now. He finished filling his pipe, lit it, and put the spent match in his breast pocket. Then he crossed his legs and leaned back, puffing clouds of smoke.

"Major Wigley," he said, in measured tones, "I have solved the Tiddenham case. I hereby offer you the solution as on a plate. To you will go most of the honour and glory that accompany it. As an insignificant token of your appreciation all I ask is a trifling favour."

"Hm," grunted the Major." And what the devil makes you so sure that we won't solve the mystery—if we haven't done so already?"

Ray smiled. "To answer that question with strict honesty would,

I'm afraid, amount to rudeness. However, if it turns out that you have arrived at the complete solution, I shall, of course, withdraw my little request."

"And what is this little request, as you call it?"

"That you, sir, and the Inspector, and, let us say, one or two of your stalwart constables, jump in a car and come along with me to Tiddenham, collecting Mr Sothern on the way. I can promise you an entertaining morning that will leave no regrets. On the contrary, you'll probably be promoted as a result."

Major Wigley pounded the table. "Confound you, sir! Stick to facts and don't poke your nose into my affairs. I'll do what you ask only if you can prove to me beyond doubt that you have the correct solution, and that I haven't."

"It's a bargain, Major. I'll demonstrate conclusively the correctness of my solution within half an hour from now, provided you'll give me leave to ask your Inspector to carry out a little investigation."

The Major made a gesture of despair. "Go ahead," he sighed.

Ray got up and went through to the Inspector's office.

After a couple of minutes he came back and sat down.

"While we're waiting for Inspector Hines' report, sir," he said, "would you mind telling me what came of my hint to you yesterday in the matter of the fingerprints?"

"Hm. Sothern's alibi was easily exploded. Hines tells me you suggested investigating this fellow who calls himself Hogg. Well, we've connected him definitely with Sothern. His name, by the way, isn't Hogg, and he has a long police record. The Metropolitan Police have sent me full particulars. Theft and burglary mainly, and in some instances Sothern has definitely been involved, though so far nothing has been proved."

"That's interesting. What are you doing about Hogg?"

"He's got two or three hide-outs, apparently, and the police are on his trail now. I expect to get a telephone call any moment to say they've got him. I feel certain he's mixed up in this case somehow, though exactly how I can't say yet."

"I see you have been busy, sir," said Ray, getting up. "And since you will spend most of to-day out of this office, I will leave you to your papers. I've some 'phone calls to make, but I'll be back by the time the inspector arrives with the good tidings."

"All right," growled the Major, "but if you can't back up what you've just told me, by God you're in for it, young man!"

*   *   *   *

Some twenty minutes later Ray opened the door of Major Wigley's office, advanced a couple of paces into the room, and stopped.

The Major, with apoplectic but radiant features, was bearing down on him, hand outstretched. The Inspector, looking like one whose cup was running over, stood to one side gripping a chair-back.

"Good work, my dear fellow!" the Major was exclaiming. "Heartiest congratulations!"

Ray laughed laconically. "Thanks awfully, Chief. But I should be grateful if you would show your appreciation by ceasing to dislocate my arm."

"Who will you have at the house? When do we start?" cried Major Wigley.

"The answers to those questions, in the order asked, are: *(a)* Ellen Briggs, Joshua Briggs, Groves, Mrs Groves, Sothern, Dr Storr, Margot Fayette, and myself, and *(b)* right now."

"Come on, Hines!" bawled the Major. "What the devil are you waiting for? And bring a gun. We may need it."

CHAPTER XVII

YES, Groves," Joshua was saying, "I think Mr Ray will like the desk put over here by the window. He will sit here, behind it. His notes will be ranged before him, thus. And the chairs for—let me see—nine people, including the two policemen, we'll put over there in a semicircle, with himself at the centre. I'm sure he will approve of that arrangement."

"What about that there bloodstain?" inquired Groves, pointing at the study carpet. "Hadn't I better put a bit o' newspaper over it?"

"No. We'll leave it exposed, and let it work on the murderer's feelings."

Groves shuddered and carefully walked round the spot. "I can't see what you want me and the missus 'ere for," he complained. "We ain't suspects, are we?"

"We're all suspects, Groves. But don't let that trouble you. The main thing is that Mr Ray will make a very long and interesting speech, and he wants as many people as possible to hear him. Now you'll sit here, and Mrs Groves will sit next to you."

"An' what about the lunch, I'd like to know?" protested Mrs Groves, who had appeared in the doorway.

"Cut it out," replied Joshua. "On second thoughts, however, a plate of sandwiches might come in useful for some of us. Though most of the audience will, I'm afraid, forget about food."

Joshua joined Mrs Groves in the doorway and turned to look at the arrangement of the room. All the furniture had been put up against the walls, except for the semicircle of chairs facing the desk.

"As the finishing touch, Mrs Groves, you might put a glass and a jug of water on the table, for the lecturer."

There came a ring at the front door. Mrs Groves went to answer it. Dr Storr stood on the step. The housekeeper was surprised at his paleness. The doctor looked ill and careworn, and his eyes were baggy, as though he had not slept for several nights.

"I have an appointment here with Mr Ray," he explained. "But I'm rather early. Is he in?"

"No, doctor. But Mr Joshua is. I'll call him, if you'll wait in here." She showed him into the sitting-room. "Excuse me," she added, after the doctor had sat down, "but aren't you feelin' queer? Should I get you somethink to drink?"

Dr Storr drew his hand across his forehead, which was damp with perspiration. "It is over-work, Mrs Groves. I shall be better in a moment. . . . A drink? No, thank you. Unless—perhaps—a sherry. Ah, thank you! That is very kind."

Mrs Groves produced a bottle and a glass from the sideboard and poured out a drink.

"Now I feel quite all right," he said, after having drained the glass. "And how is the patient upstairs?"

The housekeeper shrugged her shoulders. "Well, if you was to ask me, doctor, I'd say there was nothink much wrong with 'er."

"Quite true, Mrs Groves, as far as the body is concerned. Her trouble is—what you say?—nerves. The death of her husband, you know. . . . I may as well see her now, while I'm waiting for Mr Ray."

Mrs Groves led the way upstairs.

Ten minutes later another ring brought Mrs Groves from her kitchen, where she was cutting sandwiches, to the front door. Ray, on the doorstep, greeted her with a grin.

"Apologies, Mrs Groves, for throwing a party so early in the morning. I've brought some of my guests with me."

He indicated the Major and the Inspector, and between them Sothern, whose red face bore a defiant expression. He stood glowering at Ray, till the Inspector tugged at his coat-sleeve and urged him into the house.

At that moment there came a tooting and a churning of gravel, and a taxi pulled up at the door. Margot stepped out on to the drive.

Ray came forward. "So nice of you to come, Miss Fayette. Allow me to introduce Major Wigley, Chief Constable of Stokeby, and Inspector Hines, his right hand. Mr Sothern and Mrs Groves I think you know. . . . Gentlemen, Miss Margot Fayette, the late Mr Briggs' private secretary."

Wigley and Hines nodded stiffly, Sothern stared blankly, and Mrs Groves scowled. Margot, in short fur coat and hat like a large cream-horn, looked more attractive than ever. The drive in an open car had kindled her cheeks and tossed her dark brown curls into a sweet disorder. Nevertheless, Ray thought he detected traces of the haggardness that he had noticed on the previous day.

"Ha!" he cried, as Joshua came up. "Here you are at last, Briggs. No need to introduce *you*. . . . Well, what are we waiting for?"

In the study they found Groves, busily disarranging and arranging the chairs.

"A perfect set-up, Joshua," was Ray's comment on the lay-out of the room. "Nice warm fire, sun pouring in, and the bloodstain to remind us all what we're here for. . . . But I miss the good doctor and his patient."

"I'll go upstairs and tell 'im," volunteered Mrs Groves, departing.

"Well," said Ray, "take your seats, everybody—yes, including you, Groves—and make yourselves comfortable. Smoking is permitted." He lit his pipe.

Every one in the room sat down, with the exception of Ray, who stood behind the desk polishing his spectacles. This done, he removed a bulky sheaf of papers from his pocket, and arranged them in neat piles on the desk. No one spoke.

The door opened. Dr Storr stood in the opening, evidently startled. Mrs Groves stood behind him.

"Where's Mrs Briggs, doctor?" Ray asked. "We would like her to be present."

"Mrs Briggs," replied Dr Storr, "is unfortunately not in a fit condition to leave her room."

"Are you sure of that?" Ray's tone conveyed doubt.

" I am," said the doctor, in a firm voice. "Do you doubt—"

"Yes. I'm very much inclined to. . . . Never mind. Please take your seat, Dr Storr. Perhaps Mrs Briggs will be able to join us later on."

The doctor did not move. He said: "I'm afraid I must be going. My patients are expecting me, and I have an urgent—"

"Excuse me," Ray interrupted, addressing the others. He got up and walked over to the door. "A word in your ear, doctor, out here," he said, leading the doctor out into the hall and closing the door behind them.

After a brief interval the door opened again, admitting Ray, followed by Dr Storr, whose objections had apparently been overcome. He took a chair next to the vacant one intended for Ellen Briggs, and sat fingering his beard nervously.

"Why not smoke?" said Ray, offering the doctor a cigarette, which he accepted. Sothern and Margot were already smoking.

"Well," inquired Margot huskily, "when does the oracle start to function? I didn't come here to admire your face, Mr Ray. Nor your tie."

This observation seemed to break the tension for a moment.

"That goes for me too," Sothern growled.

Mrs Groves started to giggle hysterically, and the Major shuffled uneasily in his chair.

Ray laid his pipe on the desk, took off his glasses, and tilted back the chair in which he was sitting. His face betrayed no emotion of any kind, and the tone of his voice was as matter-of-fact as if he were lecturing to a meeting of archaeologists on the subject of Saxon architecture.

CHAPTER XVIII

FROM what I have read," he began, "it is the habit of certain detectives, at such moments as these, to whet the appetites of their audiences by expatiating on the dastardly nature of the crime, or its amazing ingenuity, or the super-human intelligence that has gone to the solving of it.

"I shall spare you all this—in any case, such *apéritifs* are apt to make the ensuing intellectual feast seem pretty poor fare—and shall get down to brass tacks with a minimum of preliminaries.

"One main feature of this case, however, is worth noticing. I refer to the multiplicity of the possible solutions. The suspects are few, it is true. The ways in which the deceased could have died, whether by accident, suicide, or murder, are obviously limited. But the number of solutions, involving not only the suspects, individually and in collusion, but also these three modes of dying, is interestingly large. From my point of view, this fact has made the case a fascinating one.

"Before arriving at the correct solution I approached the problem—or rather problems—of how Briggs died, and of who killed him, from several different starting-points in turn. The first line of investigation is clearly indicated by the three questions: Did Briggs accidentally press the trigger while he was cleaning his loaded gun? Did he deliberately shoot himself with it? Or did some one murder him, and contrive things in such a way that the murder appeared as either accident or suicide?

"Let us tackle the three questions in that order, and precisely in the manner in which I tackled them before arriving at my solution.

*　　　　*　　　　*　　　　*

"First, accident. The gun belonged to Briggs. He had bought it recently, and, according to all the evidence available, he knew little or nothing about firearms. The rags, slightly stained with oil, that were found near the body suggested that he had been cleaning the gun. He was to have gone shooting on the following day, and it seems natural that he should take out the weapon that evening and examine it, get the feel of the thing, perhaps, and polish it up a bit. The fact that the gun probably did not need cleaning is irrelevant—as every man who is intrigued by a new gadget will testify.

"So far, then, I had found nothing to discount the theory of accident. The fact that the gun was loaded raised some doubts, however. James Briggs, from what I had gathered, was not an unintelligent man, though all men, of course, are stupid now and then. It occurred to me that he might have loaded the gun just to see how it was done, forgotten about the cartridge, and then started to fiddle about with the trigger. Improbable, perhaps; certainly not impossible.

"I was also doubtful about the likelihood of his pointing the gun at his head, while cleaning or examining it. Laying the gun across, the knees would be the natural thing to do in the circumstances, especially if one were cleaning or manipulating the portion round the trigger.

"That these two improbabilities—*(a)* the gun being loaded, and *(b)* its position and direction at the time it went off—should occur together seemed to me to be, in itself, an improbability which went far towards ruling out the accident theory. I say 'tended,' because far more surprising coincidences can and do happen daily. And the fact that I was naturally biased against such an easy solution made me all the more careful not to discard it altogether.

"Accordingly I shelved the accident theory, reserving it for future examination should no more satisfactory solution offer itself. Until six o'clock this morning, in fact, I was still prepared to adopt this simple, but intellectually sterile, explanation of how Briggs died.

*   *   *   *

"Having temporarily disposed of the death by misadventure idea, I turned to the more complex question of suicide. Inquiry into this question naturally divided itself into the investigation of motive, and then of method.

"Now, generally speaking, there is but one motive for suicide, and that is a suicidal frame of mind. Was Briggs in such a mood before he died? At about half-past nine in the morning, according to Groves, he was not. In fact, he was unusually cheerful. Both Mrs Briggs and Mrs Groves say that they didn't notice anything unusual in his manner at breakfast. Miss Fayette reports that his behaviour at the office was normal. I wondered whether something to upset him had occurred during the lunch party which, Miss Fayette testifies, he attended on the day of his death. But she assured me that his manner after that lunch was in no way changed.

"At first sight, all this evidence seems clearly to show that James Briggs was not in the mood to kill himself. Actually it proves nothing of the kind. The immediate or proximate incentive to suicide may have arisen after he left his office. For instance, it is quite possible that he received bad news over the "phone on his arrival here—news, possibly, about the loss of a big sum of money, or news, let us say, concerning some woman, whether his wife or another. Remember that he was a secretive man who might have been involved in affairs of which we know nothing.

"The fact is that there is nothing whatever to show what sort of mood Briggs was in when he died, and research into the question can be abandoned as unprofitable.

"We turn next to general or long-term motives. At once we have a most excellent reason for suicide. Briggs was broke. He had squandered a small fortune on betting and other frivolities. His bank balance was insufficient to meet his debts. It is not impossible that he learnt by 'phone, just before he died, of his final ruin, of the utter collapse of some scheme for recouping his losses.

"The possibility of another motive occurred to me. It was alleged by Mrs Briggs that her husband and Miss Fayette quarrelled violently during Miss Fayette's last stay here. I had certain reasons for doubting the truth of this story. In addition, Miss Fayette herself denied it, though her evidence on this point carries little weight. I concluded that it was just possible, though unlikely, that Briggs had killed himself on account of a jealous quarrel with the woman he loved.

"Passing now to the *method* of the suicide, the use of a shotgun immediately struck me as odd. Why not a revolver, a razor, the gas-oven? But we have already come to the conclusion that if Briggs killed himself he probably did so on the spur of the moment. In that case he would have had no time to buy a revolver. As for the cut-throat razor and the gas-oven—Mrs Groves here will, I imagine, confirm that there is neither in the house. In an emergency, then, the shotgun is the obvious weapon—the only weapon to hand.

"It might be argued that the rags, presumably used for cleaning the gun, upset the suicide theory. They don't. Many a suicide has been staged to look like an accident. Briggs may well have wished to avoid posthumous unpleasantness by killing himself in such a way that a jury would bring in a verdict of death by misadventure.

"In short, the suicide theory definitely worked. There was an adequate motive, plenty of opportunity, and the method was the natural one in the circumstances. Why, then, go further? I'm indebted to my friend, Joshua Briggs, who felt that there was something queer, something unexplained, and called me in to investigate this queerness. It was not very long before I agreed with him. But the odd facts about the case, which suggested passing on to the murder theory, did not invalidate the suicide theory. They left it unaffected. On the other hand, it left them unexplained. And I yearned for a solution that explained everything, into the framework of which every fact would fit perfectly.

"The suicide theory yielded no such neat solution—which is not to say, of course, that it is incorrect. Along with the accident theory,

I shelved it for future reference.

*   *   *   *

"We come now to murder.

"Before considering the question of who had motive and opportunity for killing James Briggs, I propose to look to the nature of the murder—if murder it was.

"It would seem fairly certain that the killer intended us to believe that Briggs had killed himself, whether accidentally or deliberately. This intention would explain the murderer's choice of weapon and locale.

"Now let us try to reconstruct his procedure—and by his I also mean her, of course. He is in the house when Briggs arrives; or he comes to the house with Briggs; or calls after Briggs' arrival—which of these alternatives was actually the case is immaterial at the moment. Now, it is plain that the murderer-to-be cannot sit Briggs down on a chair, and promptly kneel down and shoot him from below at a range of a few inches, unless indeed they are playing some sort of a game—an unlikely eventuality. Can the murderer take Briggs by surprise and shoot him before he has time to dodge, or to put up some resistance? I think not; because it is essential to the accident-suicide fake that the shot shall be fired from exactly the right angle, and from exactly the right distance, at exactly the right spot. A small variation from these requirements would show accident or suicide to have been impossible, and would set the police looking for the murderer.

"In other words, we may fairly conclude that Briggs was unconscious or semi-conscious when he was shot.

"A drug or a knock-out blow on the head are at once suggested. (That neither you, Dr Storr, nor the police surgeon found traces of such a blow is of course easily explained by the fact that the head was very badly injured by the shot.) We will assume that, by one or the other means, Briggs has been rendered unconscious. If he is not already seated in the chair he is put there. The murderer then presumably puts on a pair of gloves, picks up the gun, takes careful aim, and fires.

"Was this crime premeditated, in the sense that it was carefully planned in detail beforehand? There appears to be no evidence either for or against this view. The murderer may well have known that Briggs had the gun, and have devised his method accordingly. On the other hand, the murderer may have come intending to kill, but without any preconceived plan, seen the gun, and improvised the scheme on the spot. And, of course, it is just possible that he came with no intention to kill, and that something occurred while he was with Briggs, inciting him to murder. At this stage we cannot choose for certain from these alternatives. All we can say is that the efficiency of the crime suggests but does not prove the existence of a plan.

"Among the many vaguenesses of this rather sketchy reconstruction one or two interesting certainties stand out. Firstly, the murderer was no fool. An unintelligent man or woman might very well have conceived the idea of staging a suicide; it required a more than ordinarily clever individual to carry out the actual job without bungling it. Secondly, few people are at their mental and manual best when committing a murder, and I think we can safely say that our man or woman must have been above the average not only in wits, but also in cool-headedness. And, thirdly, he or she was not squeamish. Deliberately to make such a mess of flesh and blood must have required uncommon sangfroid. Possibly the indifference of the surgeon who is used to such sights. Possibly the insensitiveness of a man driven to the extremity of hate or despair. Possibly the hardness of a practised criminal. Possibly the blindness of a man or a woman driven mad by sexual jealousy.

"So much for the preliminaries. They appear, it is true, to have muddied rather than clarified the issue—inevitably, for the case is complex, and it would be foolish artificially to simplify what is far from simple."

*　　　　　*　　　　　*　　　　　*

Ray paused to take a drink of water, light a cigarette, and rearrange his papers. "Well," he inquired, looking up at his audience, "has anyone anything to say?"

Margot, who had been getting more and more restive, took up the challenge.

"Certainly I have," she said. "This is all very amusing for you, Mr Ray. But if some poor devil in this room killed James Briggs, why don't you say so and have done with it? What's the use of making things worse for him by drawing out the agony? And, what's more, the rest of us would be able to get out of here."

"I second that," growled Sothern.

Dr Storr turned to Major Wigley and said: "Are we obliged to stay here, sir? My work is important to a number of people, and I cannot see by what law we are forced to remain."

The Major looked uncomfortable. He shifted in his chair, and finally got up, went over to Ray, and bent down, whispering something in his ear. There was a brief conversation.

"Anybody here," announced the Major at length, addressing the company in general, "is at liberty to go at once. Neither Mr Ray nor I can stop you. But perhaps I should say that suspicion will naturally fall upon anybody leaving this room."

Nobody got up. Margot heaved a despairing sigh, Sothern scowled, and Dr Storr settled down, apparently resigned, to a cigarette. Ray said:

"I'm sorry, but I'm afraid the session has only just begun. But please make yourselves as comfortable as you can." He turned to the housekeeper. "Mrs Groves here will, I'm sure, fetch anybody a drink who wants one."

"That's an idea," said Margot. Mrs Groves went out, reappearing after a minute or two bearing a tray laden with glasses, a bottle of whisky, a bottle of sherry, and a siphon, which she laid on the desk. Sothern got up and poured himself a generous whisky, which he drank all but neat, in one gulp. Dr Storr, more polite, poured out a sherry for Margot, and another for himself. The others abstained.

When every one had sat down again Ray crushed out his cigarette and said:

"Before getting down to things again I must reply to Miss Fayette's wholly justifiable criticism. What she says is perfectly true. This protracted ceremonial is no doubt tiring for all of you, and it's keeping you from your jobs. And if Briggs was murdered, and if his murderer's in this room—mind you, I say *if* in both cases—I don't envy him his feelings. But, after all, he or she can hardly complain of lack of consideration in others. Murderers have to put up with these little inconveniences—it's one of the snags of their calling. As for myself, Miss Fayette, you are quite right when you say I'm enjoying myself. Of course I am."

He turned to Joshua with a smile. "I'm not at all sure that I shall get paid in any more substantial way than this, for all my trouble. In any case, I need money less than the gentleman who engaged me. After this morning I vanish, and the Major here—forgive me, sir—gets the credit for having solved the Tiddenham mystery. Not without some justification, I hasten to add, for without him I would probably have failed. . . . In short, Miss Fayette, every dog has his day, this is mine, and I'm going to make the most of it."

Margot finished her sherry and laughed huskily. "Oh, all right, all right! Only get on with it, please."

"Before I do that," said Ray, "let me warn you all that I'm going to get personal. You will no doubt be annoyed, but don't show it too much. Remember that I may have no *proof* of my case, and that I may be counting on an emotional display by the villain to clinch the matter. An attentive silence will pay."

"Now you're talking tripe," Margot sneered. "If you were counting on the murderer giving himself away like that, would you warn him not to?"

Ray smiled indulgently. "You never can tell, Miss Fayette. Wheels within wheels, you know, and—"

"Nuts," said Sothern.

CHAPTER XIX

STEP by step I am taking you," Ray resumed," along the tortuous tracks I followed last night which led me this morning to my goal. We have explored the avenues of accident and suicide and found them to be blind alleys. Now we are investigating the possibility of murder.

"We have made one or two deductions concerning the hypothetical killer. Now we come to look for him among our suspects, and to apply the familiar tests for motive, opportunity, and temperamental capability to each suspect in turn. The order in which we proceed is immaterial, but let us start, as I started, with the simple, leading up to the complex.

"Mr and Mrs Groves . . . ."

At the mention of his name the gardener sprang out of his chair, protesting incoherently. Mrs Groves emitted sounds that were neither giggles nor sobs, but partook of both.

"Don't make an ass of yourself, Groves," said Ray, motioning him to sit down. "Take your seat and listen. . . . That's right. . . . And don't get excited, Mrs Groves. Nobody's accusing you of murder. You are, I'm sure, much too good-natured.

"To resume, I didn't come across any reason why you, Groves, or your wife should want to kill your employer. He made you no bequest in his will, and I heard of no feud between you and him. In the absence of any evidence pointing to some dark secret of the past that linked you with him, and of any present justification for violence,

I was bound to regard you to be innocent. I didn't look into your alibi, but the efficient Inspector here did, and found it to be beyond criticism. Add to this that the murder—if any—was committed by some one with a temperament which I didn't find in either of you, and I felt justified in saying that the probability of your innocence practically amounted to a certainty.

"Even so, I took nothing for granted, but labelled what we may call the Groves theory 'extremely improbable,' put it to one side, and proceeded to my second suspect, who is you, Briggs.

*   *   *   *

"At this point I appear in a different role—not as detective, but as witness. Joshua Briggs and I spent the afternoon and the evening of April the first at Bingly. Most of the time we were in each other's company. The interval between tea and dinner, however, was spent in our own rooms, he completing a sketch of the church and I writing up notes. I saw his half-finished drawing just before he went to his room, and again at about eight o'clock, when he had completed it. The amount of meticulous drawing done in the interval could not, in my opinion, have been carried out in a shorter time. Unless I was prepared to believe that he had by some miracle come here to Tiddenham, murdered his brother, returned to Bingly, and drawn what would take a practised hand at least three hours to draw, and all between five and eight o'clock-unless I could believe in such a miracle I was bound to admit that Joshua Briggs was innocent.

"On the question of motive the evidence only served to confirm me in this opinion. I have heard of no quarrel between the brothers. If they were not on cordial terms, at least they were not enemies. Nor did Joshua stand to gain materially from James's death. I considered the possibility of a jealous feud between them concerning a woman—concerning you, Miss Fayette. But I could find no evidence in support of such a view. As for temperament, Joshua Briggs seemed to me to be no more and no less capable of committing the crime than were the two remaining male suspects.

"The Joshua Briggs theory went the way of the Groves theory: it was marked 'highly improbable' and filed away.

*   *   *   *

"My third suspect was one Stephen Hogg, a shabby individual of middle age and intemperate habits, who stayed at the Tiddenham Arms from the 29th of March till the evening of the tragedy. I knew practically nothing about this man, but what little I did know was interesting enough.

"The purpose of his visit to these parts was obscure. If it were merely to enjoy a three days' drunk I could think of more congenial places for that purpose than our local pub. His sole occupation appeared to have consisted of playing cards with himself, drinking, and visiting friends—or shall we say acquaintances?

"Those acquaintances were James Briggs and Martin Sothern. Concerning what transpired during his interview with Briggs we know nothing, save that there was a quarrel. He found you to be out, Sothern, when he called at Honeysuckle Cottage, though I dare say he favoured you with another visit. It's a pity you're so reticent on the subject."

"Never heard of the man in my life," said Sothern stubbornly.

Ray continued: "My friend Major Wigley begs to differ from you, sir. He believes you were connected with Hogg in a certain professional capacity. Perhaps I should explain to those of you who don't know him that this Mr Hogg is a man with a long record of burglaries, thefts, and petty misdemeanours, and the police are now after him. They feel that he may be able to throw light on the Tiddenham case.

"I took it for granted that Hogg did not come down here for pleasure or for the good of his health, but on business. I had got wind of no burglaries in the district and I concluded that another side of the business had brought him here. Three obvious guesses as to the nature of this business were: *(a)* planning some new haul, *(b)* blackmail, *(c)* murdering James Briggs. Just three shots in the dark, admittedly, but worth following up.

"The first seemed very unlikely. An intending burglar could hardly advertise himself better than by staying in the local pub and behaving as queerly as Hogg had behaved. For precisely the same reason it was unthinkable that he had come down to murder Briggs. Blackmail, on the other hand, seemed to be a reasonable explanation of his visit. His calls upon Sothern and Briggs suggested it. And Sothern, at least, had a past.

"To imagine grounds for blackmailing Sothern was easy. Briggs was another matter. I had no real evidence to show that Briggs was a man with shady antecedents. His secretiveness, however, tended to encourage the idea, and it occurred to me that his money losses might have been due partly to blackmail.

"Anyhow, pending the arrival of an alternative explanation, I assumed that part, at least, of Hogg's business in Tiddenham was to put the screw on Briggs. But blackmailers are not, I imagine, in the habit of killing the goose that lays the golden egg, and I felt that the notion of Hogg the blackmailer automatically cancelled the notion of Hogg the murderer. Or, rather, tended to cancel. For Hogg and Briggs had quarrelled at their previous meeting. They might have quarrelled more violently on the night of April the first, with fatal results. I supposed, however, that blackmailers as a class do not kill their victims when they cannot or will not pay. Exposure is a simpler and safer vengeance.

"If Hogg had killed Briggs it was for a motive unknown to me. Evidence on the subject was lacking. But there was evidence of a sort that pointed to Hogg's innocence: *(a)* Briggs' wallet, containing £5.10s. was unrifled, and Hogg, I felt sure, would have taken the money; and *(b)* petty criminals like Hogg do not commit murder—I distrust this sort of argument myself, and merely state it for what it is worth.

"As regards opportunity there was a shade of doubt. According to your testimony, Dr Storr, Briggs died before six o'clock. According to Mrs Greene, the landlady of the Arms, Hogg did not leave the pub till well after then. If Dr Storr and Mrs Greene are right Hogg couldn't have murdered Briggs. On the other hand, the police surgeon, whose opinion I valued more than Dr Storr's, placed the death between six o'clock and seven-fifteen. In that case, Hogg had ample time in which to kill Briggs.

"Hogg was seen walking that evening not in the direction of the station, but towards the crossroads, one of which leads to this house. This, I realized, could be accounted for by the hypotheses that he had lost his way through unfamiliarity with the village roads, or that he was somewhat drunk, or both. The other explanation was that he was on his way to this house.

"The case against Hogg, as well as his defence, was extremely unsatisfactory, beset with ifs and ands. Lacking facts, I was driven to guesswork.

"All things considered, however, I felt justified in concluding that, while it was unlikely that Hogg committed murder, it was not so unlikely that he had been involved in some way, roundabout or direct, in the crime. And it seemed even less unlikely that by blackmail he had driven Briggs to suicide."

CHAPTER XX

NOW, Miss Fayette, we come to you. Frankly, I did not trust you.

"For instance, I was sure that you knew more about James Briggs than you were prepared to tell. Considering the closeness of your relationship with him, I could not believe that you were as ignorant of his financial difficulties, and of the names of the men with whom he lunched on April the first, and of where he lunched, and of several other matters, as you pretended to be. Nor could I believe that you knew as little about Sothern as you professed to.

"Again, your cheerful mood on the day following Briggs' death puzzled me. I would have expected a show of sorrow, at any rate.

"Such hints and inconsistencies were not evidence, however; they merely aroused my special interest in the case against you.

"You have an alibi. Let us examine it. You say that, at about six o'clock on April the first, you left the office in Fitzwilliam Street and went at once to your friend's flat in Kensington, arriving at about six-thirty. There you stayed for the rest of the evening with Miss Starke, who corroborates your story. A convenient circumstance. So convenient that I decided to look into it more deeply. First of all, I was not inclined to accept Miss Starke's word without confirmation. What's the use of a girl friend who won't do one a good turn occasionally?

"So I went to Kensington and investigated. Yes, the porter remembered Miss Starke arriving at about six-thirty with a friend, who stayed there the whole evening. He did not look closely at this friend, and could not recognize her when he was shown a photo of Miss Fayette. It might have been she, and it might not.

"I had very little doubt that Miss Starke's visitor that evening was you, Miss Fayette. When I went to Kensington I did not expect to explode your alibi; I went to investigate its details—and not in vain. I learned from the hall-porter that Miss Starke had never before, to his knowledge, stayed indoors with a girl friend for a whole evening. On most nights she was out with her friends, and she did not spend evenings alone at home.

"Now, even the gayest of young ladies must occasionally have a rest, and the fact that, according to William, the porter, Miss Starke seldom or never took one in the evening is of little consequence. We all do something uncharacteristic now and then. What is significant is the fact that Miss Starke should, contrary to established custom, decide to spend that particular evening at home with Miss Fayette. Miss Fayette, whether she knew it or not, needed an alibi on the evening of April the first. Was it a coincidence, an amazing stroke of luck, that Miss Starke should choose that evening of all evenings to depart from her usual practice, and invite her friend round to the flat?

"I doubted it. The chances were all against such good fortune. Provisionally I rejected the coincidence explanation, therefore, and looked for others. There were three : One, that Miss Fayette knew that Briggs was going to kill himself and contrived the alibi for herself in case she should be suspected of murdering him. Two, that Miss Fayette, knowing that some third person was planning to kill Briggs that evening, contrived the alibi to clear herself. Three, that she herself killed or helped to kill Briggs, and arranged with her friend Miss Starke and a 'stand-in' that they should remain in the flat that evening.

"Quite obviously the first of these alternatives was highly improbable, while the second and the third were equally probable. If my reasoning were correct, then, Margot Fayette was almost certainly a murderess or an accessory to the crime of murder.

"Incidentally, intending criminals would do well to note that having an alibi can be more disastrous than not having one.

"The time was not ripe for me to consider whose accomplice Margot Fayette might have been, supposing that she had not worked alone. I may say, however, that Sothern struck me as the most likely person, since he was, I believed, the only remaining suspect who knew her intimately.

"So far the case against you, Miss Fayette, is a strong one."

Margot laughed. It was not a pleasant sound. "I've let you go on up till now," she said, in a strained voice, "with this nonsense, and I haven't interrupted you. Now I'm going to. . . . Let me tell you that you haven't got a shred of evidence against me that a court would even look at. I tell you I was at the Starke girl's flat, and we'll both swear to it. Until you can produce some liar who says he saw me elsewhere all your theorizing cuts no ice whatever, and you know it."

"Why did you spend the evening in Miss Starke's flat?" asked Ray slowly, articulating every word.

"Because we wanted a rest and a talk," she snapped. "And if you can make that statement the grounds for accusing me of Briggs' murder, then you're crazier than I thought-and that's saying plenty."

Ray beamed. "At least you'll admit that my craziness is not of the harmless kind, which I suppose is some consolation—it's a fascinating subject, but we really must get on with the agenda. . . Yes, Miss Fayette, I readily admit that, at the present stage of our inquiry, I have nothing on you in the strictly legal sense. But I'm not a lawyer; I'm a man who's interested in the truth. You will appreciate the distinction."

"What is this," cried Sothern, "the fourth-form debating society? This lecture of yours is damned offensive, but for God's sake carry on and get it over."

"And when you do carry on, Mr Ray," added Margot, "you might just explain why I should want to kill Briggs."

"I was just coming to the question of your motive, Miss Fayette. Mrs Briggs told me that she overheard you and James Briggs quarrelling in this room about a week before he died. You accused him of unfaithfulness to you and threatened to kill him."

"My God!" Margot gasped. "What a lie!"

"Possibly," said Ray suavely, "and possibly not. Time will tell. At any rate, I had one working motive to carry on with. Others? Well, you don't gain by the will, and his death meant that you lost a job—though I imagine you'll get another easily enough. No, I saw indications of no other motive than jealousy, supposing always that you had been working alone. But if you had functioned as an accomplice, as a mere tool in the criminal's hands, then your motive may well have been a strong desire to help that criminal, and you may have borne no grudge whatever against James Briggs. Further speculation as to your possible motives was useless.

"Then I asked myself whether Miss Fayette were the sort of woman who had the brains to plan such a murder, and the nerve to execute it. Not being one of those detectives who work by intuition and instinct rather than by reason, I couldn't answer this question. I had a vague feeling that this was not a woman's sort of crime, or, rather, not the sort of crime any ordinary woman would commit. I also felt, with equal vagueness, that Miss Fayette's intelligence was acute, her nerves strong, and her character forceful. I set no store upon these feelings, however. The modern man or woman is such a complex organism, so unpredictable, so overlaid with the veneers of training and convention, that I am quite incapable of saying what he or she is capable of doing, or is really like inside. Such people remind me of a bit of wood that has been painted again and again, and become at last so encrusted that there's no telling what the wood inside is really like.

"Summarizing my case against Miss Fayette, I felt fairly sure that she knew who the murderer was, and that she knew that the murderer had chosen April the first for the deed. I considered it possible that Miss Fayette herself was the murderess. So far as I could tell she had both opportunity and motive. I saw nothing in her character to contradict these views.

"But I realized that there might be other suspects, against whom an even stronger case could be made out, and accordingly I went on to consider Martin Sothern.

"But before we leave Miss Fayette there is one very interesting point to note. According to Dr Storr, Briggs may have been killed as early as five o'clock. Could Miss Fayette have committed the murder at five and got to Kensington by six-thirty? I satisfied myself that she could not have done so, whether by car or train. But if Miss Fayette had believed that Briggs was to die between five and six, would she not have contrived that her alibi should cover that period of time? Surely she would have done so, in order to be on the safe side. The fact that her alibi covered the period from six-thirty onwards indicated that she believed that the murder would not be committed before then.

"The inference is that Dr Storr's estimate of the time of the death was incorrect, and that the police surgeon, who placed the death between six and seven-fifteen, was nearer the mark.

"When we come to consider Ellen Briggs and Dr Storr, this inference, tentative though it is, will be of importance."

CHAPTER XXI

IF you will overlook the impertinence, Mr Sothern, I propose to make a few general remarks about you, as a preliminary to putting the case for the prosecution. I would stay and hear them if I were you, to correct any mistakes I make."

"I'll stay all right," said Sothern, "but I tell you I'm innocent."

"Then you'll have no difficulty in putting up with what I have to say.

"Why, I asked myself, does this man live in Tiddenham? His professional activities lie in London, and must require his presence there at odd and unpredictable times of the day and night. Surely to live so far away must be an intolerable nuisance, only to be explained by the supposition that some compelling influence draws him to Tiddenham. What could that influence be?

"I could think of no reason for his living here, unless it were to be near his friends; and the only friends that he had in the neighbourhood were the Briggses. So far as I knew, Ellen was not the attraction, and I was left with her husband. Now, Sothern's connexion with Briggs was of long standing. Nevertheless, neither Ellen nor Margot, who was intimate with both of them, nor Sothern himself, vouchsafed any but the vaguest information about the nature of that connexion.

"This reticence served to confirm my suspicion that Briggs, the respectable bourgeois, was not all that he seemed to be. His secretiveness, Hogg's visit, his friendliness with Sothern, and finally his death—all hinted at an unknown and perhaps shady past, and possibly at an equally dubious present. Did the key to the mystery lie somewhere within this triangle of men? And was Sothern in Tiddenham because he was a member of that triangle?

"The only hope of answering such questions was to get down to the details of the evidence against Sothern.

"Taking motive first, I had not far to seek. I had it on the authority of Ellen Briggs and Joshua Briggs that Margot Fayette had been Sothern's mistress until about three months ago, when she switched over to James Briggs. This, Miss Fayette herself tells us, led to violent quarrels between the two men."

At these words Sothern shot up and started advancing towards Margot with threatening hands.

"Why, you dirty little liar!" he fumed.

Margot, placid but pale, looked on with scorn, while Inspector Hines dragged him back to his seat.

"Behave yourself, Sothern," warned the Major, "or I'll have you put under arrest."

The Inspector, after a whispered conversation with his chief, sat down next to Sothern, and Margot shifted into the seat he left vacant next to the Major.

"To resume," said Ray, picking up a paper that lay on the desk, "I had no trouble looking for a motive for murder. For confirmation, if confirmation were needed, I had this blotting-paper impression of a letter from Briggs to Sothern. Some of the words of this letter are missing, others are incomplete, but I was able to reconstruct, from what was given, the following:

"*March 31st*

"DEAR MAR*tin*,

"I'm *sorry* you feel *as you do* about Margot *and* me. I'm afraid *nothing can be done* about it, and it *certainly was n*ot my fault *that she fell for* me. *But I feel we* should remain friends.

"I will be in *at* 6.45 *to-m*orrow night. *Please come* and see me and have a ch*at. I*'ll be alone,

"Yours,

"JAMES BRIGGS" [1]

"It's a frame-up," Sothern gasped, when Ray finished reading the letter. His lips trembled as he spoke, and sweat stood out on his forehead.

"I swear I never got that letter," he went on. "What's more, Briggs didn't write it. The devil that killed Briggs planted that letter to put me on the spot." The last sentence was addressed to Margot. The Inspector laid his hand on Sothern's arm, and he ceased speaking. Margot's expression was one of complete indifference.

"For God's sake give me a drink!" cried Sothern.

Ray poured out a neat whisky and handed it to him. He swallowed it at a gulp.

"Now," said Ray, back at the desk, "let's continue. I filled the blanks in this letter, having regard firstly to the sense of the context, and

---

1   The italicized letters and words are those filled in by Ray.

secondly to the sizes of the gaps. There are, no doubt, alternative reconstructions, but I think they would leave the sense of the letter more or less unaffected. It seemed to me reasonably certain that the letter was intended for Martin Sothern, since none of Briggs' other friends (except Margot, who was ruled out by internal evidence) had a name beginning with *Mar,* so far as I could discover. In addition, the sense of the letter, taken along with the rest of the evidence, confirmed the view that it was addressed to Sothern.

"In this letter, then, I had confirmation of Miss Fayette's statement—for what that statement was worth—about the strained relationships between the two men. Sothern, it would appear, had killed Briggs out of jealousy.

"I put it to myself that Sothern would have been more likely to kill his rival in a fit of jealous rage at the time when, three months before, Margot had left him for Briggs than to defer vengeance for so long. But I saw that there might have been several reasons for this delay. For all I knew to the contrary, it was possible that the girl had not finally broken with Sothern until recently. It was even conceivable that he had not known of her affair with Briggs until just before Briggs died.

"I realized, of course, that the writing of the note was no proof that the addressee had received it. Sothern's maid could not remember whether a letter had arrived at the cottage on March the thirty-first or on the following day. But the evidence of the letter as to Sothern's *motive* for killing Briggs held good, even if the letter had never been delivered. The same cannot be said of the letter's evidence regarding the appointment at the house and Sothern's *opportunity* to commit the crime.

"But in that respect we have plenty of evidence from other sources. Sothern's alibi was so shaky that it collapsed as soon as it was examined. It's no good, Sothern, relying on sub-normal maidservants in these vital matters. They let you down. Why not admit you were out that evening, and tell us where you were?"

All eyes were fixed on Sothern, who sat twisting his fingers in silence.

"I went out for a walk," he mumbled lamely.

"In the dark, alone?"

"Why not?"

"I can think of as many reasons why as why not," replied Ray. "But since you won't tell me them, you can't blame me for drawing the obvious conclusions. Not only have we the faked alibi, *plus* your refusal to substitute for that alibi a reasonable account of your actions that evening, *plus* a letter asking you to come to this house on the evening of April the first—but, to clinch matters, we have evidence that you, or someone like you, was seen outside the window of this room between seven and half-past seven that night. Strong evidence, Sothern. What have you got to say?"

"All thundering lies," cried Sothern, "like everything else you've said about me! I tell you I've been put on the spot. If I could only get hold of the man . . . . or the woman"—he glared at Margot—"who did it I'd—"

Ray broke in: "Unfortunately for you, Sothern, the man who said he saw you, or someone like you, is, I believe, an independent witness with no reason for wanting to frame you.

"And finally, as further confirmation, there are the fingerprints on the gun—your prints. What more could a detective want? Or a jury?

"Having put the case for the prosecution, I searched about for a possible defence. The argument that Sothern, intending murder, would have provided himself with a more specious alibi cut no ice, for I had already decided that the crime was not necessarily planned in advance.

"But Sothern was, I understood, not unskilled in evading the lawful consequences of his deeds. Neither did he impress me as a fool. Was it conceivable, I asked myself, that such a man, having shot Briggs and staged the suicide-*cum*-accident, would have been so careless as to leave his fingerprints on the weapon and to allow himself to be seen on the scene of the crime? On the face of it the thing was unlikely.

"Probing deeper, I was not so sure. Sothern drank pretty heavily. Sometimes he got drunk. It was perfectly possible that he had been not drunk, but sufficiently intoxicated to bungle the job that night. It was equally possible that, accomplished as he doubtless was in the technique of lesser misdeeds, murder, and particularly a messy murder, was too much for him. Perhaps he had lost his nerve when he needed it most, and left the evidence that would, in the fullness of time, hang him.

"So far my defence of Sothern had failed. There remained to be considered the possibility that he had been framed."

"Ha!" cried Sothern. "I knew you'd come to that. Tell us who did it."

"I did *not* say that you had been framed," Ray retorted. "I could see no real flaw in the case against you, and I saw nothing to suggest a frame-up, much less to prove one. I merely felt it necessary to look into the possibility. And even if I privately believed that you had been framed, Mr Sothern, that would in itself be small cause for jubilation. Judges and juries, not private detectives, have the last word in these matters.

"As I say, I embraced the frame-up hypothesis just to see where it led to. It led exactly nowhere. Who, I asked myself, could have contrived to get you out of your house alone and at night, got you then to Briggs' house, obtained your fingerprints on the gun, made sure that Briggs was in the house at precisely the right time, made sure that he was alone, and planted the blotting-paper impression? And who, among men or angels, could have done all this without arousing your suspicions and *without revealing to you his or her identity?*

"It is untrue to say that the frame-up hypothesis led nowhere. It led me, via a patent absurdity, right back to my old position—that Martin Sothern was indeed guilty of the murder of James Briggs."

Ray paused for a drink of water. Everyone was looking at Sothern, who sat quite still. The fear and fury in his face had died out like a flame that had spent itself, leaving only ashes. . . .

"Look out!" screamed Ray.

The gun had barely left Sothern's pocket before the Inspector had his wrist in an iron grip. There was a brief struggle. Sothern was tall and strong, but Inspector Hines was taller and stronger, and it was not long before Sothern was back in his seat staring blankly down at handcuffed hands and making choking noises in his throat.

"For God's sake," said Ray, "give him a drink! And give another to Mrs Groves, who appears to be unwell."

CHAPTER XXII

"NICE work, Ray! Clear-headed and all that," exclaimed Major Wigley.

"Hear, hear!" endorsed Joshua, getting up and stretching himself. "But by the expression on her face I see that Miss Fayette doesn't agree with us."

"I do not," came the caustic reply. "Nine-tenths of this precious lecture was unnecessary. Any fool who knew what this so-called detective knew about Sothern would have been able to prove him the murderer in two minutes. It takes this master-mind two hours. Two hours wasted over pettifogging details intended to conceal the fact that all he has done is to detect the obvious. . . . Mr Ray, when you don't make me sick, you make me laugh!"

Dr Storr, smiling, went up and shook Ray's hand. He said: "I do not agree with Miss Fayette. It was a beautiful analysis. It is necessary to be thorough in such a serious matter as murder. . . . Now, sir, I must wish you good day. I hope we will meet again."

Ray smiled his appreciation, and detained the doctor with a gesture of the hand. "Don't be in too much of a hurry, doctor," he said. "We haven't finished this meeting yet. As you justly observe, one must be thorough when dealing with murder, and when you've all finished your premature reviews of my performance to date I'll continue it."

The doctor's troubled look returned, Margot groaned, and Sothern began to show a dawning interest in the proceedings again. The whisky had partially revived Mrs Groves, who sat upright in her chair, staring into space.

"A knowledge of English law and judicial procedure," said Ray, "is not one of my accomplishments. I imagine, however, that when the counsel for the defence has utterly failed to demolish the arguments of the prosecution, and the prisoner is virtually proven guilty, there is still one last desperate chance of saving him. If the defending counsel can prove that some other person, unconnected with the prisoner, might equally well have committed the crime, then he has saved his client.

"I had made out a case against Sothern that was, I believed, watertight from the legal angle. But because this solution of the mystery was to me unæsthetic, because it left loose ends trailing, and because I had still two more suspects on my list, I could not let the matter stop there. Accordingly I temporarily pigeonholed the Sothern theory, and went on to consider the evidence against Dr Storr and Mrs Briggs. It was not inconceivable that one of them, or the pair of them acting jointly, had killed Briggs. At any rate, I had to find out."

"This is a joke!" cried Storr. "What connexion could I have with Mr Briggs, and what reason for wanting to kill him? It is absurd."

Ray nodded. "Nevertheless, sir, correct professional procedure demanded that the absurdity should be duly demonstrated. You ask me, Dr Storr, what connexion you had with Briggs. It doesn't need a detective to tell you that the answer to that question is—Mrs Briggs. She is your patient, and—this is no time to mince words—your mistress."

"You will take that back or I—" Dr Storr's face was livid.

"You'll do nothing, because it's true. Ellen Briggs went to your house, not for the first time, between six and eight on the night of Briggs' death. She left her cigarette-ends there to prove it. On the following morning I happened to overhear words that passed between you, in her bedroom. They did not suggest the doctor-patient relationship. On the evening of the same day I intercepted a note from her to you, advising you to give support to the idea that Briggs had killed himself, and urging you to think of a way of getting me out of this house without arousing suspicion. It was a note written by a frightened woman. So you see, doctor, I know quite a lot about you and Mrs Briggs. Why not tell us the rest, and clear yourselves, if you are innocent? For example, why not tell us where you were that evening?"

"I was at my house."

"Alone?"

"Yes. From six o'clock."

"And where was Ellen Briggs?"

"I understand she was at the cinema. I did not know then where she was. As for the letter you intercepted, do you think I am responsible for what a hysterical patient puts on paper?"

"And the cigarette-ends in your dustbin, and the conversation in the bedroom?"

"All lies."

Margot interrupted: "What's the use of all this? If you know who murdered Briggs all this back-chat is a waste of time."

"On the contrary," said Ray. "I'm learning a lot of interesting things about Dr Storr. However, you recall me to my present purpose, which is to lead a conducted tour along the paths by which I actually investigated and solved the case. Any further information now forthcoming, such as what I've just gleaned from my conversation with the doctor, is purely corroborative. I asked myself why Storr should want to kill Briggs.

"Eventual marriage to Ellen Briggs? Possibly. While it was, I thought, very unlikely that an ordinary layman would go to such lengths when a divorce could probably have been arranged, a medical man might consider himself forced to take extreme measures. A breath of scandal, and his practice melts away; perhaps he is eventually struck off the register. Did Storr kill Briggs to get his wife without risk to practice or professional status? Men have done such things for love; more often, I thought, for money. Storr may well have known nothing of Briggs' virtual bankruptcy, and have believed him to be a rich man. Did Storr, who was relatively poor and with difficulty building up a practice, kill Briggs for his money, which he intended to acquire via Ellen Briggs?

"At any rate, whether it was love alone, or greed alone, or a blend of the two, the doctor had a good and sufficient motive for murder. You have heard for yourselves what sort of an alibi he has. As for temperament, he is a surgeon, used to the sight of wounds and blood. Whether he was actually capable of murder I could not tell.

"Positive evidence against the doctor was lacking. There were two suspicious circumstances, however. The first of these—I refer to the fact that his opinion as to the time of Briggs' death differed so markedly from that of the police surgeon—was capable of several explanations. Storr might have lied to shield Ellen Briggs, who had an alibi until six o'clock. You will remember that Storr placed the death before that time. He might have lied not because of his guilt, but because he feared that his lack of alibi for the period after six o'clock would make it difficult to prove his innocence. He might not have lied at all. He might have made a genuine error.

"You will notice that I took it for granted that the police surgeon was right, and Storr wrong. My principal reason for doing so was that Storr probably had an axe of some kind to grind, whereas the police surgeon obviously had none. As though to confirm my view, there was the time—six-forty-five—mentioned in the blotting-paper note to Sothern; there was Miss Fayette's alibi, which, as we have seen, seemed to show that she believed the crime would be committed after six o'clock; there was the fact that Sothern (or some one like him) was seen outside this house well after six o'clock; and finally there was the fact that Storr and Ellen have no alibis after six o'clock. All after six o'clock. After six things started to happen, and not before. Whoever killed Briggs, I felt sure the deed had been done, as the police surgeon says, between six and seven-fifteen.

"I tried the hypothesis that Storr had deliberately lied regarding the time of Briggs' death, in order that he and Ellen should have *separate* alibis. After six they were together—for how long I don't know—in Storr's house, and any alibis for the period after six would have to be *mutually* provided; in other words, if Briggs' death were placed after six by the police, then the doctor would have to provide Ellen with her alibi, and she, in turn, would have to provide Storr with his. But if they were accused of *jointly* killing Briggs these alibis would be useless. That might be one of the reasons why the doctor lied.

"Another possible reason was that he feared scandal. He was desperately anxious to keep Ellen's visit to his house a secret. It almost seemed as though he would rather see her hang for the murder of her husband than give any evidence which would clear her but damage his practice.

"The second suspicious circumstance concerned the letter which my friend Joshua Briggs found in the doctor's study—by what deplorable means I need not say. He ransacked the room thoroughly. Only one letter from Ellen Briggs came to light, in an unlocked drawer. It was a letter, purporting to have been written on the day before the murder, telling him that she was going to the pictures on the following evening.

"The letter was an obvious plant. Why only one letter in the study? Why in an unlocked drawer, where his admittedly inquisitive housekeeper would be certain to find it sooner or later? Because Storr knew I was interested in his correspondence; because he wanted me to find this letter.

"The letter was not only planted, it was faked. The wording was unconvincing. Lovers don't write letters as that letter was written, even in a tearing hurry. In addition, the letter itself was superfluous. Why on earth should Ellen write to her doctor to say that she was going to the cinema?

"I don't yet know whether the letter was forged by Storr or written by Ellen at his instructions. In either case, I assumed that it had been written *after* Briggs' death, and put in an old envelope which bore the required postmark and the date of March 31st.

"If Storr, acting alone, had killed Briggs, would he have planted this letter? Surely not. He would hardly have risked his own neck for the sake of his reputation. He would surely have sworn that Ellen Briggs had been with him that evening, and taken advantage of the alibi, defective though it was.

"It appeared, then, that Storr, acting on his own, had not killed Briggs. But supposing he had committed the crime in conjunction with Ellen Briggs: in that case, as we have seen, mutually furnished alibis would be valueless, and both the planted letter and the lie regarding the time of Briggs' death would be called for, to help to divert the suspicions of the police and myself.

"And finally, suppose that Ellen Briggs, acting on her own, had killed Briggs in order to be free to marry Storr. Had Storr, discovering this, refused to become involved in any way, even to the extent of furnishing her with an alibi? Had he agreed to furnish the alibi, and then backed out after the deed was done? Had he merely suspected Ellen of murder, and, to avoid the risk of being charged as an accessary, refused to admit that she was in his house at all that night? Or had she been with him in his house the whole evening, including the period during which Briggs was killed, but he would not admit the fact, preferring to avoid scandal even at the risk of his mistress's life?

"I could not answer these questions. Three tentative conclusions, however, emerged. One, that Storr did not kill Briggs independently. Two, that he may have believed that Ellen killed Briggs. And, three, that Storr and Ellen, acting jointly, may have killed Briggs.

"In conclusion, I may say that I had an irrational feeling that, after Dr Storr, the murderer or murderess might seem quite a pleasant individual."

"What do you mean by that, you swine?" Storr cried.

"I mean that I don't like a man who lets down a woman to save his own skin, especially when that skin is in no great danger, and he happens to be the woman's lover.

CHAPTER XXIII

ELLEN BRIGGS, the last on my list," Ray continued, "had, so it seemed, more compelling motives than any other suspect for killing Briggs.

"Firstly, her husband had approached his lawyers with a view to changing his will—a will which left her all his money. Ellen, while ignorant of James's virtual bankruptcy, may possibly have known of his intention to alter the will, and have killed him to prevent him from doing so."

"Secondly, her husband was not only consorting with another woman, he had the effrontery to bring that woman to her house. The human mind is an ill-designed machine; and one of its flaws is the almost universal desire for *unilateral* polygamy. Wherefore I assumed that, though Ellen herself was in the midst of an affair, this was no reason why she should tolerate similar behaviour on the part of her husband.

"When I first met Ellen Briggs I noticed that she owned a rosary, and I inferred, rightly it seems, that she was a Catholic. Now, as a Catholic, she would not be able to divorce her husband. Only his death would leave her at liberty to marry her lover. By killing Briggs she would wreak her revenge on him, and she would, in addition, free herself to marry Dr Storr and to bring to him her husband's money —money that Dr Storr needed.

"Whether it was because Storr had failed her at the last moment, or for some other reason, Ellen Briggs had no alibi. The cinema story could not be substantiated. I had not the slightest doubt that she could have left Storr's house, say at six-fifteen, motored to this house, killed Briggs, returned to Stokeby, and come back here again at eight o'clock. She might have told Storr what she was going to do. On the other hand, it appeared more likely that she had not done so, reasoning that men do not care to marry women who have murdered their husbands. In that case, Storr, finding Briggs dead, and well aware of Ellen's motive for killing him and her opportunity to do so, had no doubt put two and two together and made murder.

"While putting the case against Sothern I asked myself who could have framed him. The answer was—nobody. That conclusion was premature. For it now appeared that Ellen Briggs could have done so.

"Firstly, take the note inviting Sothern to the house. Ellen Briggs, before her marriage, had been an engraver, therefore the forging of the note would present no difficulty to her. The original she would destroy, leaving only the blotting-paper impression for me or the police to find.

"Secondly, she could have lured Sothern from his house by means of another forged note, purporting to come, let us say, from Margot Fayette, inviting him to meet her at some lonely spot. If Sothern were still under Miss Fayette's spell, no doubt he would respond. Ellen might even have 'phoned him, imitating Margot's voice, to make such an appointment.

"Thirdly, we come to Sothern's prints on the gun. For a long time I could not see how Ellen could have contrived this item in the frame-up. At length I remembered what Sothern had told me—that on the occasion of his last call on Briggs he had inspected the gun. Ellen might well have noticed Sothern handling the gun, and have kept watch to see that no one cleaned or handled it subsequently. In that case, she would have at the time of the murder a weapon bearing the fingerprints of her victim and of the man she intended to frame. All that would remain to be done would be to handle the gun with gloves, and leave it as it was for the police to find."

"There you are!" cried Sothern. "What did I tell you? . . . Here"—he turned to the Inspector—"take these things off me." He held up his hands.

The Inspector sought his chief's eye.

"All right," the Major agreed. "On condition you behave yourself. Take his handcuffs off, but keep a good eye on him, Hines."

"Well, Sothern," inquired Ray, after the handcuffs had been removed, "will you tell us now what took you out of your cottage that night?"

"As you say," he replied, "a note from Margot Fayette. But what was the use of telling you that when she'd have denied it?"

"If you'd said so before I put the idea into your head, you would have stood more chance of being believed. And remember that you're not acquitted, and that I'm merely showing why I decided that Ellen Briggs *could* have framed you."

"To resume, I have shown that the three vital parts of the machinery of this alleged frame-up could have been engineered by Ellen Briggs. The rest seemed easy. Briggs had told her that he expected to be back early that evening. She knew that Groves and

Mrs Groves would be out, and that there was every chance of Briggs being alone in the house. All she had to do was to send a forged note, purporting to come from Margot Fayette, to Sothern, turn up at the house, drug Briggs, and shoot him."

"One moment," interrupted Joshua. "How do you account for Sothern being seen outside the study that night?"

"In the first place," answered Ray, "we aren't absolutely sure it was Sothern. It may have been some one else. But even if it were Sothern, why shouldn't he look in at the house on his way back from the rendezvous that didn't come off, to see whether Margot were there? Perhaps Sothern himself has something to say?"

"It wasn't me," said Sothern.

"The point," Ray continued, "is not of vital importance, and we will proceed. . . . Why should Ellen Briggs choose Sothern as her scapegoat? Not, I felt, on account of any particular dislike of the man, but merely because his motive was adequate, and because, by a stroke of luck, his prints were on the gun.

"Having got thus far, I turned to the deed itself. If Ellen had killed her husband she had no doubt drugged him first. I could not imagine her hitting him on the head. The shooting was perhaps not what one would expect of a woman. But I saw Ellen Briggs as a woman consumed with jealousy, and such a woman is capable of extraordinary deeds.

"In the eyes of the law, no doubt, the evidence against Sothern was more damning than the evidence against Ellen Briggs. In my own view, however, I felt that, to date, Ellen was at least as likely to be guilty as Sothern.

"But my self-appointed task was not to secure a conviction at all costs; it was to arrive at the truth. Therefore it was incumbent upon me to try to defend Ellen against my own onslaught. My defence was subdivided into two parts.

"Firstly, why, if Ellen had framed Sothern, should she bring evidence, faked or genuine, against Margot? Merely in order, I imagined, to harass Margot, and to divert any suspicion that Sothern had been framed.

"The second line of defence was less easily disposed of. I had already demonstrated that, in all probability, Margot either knew that Briggs was to die that night, or had herself killed him. Ignoring the latter possibility and assuming Ellen's guilt, how could Margot have got to know of the impending murder? I could not believe that the two women were working together.

"I was faced, then, with the following proposition: *either* Margot's alibi was a genuine coincidence and my indictment of Ellen held good, *or* the alibi was a fake and the case against Ellen fell through.

"The defence of Ellen Briggs had partially succeeded. I was bound to admit that the circumstances of Margot's alibi had, oddly enough, gone far towards taking the sting out of the case against Ellen. The chances of Margot being aware of any murderous plans of Ellen's were less than the chances of her being aware of similar plans of Sothern's. That was one of my reasons for placing Sothern at the top of the list of suspects.

"But I was careful to add and to underline the footnote that, if

Margot's alibi should prove to be a genuine coincidence, then the evidence against Ellen Briggs would be damning indeed."

*   *   *   *

"What's the matter, Mrs Groves?"

"Oh, sir," she cried tearfully, "I'm sure Mrs Briggs couldn't have done such a thing! And, sir, please excuse me so as I can go an' see if she wants anythink."

"Of course, Mrs Groves, do go. And ask her, if you please, whether she feels well enough to join us."

Mrs Groves nodded and bustled out of the room.

"So," said Margot, "your delightful conducted tour has brought us round again to Sothern. Are we ever going to get any farther, or do we go on chasing our tails all day?"

"We'll get far enough too soon for some one in this house," was the cryptic reply.

As though in fulfilment of this threat, there came a woman's scream from the upper part of the house.

There was a stampede for the door. The Major was there first, issuing terse orders:

"Hines, stay here. See that no one leaves this room. Ray, come with me. . . . Yes, Groves, you can come with us."

The three men raced upstairs to Ellen's bedroom. The door stood open. Ellen, clad in a nightdress, lay on the bed with closed eyes and face drained of colour. Mrs Groves, holding with one hand on to the bedpost for support, pointed unsteadily with the other to the woman on the bed. Major Wigley bent down over the body.

"Dead?" asked Ray.

The Major nodded.

He said: "Take your wife downstairs, Groves, and tell the Inspector I would like Mr Briggs and Dr Storr to come up here at once."

Ray pointed in silence to a half-empty tumbler of water and a bottle of aspirins that lay on the table beside the bed.

Then he walked over to the dressing-table, picked up a little pile of letters that lay on the glass top, and glanced quickly at their contents. At the bottom was a single sheet of notepaper. He read out aloud what was written on it:

"I killed James Briggs and framed Sothern. But it was no use. The man I did it for, and who planned it, let me down at the last moment. Now there is only one thing to do.

"ELLEN BRIGGS"

CHAPTER XXIV

AN hour later Joshua and Ray entered the study. Margot and Sothern were sitting by the fire, smoking in silence. The Major and the Inspector were conferring outside in the hall, and Mr and Mrs Groves had vanished into the back parts of the house.

Sothern jumped up as the two men came in.

"For God's sake," he cried," tell us what happened!"

"Sit down, and we'll join you by the fire," said Ray. "Well, what's happened is plenty. Ellen Briggs has been found dead in her bed. The police surgeon says she died of some kind of poisoning about two hours ago. A note in her handwriting confessing to the murder and virtually naming Storr as her accomplice was found on her dressing-table. There were no fingerprints on the glass from which she drank the poison, except her own and those of Mrs Groves, who put the glass by her bedside early this morning. Dr Storr is lying on the sofa in the next room in a state of collapse. Incidentally, Sothern, she says in her note that she framed you."

"Well, that's what I call a bit of good news!" cried Sothern. "I'm going to have one on the strength of it. One for you, Margot?"

"Definitely." She laughed, and turned to Ray. "Well, Mr Ray, I guess that takes care of what you were pleased to call my faked alibi?"

Joshua poured out drinks all round. Handing one to Ray, he said: "Clever bit of reasoning, Ray, to work out that Ellen had framed Sothern. I'm sorry, though, that she stole a march on you and proved herself guilty before you had time to finally work up to that conclusion. Of course, you were obviously heading that way."

Ray smiled and said: "That's a really nice speech, Briggs. Now that the tumult and the shouting have died, would you care to hear just how I worked things out?"

"Rather!" cried Margot, with a wink at Sothern which was not lost on Ray.

Sothern agreed. "Certainly. Having got so far, I'd like to hear it all, now that I'm cleared."

*   *   *   *

Ray walked over to the desk and brought back a sheet of paper.

"This, "he said," is a list I made early this morning, after having put the case against each of my suspects in turn."

He handed the list round. It read:

1. ACCIDENT .... ***
2. SUICIDE .... ****
3. MURDER by (a) Mr and Mrs Groves ...... *
                (b) Joshua Briggs .... *
                (c) Hogg .... ***
                (d) Margot Fayette .... ****
                (e) Sothern .... *****
                (f) Dr Storr .... **
                (g) Ellen Briggs .... ****

"It looks like an A.A. publication," laughed Margot. "What do the stars mean? Pubs?"

"Very roughly, to the nearest star or two, each group of stars indicates the degree of probability of the theory it appears against."

Sothern grinned. "Well, you slipped up there a bit, old man. You've made me the winner with five stars, and Ellen Briggs has only got four—the same as Margot. Not so hot!"

"I know, Sothern. I admit that the table proved to be wrong. But then, you see, I hadn't finished. The stars simply registered progress to date. They weren't final."

"Now you're cheating," reproved Margot, "and being wise after the event. We've only your word for it that you solved the mystery before it was solved for you by Ellen Briggs herself."

"Odd thing," observed Ray, "but I can prove to you I saw the light before Ellen Briggs died."

"I'd like to hear you do that," said Margot. "Carry on."

*   *   *   *

"The table I've just shown you," said Ray, "summarized in a rough and ready way my detailed investigation. As you say, Sothern, you won on points. I had private reasons for being depressed with the result. For one thing, it looked as though I would have to undergo the bitter ordeal of admitting that you, Joshua, had been right almost from the start, and that all my finesse had gone for nothing.

"More devastating still was the inconclusiveness of the result. I had four solutions on my list with four or more stars against each of them: suicide, murder (or more probably complicity in murder) by Margot Fayette, murder by Sothern, and murder by Ellen Briggs.

Sothern no doubt was a likely winner, but the others were well in the running, and such a situation irritated my tidy mind.

"A solution of this kind was as bad as utter failure. I wanted to prove my villain guilty without the shadow of a doubt, and the remaining accused innocent beyond all question. Above all, I desired a solution which, like magic, would put every person and every fact in the proper place and make a satisfying picture. You, Joshua, will appreciate what I mean, because the issue is partly an aesthetic one. My solution, if you can call it that, filled me with repulsion.

"And, most sickening of all, this so-called solution was probably correct. Real life is just like that: uncertain, uneconomic, and untidy. That is why art is so necessary—to overcome these defects. Would that this were a story, I said to myself, and I'd see we had more satisfaction than this.

"Such was the situation at four o'clock this morning. Hoping against hope, I went through the whole of the evidence again. I arraigned each suspect for the second time. I found that in every instance much more could be said for and against, and neither this way nor that—far more than I have burdened you with this morning. I found that I had not exhausted the possible combinations of suspects working jointly. I found that I could go on building up and demolishing hypotheses enough to fill a fat volume. But all was vanity and vexation of spirit because I lacked that touch of inspiration, that magic password—"

"Sometimes I wonder," Margot broke in, "why you didn't go in for the Church."

"Madam," said Ray, "I did. But it didn't go in for me. Haven't you noticed how Biblical I become when I'm in the vein?—As I was saying, from four till six I wrestled with the evidence like Jacob with the angel. Now Sothern, the title-holder, won on points—forgive the tangled metaphor—now Ellen Briggs, and then another challenger would arise. The knock-out blow, or winning hold, or whatever it is in wrestling, never came off.

"I feel in the mood to go on harrowing your feelings indefinitely, but I will considerately take you by a short cut to six o'clock, when physical light began to dawn outside and mental light within this brain.

"You remember the composite question that I have already put twice this morning. It runs like this: who could have contrived to get you, Sothern, out of your house alone and at night, got you to Briggs' house made sure that Briggs was there at the right time and alone, obtained your fingerprints on the gun, and planted the piece of blotting-paper? What mere mortal could have done all this without revealing his identity to you and without arousing your suspicions?"

"Easy," said Margot. "Ellen Briggs, and nobody else."

"Try again," said Ray. "Remember that the author of the frame-up must have lived in this house."

Joshua laughed. "Look here, Jethro, this case is getting you down. I don't know much about Groves and his wife, but"—he appealed to Margot—"I ask you!"

"You'll be telling us next, Mr Ray," said Margot acidly, "that James Briggs, knowing his wife was going to murder him, framed Sothern to oblige her.

"By God," cried Ray, "I'll be damned if you haven't almost got it right!"

He stood with his back to the fire, facing the two men and the girl. In a calm, detached voice he announced: "It WAS James Briggs who framed Sothern."

CHAPTER XXV

INSPECTOR HINES poked his head in at the study door.

"Mr Sothern," he announced, "the Chief would like a word with you out here, if you please."

Sothern replied, "Well, since our detective's mind's gone, I don't mind seeing whether the Major's still sane," and followed Hines into the hall.

"You know," Margot remarked, "this party reminds me of the ten green bottles hanging on the wall. We started off with nine of us, and now we are three. You're for it next, I think, Mr Ray. In a sense, you've gone already. Up here, I mean." She pointed to her head, and bit a large lump out of a ham sandwich.

Ray grinned. "You know, Margot—I may call you Margot? . . . thanks—I think I have a happy knack of drawing out the best in you. It's the same with dear old Joshua here. I'm always making him furious, and then he gets quite amusing."

Joshua did not return Ray's grin. "You're a fool, Ray. You're the sort of man who cracks jokes at deathbeds, botanizes on his mother's grave, not for science, but for fun, and wears the motley on such an occasion as this. What do you mean by saying that my brother framed Sothern? I never heard such drivel."

"There!" cried Ray. "You see what I mean, Margot? In this sort of mood he speaks with tongues."

Ray helped himself to a glass of sherry. "For the first time today," he explained, "and I think I've earned it. And if you really want to know how I concluded that James Briggs himself framed Sothern, here goes.

"For Briggs it was easy—easier than for anyone else. *(a)* Unlike the others, he had not to forge the appointment note; he had merely to write it in his own handwriting, blot it in such a way that the vital words appeared on the blotting-paper, and destroy the original. *(b)* With the exception of Sothern himself, Briggs was the only person who, for certain, knew that Sothern's prints were on the gun—Ellen may have been aware of them, but Briggs could not help but know. *(c)* Briggs had more facilities than Ellen for enticing Sothern out of his house that night. And *(d),* who could be so sure of the victim being alone and in the right place at the right time as the victim himself?"

"Well," said Margot incredulously, "I knew that James was fairly good-natured, but, really, I think that's going a bit far, even to oblige a wife."

'Hush!" Ray admonished. "Let me tell this in my own way. . . . Absurd though the hypothesis seemed, I decided to try it out. As you say, it was going a bit too far to suppose that Briggs had let his wife or someone else kill him, just like that. Yet, if he had framed Sothern, what other conclusion could I draw?

"This—*that Briggs killed himself.*"

*   *   *   *

"I never heard such nonsense," protested Margot. "Why should he? And what about Ellen upstairs and her confession?"

"All right," said Ray, "I'll take the first of those questions. Why should he commit suicide?

"I had already concluded that Hogg had probably been blackmailing Briggs, and I was quite prepared to believe that Sothern was doing likewise. I could think of no other adequate reason for Sothern's presence in Tiddenham. Briggs' dwindling bank balance was attributed to betting. But on what grounds had I concluded that Briggs' money had gone on horses, except that Briggs had said so? None. Blackmail was the more likely explanation. I proceeded on that assumption.

"Briggs, then, was ruined. One of the men who had helped to ruin him lived here in Tiddenham. And that man was the one who—according to Ellen—was a dangerous rival for the affections of Briggs' mistress. Briggs may have believed that, having lost his money to Sothern, he was about to lose his girl to the same man. Supposing he decided to end the whole wretched business by killing himself, and—this is where the ingenuity comes in—*by killing himself in such a way that his tormentor is hanged for murder.*"

"My God," exclaimed Joshua, "I do believe you're on to something!"

"Of course I am. The pattern I had been seeking was beginning to emerge. I liked the look of it. Here was a murderer with ideas, worthy of a real detective. Here was a man who planned to eliminate his victim posthumously, by judicial murder. He very nearly succeeded."

"An ingenious theory, I must admit," said Margot, "but a crazy one. You had no possible means of proving it."

"You," said Ray quietly, "supplied all the proof I needed."

Margot angrily appealed to Joshua. "This is getting beyond a joke!" she cried.

"Let him explain," said Joshua soothingly.

"Yes, Miss Fayette," Ray resumed, "you supplied the proof. Don't you remember that I had more or less concluded from the circumstances of your alibi that you knew James Briggs was going to die that night? This conclusion had puzzled me more than any other feature of the case. Now at last I saw the explanation of your knowledge. *James Briggs himself had told you that he would end his life that night.*"

"You're mad!" she cried, but her voice lacked conviction.

"You knew. And to avoid the possibility of suspicion falling on you you arranged the alibi. A pity, and unworthy of your intelligence. For it was only the queerness of that alibi which enabled me to solve the case."

Margot lay back in her chair, silent.

Joshua spoke excitedly. "Amazing, Ray! I believe you're right about James killing himself"—he checked himself, and a look of doubt spread over his face—"but what about Ellen's confession?"

"I've almost come to that," Ray went on. "But first, perhaps, I should explain that, though the solution which I've just propounded to you was substantially correct as far as it went, it didn't go quite far enough. The mental dawn had broken. Sunrise was yet to come.

"It came swiftly and inevitably. As I stood by the window and watched the sun appear above the clouds the complete pattern, symmetrical and satisfying, of the Tiddenham case unfolded itself before my mind's eye. That moment was one of the high-lights in my otherwise ill-spent career.

"It is to you, *James Briggs,* that I owe that moment." The hall door burst open, and a voice commanded: "Don't move, either of you. I've got you both covered."

It was the Major, armed with a revolver. Advancing, he said:

"I arrest you, *James* Briggs and Margot Fayette, in connexion with the murder of Stephen Hogg and Ellen Briggs. Look slippy, Hines, with those handcuffs!"

PART FOUR

CHAPTER XXVI

RAY, attired in what he euphemistically called a dinner-jacket, stood with his back to the fire, propping up the Major's mantelpiece and smoking one of the Major's fat Havanas. Major Wigley himself, in a mess-jacket and cummerbund, sat sprawling in an easy-chair, staring at as much of the fire as Ray's legs did not intercept. Except for the firelight, the room was in darkness.

The Major was saying in an injured tone:

"You've made me talk about life in up-country stations all through dinner. I've told you the story of the A.D.C. and the box-wallah's memsahib, and four worse ones, and now I flatly refuse to say another word till you answer all my questions about the Briggs case."

Ray laughed. "My dear Major," he said, "let me assure you that I shall not hold my peace. I'm merely playing Antony to your Brutus, and shall speak with greater effect because I speak last, the more so because I shall not be interrupted by sounds like water running out of a bath. I prefer not to have to shout down the soup. . . . Well, sir, what's worrying you?"

"Everything. Ever since we checked up the fact, on your advice, that Hogg's fingerprints, as given in his police record, corresponded with fingerprints taken from the body, I've been wondering how to goodness you worked it out. Listening at the study door, I followed you up to the point where you concluded that Briggs had framed Sothern. From that point to the solution was rather a jump. What clues enabled you to make that jump?"

"The clue of the twin garages, the clue of the photograph with the dark background, the clue of the Moon and Sixpence, the clue of the painter's paraphernalia, the clue of the superfluous letters—and plenty more."

The Major shook his head. "I'm still in the dark. In fact, rather more so than before."

"Major, believe me, when the interpretation of these clues was revealed to me I could have kicked myself. Right from the start of the case the truth had been staring me in the face. If I had concentrated on these clues I could have dispensed with most of the reasoning which led me, by tortuous paths, almost up to the goal. I could have taken a short cut to the truth. Instead of which, the clues of which I speak merely enabled me to cover the last lap, to get from the half-truth of Briggs' suicide in order to frame Sothern, to the whole truth of James's reincarnation as Joshua."

"You did extraordinarily well, Ray. Why, even Scotland Yard couldn't have done better," said the Major warmly.

"Your compliments, sir," laughed Ray, "would to the sleuth of fiction appear so back-handed as to amount to insults. To me they are the genuine balm of Gilead. . . . But, to resume, I'll take you quickly through the evidence that convinced me that James and Joshua were one and the same person.

"Firstly, I recollected that no one except Margot had ever spoken of having seen them together. On the occasions when Joshua had called at the Tiddenham house James was always out. When Sothern met Joshua James was not there. Ellen Briggs and Mr and Mrs Groves had never seen the brothers in each other's company. Odd thing, that. Taken by itself, it might be a coincidence. Taken along with the rest of the evidence, it was something very different.

"Secondly, the letters. I was myself the bearer of one of these—a letter from James to Joshua that said so little that it need never have been written. Its purpose was twofold: to reinforce the two-brothers idea, and to 'prove' that James was in London while Joshua was with me in Bingly. There were, as you know, other letters and carbon copies of letters between the two brothers in the London office and the house. On the whole they appeared to be superfluous letters. They didn't ring true. They were, of course, part of the plan by which Joshua was created.

"The fact that the letters from James to Joshua were typewritten I had found mildly surprising. It was not until the end that the reason for this fact struck me. It was this: Joshua's writing would naturally resemble James's, and it would be embarrassing if, after James's elimination, someone discovered the striking similarity. Therefore the less of James's handwriting there was in existence the better.

"Thirdly, there was the clue of the photograph. This clue was, I think, a slight tactical error on Briggs' part. If I had been sharper it would have given the game away at the start. Joshua had told me that the brothers had had very little to do with each other for years. Yet here was a studio photograph of them together, and taken not so very long ago. And that was not all. The brothers' clothes intrigued me. Joshua was too untidy; James too smart. I could just conceive circumstances explaining the taking of the photograph; I could imagine Joshua truculently refusing on principle to spruce himself up for the ordeal; I could even pass the unnatural, out-moded posing of the subjects. All this might be capable of innocent explanation—but would James the art-dealer, the respectable bourgeois, the man who allegedly looked down on his brother as a ragamuffin artist, put that photograph, for all to see, in a prominent place in his sitting-room? No. Not unless he had a strong motive for doing so. That motive was a double one: *(a)* to establish Joshua's separate identity, and *(b)* to familiarize as many people as possible with Joshua's appearance.

"The photograph had a dark background. Some studios do go in for dark back-cloths, but the old-fashioned full-length portrait, where the subject is made to look as much like a stuffed museum piece as possible, is usually taken against a dreadful background of vignetted rusticity. Why didn't the photograph of the two brothers have such a background?

"The explanation turned out to be absurdly simple. Against a very dark background any amateur can take two or more photographs of a relatively light object on the same negative, one after the other. Such a background has little or no effect on the emulsion of the film, and if the object being photographed—say, a vase—is shifted between the first and the second exposure, the final print will show two vases. If the photographer has been careful to shift the vase the right distance there will be no overlapping, and even an expert would have difficulty in determining whether there had been two vases, or two positions of one vase. Either Briggs, by means of a simple contrivance known to all photographers, had taken the photograph himself in this way, or Margot had taken it for him. And the negative had been exposed twice—once to take James, the art-dealer on one side of the film, and again to take Briggs dressed up as Joshua, the artist, on the other side. Result: the two brothers."

"Damned ingenious!" exclaimed the Major.

"Obviously, sir, you're not a photographer. The dodge is pure apple-sauce to the keen amateur. Such ingenuity as there was lay not so much in the trick as in its application.

"Fourthly, we come to the clue of the twin garages. This was a much more difficult nut to crack. You remember how I elicited from old Groves the fact that Briggs had one car and two identical garages. Sometimes he used one of them, sometimes the other. Such behaviour seemed to me to be unnatural. Ordinarily one of the garages would have been pressed into service as a lumber-room, potting-shed, or whatnot. But supposing—what is quite likely—that an extra garage were kept as a spare one for visitors' cars, I hold that any normal man would have used only one of the two garages for his own car, and would have used it exclusively. Briggs did not. Why? I confess with shame that the reason only came to me after I had, on other grounds, discovered the identity of the two brothers.

"The reason was this. On the day of the murder, and thenceforward, Joshua had to have a car of his own. Previously he had used James's. (Forgive me when I speak of the brothers as different people, but you will get my meaning more easily that way.) After the murder James's car had to be found in the garage by the police, and Joshua must needs return to Bingly, after killing Hogg, in *another* car. That car he had kept ready in one of the garages. There were, in fact, unknown to Groves, two similar cars of the same make, one in each of the garages, on the day of the murder. In one of these cars—the one destined to become Joshua's—James went off that morning, ostensibly to London, actually to Bingly. Groves saw him drive this car out of one garage in the morning. In the evening the police found James's car—which had not been used that day—in the *other* garage. The fact that James had apparently swopped garages would arouse no suspicion in Groves' mind, because Briggs had been in the habit of swopping garages."

"Half a minute," cut in the Major, "let me get this straight. Groves saw James leave in a car that morning, in Joshua's car, and not the usual one. Then it must have had a different registration number. Groves would have noticed that."

"What's the number of your car, sir?"

"I haven't the foggiest idea."

"There you are. And it's your own car. This car had nothing to do with Groves, who isn't overbrimming with intelligence, anyway. The chances of his scrutinizing the number-plate were next to nil, and Briggs banked on the fact."

"Another thing, Ray," continued the Major. "Why couldn't Joshua, after having committed the murder, have transferred James's car to the other garage—I mean to the garage Groves had seen him drive out of that morning—instead of laboriously building up a tradition which would explain the fact that he had apparently used one garage on the night of March the thirty-first and another on the night of April the first?"

"Because *(a)* the transfer would have taken five minutes, and every second was valuable; *(b)* he might have been seen from the road; *(c)* the gravel might have retained marks of the switch-over. Moreover, the tradition was necessary so that when garaging the second car—Joshua's—at the time of its purchase anyone seeing him do so would be equally incurious whether the car were put in one garage or the other."

The Major shook his head despondently. "You've got me all tied up in knots, Ray, but I'll take your word for it all."

"Check the clue of the twin garages at your leisure, preferably with the help of diagrams…. It does seem an extraordinary precaution to have taken, but extraordinary precautions are typical of this crime.

"Then there was the clue of the painter's paraphernalia, which I found in a drawer in Biggs.' office, and Margot's unconvincing explanation of its presence there. There was the hint, which I was all too slow to take, of the well-thumbed copy of *The Moon and Sixpence* on his bookshelves. There was the clue of the method of the murder, which involved mutilating the victim's face to hide his identity. There was the clue of Briggs' lack of friends—the fewer friends he had *qua* James, and the more he had *qua* Joshua, the better for his plan. There was the clue of his frequent absences from home. And so on.

"I think, Major, that answers the question: what clues enabled me to bridge the gap between the theory of James's suicide in order to frame Sothern, and the theory of James's 'suicide' in order not only to frame Sothern, but also to reappear as Joshua?"

*   *   *   *

"Look here, Ray," said the Major petulantly, "I've got hold of shreds and patches of this wonderful scheme of Briggs', but the outfit as a whole escapes me. I don't yet know why he killed Ellen Briggs. I can't conceive why this ace-criminal was such a half-wit as to bring you of all people in as a detective. I don't know the why and the wherefore of a score of things, and yet you keep me waiting by blathering about garages. You're doing your stuff the wrong way round."

"Oh, no, I'm not," Ray laughed. "Before I spill the entire can of beans I must needs rouse your flagging interest in the tin-opener. After you're distended with the intellectual feast that I'm now about to dish up you won't give a damn for the insignificant instrument by which the meal was made available. Which in translation means: if you knew all the answers, my self-congratulatory account of how I arrived at them would fall on comparatively deaf ears."

CHAPTER XXVII

RAY'S lanky form had descended from its caryatidal position to the generous depths of one of the Major's arm-chairs, from which only a pair of legs protruded, like the antennae of some monstrous insect attracted by the warmth of the fire.

"This reconstruction," Ray began, "is going to be sketchy, and not entirely free from guesswork. Remember that my acquaintance with the case lasted only two and a half days, of which the odd half-day was spent in giving, not acquiring, information. Some of the blanks I think you can fill in, sir. In fact, you can start off by telling me what you've found out about our triumvirate: Briggs, Sothern, and Hogg."

"Certainly I can," replied the Major. "Acting on your advice, I got the London people busy on Sothern and Hogg. This is what they found out.

"About eighteen months ago there was a serious theft from one of the public picture galleries in London. No fewer than three extremely valuable old masters were stolen. Hogg, under another name, was one of the gallery's attendants. The police were never able to prove anything against him, though they felt sure that he had been involved in the theft. He was shadowed, which eventually brought them to Sothern. Sothern, like Hogg, was known to the police, but, unlike Hogg, he had never been caught. Well, after a lot of trouble—I don't know the details—they made sure that Hogg had put the safety devices out of action and had arranged a counter-attraction to divert the attention of the other attendants, while Sothern carried out his daring daylight robbery, coolly walking out of the place with the canvases wrapped round his body. But the police couldn't pin the crime on the two men. Legally the case against them wouldn't stand examination. And the stolen pictures were never found. The conclusion that the police drew was that some third person, able to dispose of the loot, had engineered the whole business."

"To wit, James Briggs," said Ray.

"Yes. We've found enough among Briggs' effects and papers to be sure that the three of them were involved, and that Briggs' job was to sell the pictures."

"From that point I can continue," said Ray. "Briggs sold the pictures and hung on to the money, probably fobbing off his partners with the story that he couldn't find purchasers. Not long after the theft he married Ellen—doubtless for her money—and shifted from London to the Tiddenham house. Then, three or four months ago, his affair with Margot started. All this time Hogg and Sothern were chasing him, and Sothern went so far as to take a cottage in Tiddenham, the more effectively to press his claims.

"At the beginning of this year, then, Briggs' circumstances were as follows: Sothern and Hogg were pestering him for money; Hogg, at least, having little to lose, was threatening to turn informer, and had to be pacified with small payments from time to time. In addition, Briggs knew that the police suspected these two of complicity in the theft, and that their association with him must at last lead the police to himself.

"Next, Briggs was married to a woman he did not love. He had got hold of her money and had no further use for her. He was in love with Margot, but he could not marry her, since Ellen, being a Catholic, would not divorce him.

"And, finally, what is far more important from my point of view, Briggs was a real painter. Not only was he possessed with a tremendous urge to make significant marks on canvas, but he had, I believe, the makings of a really great painter.

"I do not go so far as to say that Briggs was suffering from advanced schizophrenia, or that the duality of his personality was as pronounced as in the case of Dr Jekyll and Mr Hyde. Rather his prototype was Gauguin. Perhaps you remember, Major, the story of the French banker-painter?"

Major Wigley shook his head.

"Then you must read Somerset Maugham's *The Moon and Sixpence,* which is a tale based on Gauguin's extraordinary life. I won't go into details, but since the story of the hero of *The Moon and Sixpence* bears a resemblance that is not wholly accidental to the story of James Briggs, its outline is worth noticing.

"Charles Strickland, a middle-aged London broker, was outwardly an ordinary, stolid business man, an exemplary husband, and a good father to his two children. His wife, an inveterate lion-hunter, cultivated promising young aesthetes, and was in the habit of confiding to her friends that Strickland was a philistine—a virtuous man, a good-natured individual, but still a philistine. And what was worse, he was dull. He was kept in the background as much as possible.

"For seventeen years Strickland lived this sort of life with his wife. Then one day he vanished without warning, and turned up later in Paris as a painter, desperately poor, absolutely unconventional, and living for nothing but his art. His sole object in life was to become a great painter. Appeals to his 'better nature,' threats, and the world's contempt left him quite indifferent. His wife and family were nothing to him—they could shift for themselves.

"For a year before he ran away to Paris Strickland had been secretly attending art classes and planning his escape.

"He lived in Paris, and then in Marseilles, in utmost poverty, picking up a half-living anyhow, and painting. But it was in the island of Tahiti, whither he went in search of a congenial environment, that his genius flourished more abundantly. He took to himself a Tahitian wife, and lived and worked in a tiny bungalow far from the society of Europeans. After some years spent in making pictures that afterwards became world-famous of the natives and their exotic surroundings, Strickland died, blind and a leper, attended only by his native wife, and painting almost till the end.

"Now, Briggs knew this story well. The copy of the book on his shelves had been read and reread. Undoubtedly the theme fascinated and influenced him, and he found in Strickland a kindred spirit. Like Strickland, he was, outwardly at least, a respectable and prosperous citizen with an unsympathetic wife, uninspiring friends, and a hopelessly circumscribed middle-class way of life. Like Strickland, he nursed a secret longing to paint, and to paint superlatively well. Like Strickland, he hated his environment, and planned to sever himself from it at one blow. Like Strickland, his art was his only morality.

"Such, then, were Briggs' circumstances. They had become intolerable for many reasons. A lesser man would have taken the easy way out and shot himself. Briggs was made of different stuff. His way out was difficult, desperate, and chancy, but it was a courageous and exciting way, the way of an artist in crime no less than in paint. And it was much more than a way out; it was a way in—to the new sort of life he yearned to lead. Don't think of Briggs' Plan as negative. It was that, and much more than that. It was a true work of art, having value in itself for Briggs, apart from its material outcome. And don't think of the Plan as a trick, a gigantic hoax. Again, it was that, and much more than that. It was a genuine manifestation of a rich and strange personality.

"For in a very real sense two men did exist—Joshua the painter, and James the man of business, and Joshua gradually became the more genuine of the two. In the end James died, leaving only, as it were, the desiccated shell that had given birth to Joshua. In a fundamental sense Joshua Briggs was not the same man as James Briggs, and we were not hoaxed. Mark that point, Major, for it is of the essence.

*　　　　　　*　　　　　　*　　　　　　*

"Briggs' Plan you already know in outline. Like most works of art, it can be reduced to a simple broad pattern, which, so seen, must appear bare, unoriginal, naïve. The working up of the Plan, the subtlety of its detailing, above all its manifold application—in these lie its peculiar virtue.

"The broad pattern or *leit-motif* of the Plan was the gradual creation of a new man—Joshua Briggs. Step by step this new individual was to be built up. Evidence of his independent existence was to accumulate until it became overwhelmingly convincing. Joshua's Galatea was eventually to become more alive than James's Pygmalion, and finally to oust him. It was a painfully slow process, requiring infinite care and judgment, but the utter satisfactoriness of the end justified the laboriousness of the means.

"'Satisfactoriness' is hardly the word I want—'polyvalence' is nearer the mark, if the chemists don't mind my borrowing their term. The Plan, in its final form, not only lifted Briggs right out of a tight spot, but out of several tight spots, and deposited him on the threshold of a new, spacious, and promising life. I was so impressed with this polyvalence, this many-sidedness of the Plan, that I made a list of its objects. The list read like this:

"1. The police, who, apart from the Plan, are bound to track him down sooner or later, are put off the scent for ever.

*2. He is able safely to decamp with the money for which he sold the pictures.

3. Likewise, he is able safely and without reproach to appropriate Ellen's money, leaving her unsupported.

* 4. He rids himself of his wife, from whom he could not obtain a divorce.

*5. He does this without killing her, which, apart from the Plan, would have been the only way to free himself. (The fact that he did find it necessary to kill her in the end was no part of the Plan, but was due to a hitch.)

6. He is left free to marry Margot.

7. He revenges himself on Hogg.

*8. In removing Hogg he not only prevents further blackmail, but he removes one of the two men who have most reason for suspecting the existence of the Plan, and are most likely to upset it.

*9. Similarly, in framing Sothern and ensuring his conviction as the murderer, he eliminates a potential blackmailer and the other man who has most reason for suspecting the existence of the Plan.

10. By framing Sothern and ensuring his conviction as the murderer, he eliminates the man who has been Margot's lover, and who may succeed in winning her back again.

11. By fixing the date and the time of the crime to coincide with Ellen's weekly visit to Dr Storr, he is able to throw suspicion on both of them—suspicion which would lead, he hoped, to the ruin of the doctor's professional career. (I should explain here that Briggs was jealous of his wife's relationship with the doctor, though he didn't realize until after the crime just how intimate that relationship really was.)

*12. And, finally, he is able to do what otherwise would have been so difficult—to make a clean break with the old life and start anew. In a word, to be born again.

"These were Briggs' Twelve Points. A round dozen, mind you!

"You remember, Major, the case of the commercial traveller who gave a tramp a lift in his car, killed him, and set light to the car in the hope that the tramp's remains would be mistaken for his own. The commercial traveller's sole motive, if I'm not mistaken, was to avoid the consequences of excessive paternity.

Perhaps I'm wrong, but I'll warrant that he hadn't more than three or four purposes in mind. Briggs had twelve!

"I own that, in drawing up this list, I included certain minor aims and perhaps one or two mere by-products of the Plan. To distinguish the greater from the less I divided the points into six major and six minor ones.[1] Even if, to avoid the worst excesses of villain-worship, we ignore the six minor points altogether, I contend we are left with an impressive array.

"Of course, the Plan was not revealed to Briggs in a flash, as though by divine inspiration. It grew. I dare say that on some sketching excursion, dressed in unfamiliar, unrespectable clothes, engaged in a new and exciting task, feeling another man, the idea had come to him of breaking with the intolerable old life, of not only feeling a new man, but becoming one. Problem: how to get hold of enough money to support this new man. Answer: by gradually withdrawing his money from the bank, on some pretext or other, and hiding it somewhere against the day of the switch-over. How well this scheme of changing his identity got over the blackmail nuisance he must have immediately realized.

---

1   The six major points in the list are marked with asterisks.

"But if he were merely to disappear Hogg and Sothern would find him in the end. Therefore, there must be a body. Whose body? Why not Hogg's? Probably the idea of framing Sothern came long afterwards, along with Margot's appearance on the scene. From the start, no doubt, the fact that the Plan freed him from Ellen increased its attractiveness, but the scheme whereby Dr Storr became involved was perhaps the last development of all. In fact, not until a few weeks, or even days, before the murder of Hogg did the Plan crystallize into its final shape. Until then parts of it remained fluid.

"All this is conjecture, fascinating, but airy. Briggs was an artist, his Plan a work of art. And it does not do to inquire too nicely into the genesis of a work of art. Its justification lies in the finished product."

CHAPTER XXVIII

IT was a One Year Plan. It was initiated when Briggs shifted from London to Tiddenham in March of last year, at about the time when I first met him.

"The first and the chief task of the Plan was to create Joshua, and to make him familiar to as many people as possible, myself included. Above all, those who knew James must also get to know Joshua.

"Now, Joshua, as you know, had his hair brushed back—in so far as it could be said to be brushed. He had clothes as disreputable as my own, shoes worn down at the heels, and brilliant ties of coarse weave. The disguise was double-edged: as Joshua became excessively painter-like, so James became excessively respectable-looking, even to the extent of caricature. This was not only good policy, it was good psychology. Briggs was to some degree a divided personality in the process of unification. It must have given him deep satisfaction to exaggerate James's well-loathed stuffiness, to dress him in the wing-collar, pin-stripe fashion, to push the narrowness of his mind to extreme lengths, till he became, almost genuinely, the sort of man who believes in things like the Protocols of the Elders of Zion, the White Man's Burden, and the Essential Un-Britishness of Socialism. This, I say, was more than a part of the disguise necessary to the Plan. It was a revenge on a hated and soon-to-be-discarded part of the self. It was contumely poured on the wasted, uncreative years.

"The genuine differences, in mind, behaviour, and appearance, between James and Joshua, no less than the more artificial ones of dress and mere disguise, succeeded admirably. Such similarities as remained were readily accounted for by the fact that the two men were supposed to be brothers. If it should happen that the resemblance were still so close as to cause comment, notwithstanding the known relationship, people's surprise would be over long before the crime was enacted, and long before they had any reason to suspect Joshua's real identity. The frequent appearances of Joshua before the crime obviated the possibility of any awkward questions being asked after it. And these appearances served as dress rehearsals. If the disguise succeeded at the start, and succeeded with Sothern and Ellen and Mr and Mrs Groves, then the danger of exposure later was small. If the disguise failed, then no harm was done, and another plan had to be devised.

"I said that Briggs' disguise was a double one. Actually it had to become triple. James had not only to become unlike Joshua, and vice versa, but he had to become like Hogg. Now Hogg, by a stroke of good fortune, resembled Briggs in that he was dark, of similar build, and of middle height. There the resemblance stopped. Facially they were unlike, but the method of killing was to take care of that. The clothes in which Hogg was to be found were, of course, to be the clothes which James had worn on the day of the murder. All that remained to complete the illusion that Hogg's corpse was James's was to make sure that the body, apart from the face, did not markedly differ from James's body. I say 'markedly' because few people would know of any distinctive blemishes on James's body, and those few would have little reason for questioning the identity of the corpse.

"But Briggs was taking no chances. He knew that Hogg had a scar on his right forearm. So far from presenting an obstacle, this scar served to confirm that the corpse was James's, for, some time before the murder, James let it be supposed that he had sustained a cut on the arm. Actually, all he did was to say that he had cut himself, and let people see the bandage.

"One of the major functions of the Plan was to provide Joshua with enough capital with which to start upon his new life. This was easily arranged by withdrawing cash in small sums from his bank over the whole period of the Plan, so that in the end his own money, and Ellen's too, had been realized and put away, in an easily negotiable form, for Joshua's use. Hence James's reputation for betting; hence the book on racing deliberately left in his bookcase; hence the newspaper cutting of racing fixtures found in the corpse's pocket; hence the story of betting losses told to the bank manager.

"Several of the minor tasks of the Plan you know of already. You know how he faked the photograph—incidentally I prefer to look on the picture of James and Joshua as much more than a fake. I have told you how he used the two garages and, latterly, bought a car of the same make as his old one, for Joshua. You know about the letters that passed between the brothers, and of Joshua's calls at the Tiddenham house.

"Other preparations had to be made for the day of the switch-over. For instance, a picture of Bingly church had to be painted and held in readiness, to form the basis of his faked alibi. His appointment to spend the day with me in Bingly had to be arranged to fit in with the rest of the programme. Hogg had to be instructed to turn up at the correct time, no doubt to receive, as he fondly thought, a substantial sum of hush-money. The blotting-paper note had to be written to plant after the crime. The gun had to be purchased, Sothern induced to handle it, and his fingerprints carefully preserved.

"And Margot had to be coached to play her part. It was her job to post, on the day of the murder, letters written and signed by Briggs on the previous day but dated April 1st, to make it appear that Briggs had been in town that day. It was her job to ring Sothern and get him to agree to meet her at some lonely spot. The place of the rendezvous, by the way, had to be sufficiently far from Briggs' house to ensure that, after finding she had failed him, Sothern would be unable to get to the house before the murder had been committed, and Joshua had got away to Bingly. And, finally, she was instructed exactly what to tell the police and me about Briggs' fictitious lunch party and his work at the office, at the time when he was actually to be with me at Bingly.

"Such, Major Wigley, was the spadework of the Plan. Most of it could be carried out at leisure, with a maximum of care and a minimum of risk. By means of the Plan Briggs was able to spend a whole year committing his crime—an incalculable advantage. Only at the end of that year, when the dress rehearsals had reached perfection, when the stage was perfectly set, when each actor had been properly primed as to his entrances and exits, did the actor-producer give the show his final O.K. and ring up the curtain. And, as one might expect of a drama that had a sound plot, well-cast players, and an infinitely painstaking producer the show went with a bang."

*   *   *   *

"Till you bust it up," came a voice from the depths of the other arm-chair.

"Good Lord, Major!" cried Ray. "Are you still there, and awake?"

The Major laughed. "Strangely enough, I am. Only don't you think you could dispense with the oratorical effects, and get on with the twenty or thirty things I still don't know about this case?"

"This crime," replied Ray, "took a year to commit, and I'm not going to insult it by rushing you past its beauty-spots like a cicerone who's being paid on a piece-work basis. As for the occasional purple patch, I must insist on its inclusion in the colour-scheme. To change metaphorical gears, you'll have to take your jam with the pill, and like it. If you won't, no pill.

"Fortify yourself, Major, with one of those filthy things you call *chota-pegs,* give me another of your capitalistic cigars, and prepare to hear what befell on All Fools' Day."

CHAPTER XXIX

JAMES BRIGGS," continued Ray, "got up at a reasonable hour, and breakfasted with his wife. Over the eggs and bacon he announced that he intended to spend the day in town and to get back to the house early in the evening. Ellen said she was going to the cinema. At nine-thirty he took out not James's car, but Joshua's, and drove off to Bingly.

"In the back of the car was the suitcase containing Joshua's clothes. At some convenient spot between Tiddenham and Bingly—preferably nearer to Tiddenham—he changed into Joshua's clothes, took off his spectacles, brushed his hair Joshua's way, put James's clothes in the suitcase, and continued his journey.

"We met at the George and spent the rest of the morning and the afternoon at Bingly Church. At about five o'clock we went back to the pub and retired to our own rooms. At that time his drawing was half finished.

"Joshua, leaving the light of his room burning, walked out by the French windows into the yard at the side of the building, where his car was parked on a slope. All he had to do was to release the hand-brake and steer the car downhill. There was no need to start the engine till the George was practically out of earshot. In the back of the car was the suitcase containing James's clothes.

"It takes roughly an hour to drive from Bingly to Tiddenham. Joshua therefore arrived at the Briggses' house at about six-twenty or so—over an hour after Mr and Mrs Groves had left, and two hours after Ellen had gone to Stokeby.

"You may remember that Hogg left the Arms at about that time. Presumably he arrived at the house not long after Briggs. I'm sure that Briggs didn't dress up as James to receive him, but, as Joshua, took the first opportunity of knocking him out or drugging his whisky—I don't yet know which it was.

"Now work began in real earnest. He had to undress the unconscious Hogg, shave off Hogg's moustache, possibly wash Hogg's hands and clean his fingernails, dress him in James's clothes from the suitcase, and put James's glasses on him. Hogg's clothes had to go into the suitcase, and the suitcase into the back of the car. The study had to be cleaned of any fingerprints of his own, and Hogg's fingerprints had to appear on the gun. This last was simple. He had simply to press Hogg's hand to the weapon in suitable places, taking care to leave Sothern's prints intact and to avoid leaving any of his own.

"Everything had gone off smoothly according to schedule. All was now set for the *coup de grâce*."

"Just a moment," cut in the Major. "The man must have been mad. Think of the risk he took of being seen between Bingly and Tiddenham, of being seen outside his house, and of some one paying a call while he was on the job!"

"Not so mad as all that, Major. I have two suggestions to make concerning what you've said. The first sounds like melodrama, and is in any case only a guess. A man driving a car is no sooner seen than he is gone. There's no time to take in the details. Supposing Briggs had clapped on a fancy moustache while in the car—an enormous walrus, let us say—his own mother wouldn't have been able to recognize him passing at thirty miles an hour. It's ludicrously simple—no dressing up, no waste of time, just dabbing a mass of fur on the upper lip. Well, it's only a suggestion, but if I can think of it I'm sure Briggs did, or of something better.

"My second observation is this. Up till the moment before the shot Briggs was in a position to abandon the whole scheme. Supposing some one had called at the house at the last moment, or supposing he had met some one on the way who had recognized him, or supposing he had known that he had been seen leaving the George—in any of these events he would doubtless have called off the whole business. Only when all but the actual killing had been done, only when ninety-nine-hundredths of the Plan had been consummated safely and without a hitch, did Briggs add the finishing touch and fire the shot which made retreat impossible.

"You know most of the rest. How he shot Hogg in such a way as to render his features unrecognizable and drove back to Bingly, stopping on the way to cache Hogg's suitcase, containing Hogg's clothes, and how, having parked his car, he returned to his room in time to substitute for the half-finished painting the one he had completed in readiness for that night.

"It was either due to an appalling lack of observation on my part, or to amazing self-control on his, that the Briggs I dined with that night seemed to me the same unruffled, over-serious painter that I had been with all day. Not by so much as a tremor of the hand or voice, or by any unusual behaviour whatsoever, did he let fall the slightest hint of what he had passed through that day.

*   *   *   *

"Now you know the part that the principals played on April the first. I won't spend long over the others.

"In response to her telephone message Sothern went to meet Margot, found that she had not turned up, and looked in at the Briggses' house on his way home. There he saw the body, and was himself seen by the villager.

"Ellen, of course, did not go to the cinema that evening, but remained at the doctor's, leaving shortly before eight. There never was any doubt in Storr's mind as to Ellen's innocence, but he knew that he could only confirm her alibi at the risk of his reputation and his practice. It was for that reason he announced that Briggs had died between five and six o'clock, during most of which time Ellen had been in the teashop. For the same reason he denied that she had been to his house that evening."

"What I don't understand," said the Major, "is why she wrote that letter to Storr the day after—the letter you intercepted."

"There's a very simple reply to that, Major. They were both anxious that I should cast no doubt on the suicide theory, in case further investigation should bring up the question of Ellen's alibi. During their conversation on the morning of the crime it was probably agreed that a certain amount of suspicion should be cast upon Margot, so that, if the suicide theory should prove untenable, Margot's alibi, rather than Ellen's, should come in for scrutiny. Ellen's letter to Storr advised him to stick to the suicide theory, because, from the conversation she had overheard, she thought it likely that Margot's alibi was a sound one.

"Ellen was a foolish woman. She should never have written such a letter. Storr, realizing it had been intercepted, planted the second letter for me to find, in order to neutralize, as far as possible, the effect of the first. The whole Ellen-Storr business was clumsy and amateurish.

"Next question, Major?"

"Ellen and the doctor were admittedly not brilliant," replied Major Wigley, "but I don't think they compare unfavourably with Briggs. If Briggs was the intellectual giant you make him out to be, I ask you, for the second or third time, why he committed such a suicidal blunder as to get you of all people involved in his scheme at the start, and, not content with that, why in the name of goodness he dragged you in as detective? You're not going to tell me that was a part of the Plan too? Or are you?"

"I am, and I do. I was almost as flattered when I realized that I was one of the cast as when I realized that I was the only actor that had not performed according to schedule. I failed him by overplaying my part and eventually ruining the show. If I had behaved myself, done my business, and said my lines as the author-producer-actor had intended, Briggs would now be painting in Paris, and Sothern would be in the cell that Briggs occupies.

"To elucidate. For his alibi Briggs needed an independent witness, one who would be above suspicion. I answered these requirements. And what better witness to his 'innocence' could he have than the man destined to become the investigator of his crime?

"When I first met Briggs I told him I was interested in criminal investigation. I own I bragged a little. I own, further, that, to the casual observer, I look a bit of a fool—you, sir, will be the first to endorse that. Well, at the time when I first met him Briggs was in the process of planning what he thought was the perfect crime. No doubt he was intrigued with this self-confident youngster, who was so obviously an ass. It amused him to put this much vaunted brain to the test; it amused him because he felt quite safe. I believe that even with an intelligent-looking sleuth he would have felt secure from discovery. Briggs was vain—not without justification.

"But he had stronger and more practical motives than vanity for bringing me in. To engage a detective at all is at once to divert suspicion from yourself. People argue that the guilty party would be the last to do such a thing. But if the detective is as raw as I actually was, and as stupid as I seemed to be, then the criminal has everything to gain and nothing to lose by engaging me. Along these lines Briggs must have reasoned.

"In another way I was to serve his purpose. Briggs' intention was that the police should adopt the accident theory or the suicide theory. He did not want the police, who—this will interest you, Major— he believed to be more dangerous than me, to probe beneath the superficial solutions of accident or suicide as far as the theory of Sothern's guilt. That was where I came in. He preferred that I should probe, because I would do so under his observation. He would be able to control my investigation, plant additional 'clues' if required, suggest—not too obviously—each move of mine, and finally, if my probings should go too deep, put me off or get rid of me.

"If I had been the man he took me for his action in engaging me would have proved a brilliantly clever step. Remember that he wanted, if possible, to hang Sothern. Naturally he did not care to be the one to throw suspicion—that might have been dangerous. He wanted a tool, one who would, at the psychological moment to be determined by himself, lodge the necessary information with the police."

"I still don't see why," cut in the Major, "Briggs didn't frame Sothern in such a way that the police would have no difficulty in spotting Sothern as the murderer, right from the start."

"The answer to that, Major, is that Briggs was one of the subtlest criminals I've ever heard of. He knew that the police and everybody else would expect an experienced evil-doer like Sothern to make some effort to cover up his crime. To make Sothern too obviously the murderer was to lessen the chances of getting him convicted. A further reason, subtler than the last, for obscuring Sothern's 'guilt' was that the police, having jumped to the conclusion that Briggs had accidentally or intentionally killed himself, and then having seen that their theory was wrong and that Sothern had killed Briggs, would doubtless rest content with that solution. The idea that the truth lay deeper still would hardly occur to them. When a man forsakes an error for a half-truth or a quarter-truth he is apt to imagine that he has nothing further to learn. By contrast with the blackness of the original error, the quarter-truth seems to have the pure whiteness of the whole truth, whereas, taken by itself, it is grey and doubtful. Briggs' motive for concealing the evidence against Sothern for a certain time was based on acute psychological observation.

"So it was necessary, you see, to reveal Sothern as the murderer at the psychological moment—neither too soon nor too late.

"I had yet another use—to help throw suspicion on Ellen and Storr. Just as Briggs couldn't himself denounce Sothern, so he couldn't denounce his wife and the doctor. As I have already told you, Briggs had no intention of framing them, but simply of ruining the doctor. I was to be the instrument.

"I think you'll agree, sir, that Briggs had plenty of excellent reasons for putting me on the case. What's more, I served his purpose well and truly, right up to the moment when the light dawned upon me. All through my investigation, while I was playing (as I fondly believed) Holmes to Briggs' Watson, while I felt so convinced that Briggs was rather a slow-witted fellow and that I was rather brilliant—I was his pawn. It was part of his game to feign stupidity, to make no overt attempt to guide my investigation, to conceal from me, by any means, that I was his cat's-paw.

"But the Plan failed. It failed through no flaw in its structure, and by no error on the part of its designer. If Margot had not been involved in it I believe the Plan would have succeeded. For it was she who, without Briggs' knowledge, provided an alibi for herself and a master-clue for me. A woman let him down. His only real mistake was to suppose that she would do anything else."

* * * *

"I take you up there, Ray," said the Major. "Wasn't it a flaw in the Plan that made it necessary for him to kill his wife?"

"I would prefer to call it an extension of the Plan, Major. An annex need not spoil a building; occasionally it is an improvement.

"But whether you consider the murder of Ellen as an addition that mars the symmetry of the Plan, or as a complementary part of it, this much is certain: it was a necessary deed. As you must appreciate by now, Briggs was not a man to act hastily or without excellent motives. His reasons for eliminating Ellen were five:

"1. Ellen was the person most likely to penetrate Joshua's disguise. He thought that she had, perhaps, already begun to do so.

2. In the event of her being required formally to identify the corpse there was a grave risk that she would discover the substitution. In removing Ellen he removed this risk, and in planting her 'confession' to the murder of James he added confirmation to the general belief that it was James who had died.

3. Briggs was getting wise to me. I had let fall several hints that I suspected some one of framing Sothern. Early on April the fourth he realized that I had, so to say, peeled off too many skins from the onion, and was getting perilously near the central truth. His remedy was, by a sort of subcutaneous operation, to introduce an additional protective layer or skin, which, he devoutly hoped, would arrest my probings. I was after the person who framed Sothern. It was necessary that Ellen should 'confess' and die, and so appear to be that person. Only Margot's blunder

undeceived me.

4. As I have said before, at the time of the murder Briggs was not aware of Ellen's adultery. The most that he suspected was a mutual attraction and a not-too-serious flirtation. During our investigation the true state of affairs became evident. Again we have that queerest and commonest of mental aberrations—insistence that polygamy shall be unilateral. (You and I, Major, are unmarried. Let us count our blessings. I shudder to think how often marriage is a chemical process whereby love congeals into possessiveness, and possessiveness into jealous mistrust, leaving at last a hard lump of habit and hate, cemented by economic dependence.) Briggs was having an affair himself, and he didn't love his wife. But he was jealous. He killed her.

5. And in killing her he planned also, by means of her 'confession,' to frame and kill her lover.

"There, sir, is polyvalence again. Economy of means and multiplicity of ends. The annex is in the same style as the main structure.

"I prefer not to look on Ellen's murder as an afterthought. The poison 'aspirin' tablets which he put by her bedside, and the forged confession which he hid among the papers on her dressing-table, were certainly prepared long beforehand. I believe that Briggs included Ellen's murder in the original Plan, just as an architect includes in his design a story or a wing marked *To be built at a future date.* The wing or the story may never be needed, but the foreseeing planner ensures that, if it is required, the enlarged building will be as practical and as beautiful as the original one. Ellen's murder was a *provisional* part of the Plan—a part which the designer hoped would prove to be unnecessary. It was a vain hope."

*　　　　*　　　　*　　　　*

"I've only got one more question," said the Major. "Why did Briggs decide to pose as his brother? If he had posed as an outsider having no connexion with the Briggs family, he need never have returned to Tiddenham, and we would probably never have caught him."

"The reason," replied Ray, "I have already suggested. There had to be some explanation of the many likenesses between Joshua and James—likenesses of voice and face and manner. During the year's preparation Joshua the painter and James the dealer would inevitably meet the same people. Afterwards there would be a constant risk of Joshua's encountering some one who had known James. In becoming, so to speak, his own brother, Briggs had no reason to fear such encounters.

"And remember that Briggs had courage bordering on bravado, a wise recklessness, and a cunning vainglory. It was this, as much as anything else, that drove him to engage a detective, to interview his own lawyers and the bank manager, to arrange the meeting of the suspects to hear my lecture, and flippantly to suggest to me that he might be the murderer of James Briggs. And it was this that prevented him from running away from the scene of his crime. Characteristically, with sublime impertinence, he remained to face the music—and conduct it."

CHAPTER XXX

MAJOR WIGLEY uncurled himself, stood up, and stretched his portly frame.

"When you've finished culturing your abdomen," remarked Ray, "I suggest you turn on the switch and bring to light some suitably expensive liquor in which to toast our villain."

"I'll be damned if I will, sir!" cried the Major. "I'll drink with enthusiasm to you, Ray, who caught him, but you don't catch me toasting a murderer—a murderer twice over."

He switched on the light and poured out a couple of glasses of champagne.

"There's something wrong with your moral sense, Ray," he said.

Ray responded in a voice of unwonted seriousness. "I wouldn't drink to a man who murdered for gain alone, or for revenge and jealousy alone, or even for love alone. I wouldn't drink to such a man, however perfect his crime, however faultless its execution.

"Briggs killed for gain, for revenge, for jealousy, and for love, but most of all he killed for art's sake. . . . I like to look upon his crime as a work of art in itself, committed for art's sake—a double justification.

"People say that the artist is amoral. I say that his morality is more real, because it is more personal and less conventional, than the morality of ordinary mortals. To Briggs, to any man of genius, the deadly sin, the only sin, is to do violence to that genius. If, to give it scope, one or two insignificant obstacles have to be removed, what is that to him?"

"*Mein Kampf!*" muttered the Major.

"*Mein Kampf* with this difference," came the instant retort. "It was not Briggs, nor Briggs' race, not Briggs' country, *über alles,* but Art—the life of the spirit."

Ray pulled himself up with a laugh.

"I know, Major. I exaggerate. I'm an incurable villain-worshipper. And I've talked myself into endorsing anarchy and the irresponsible, anti-social use of force. But I will say this. Briggs aimed high; his means may have been ignoble, but his end was noble. He was not petty. Can we say as much of ourselves?"

"It's an odd story," mused the Major, "this story of how Briggs died. We thought he killed himself accidentally; then we were sure he committed suicide; and at last we came to the conclusion that he had been murdered. We never thought there could be a fourth alternative—judicial execution."

They raised their glasses.

The Major said: "To the man who caught James Briggs!"

Ray said: "To my friend *Joshua* Briggs, and may he die as boldly as he lived."